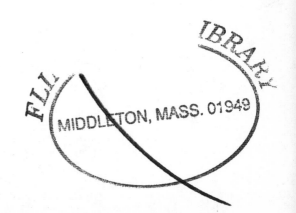

To Amelia Caroline, my sassy, strong, beautiful girl.

Ripper

Ripper

AMY CAROL REEVES

flux
™
Woodbury, Minnesota

First Edition
First Printing, 2012

Book design by Bob Gaul
Cover art © Dominick Finelle/The July Group
Cover design by Kevin R. Brown
Interior map illustration © Chris Down

Flux, an imprint of Llewellyn Worldwide Ltd.

Library of Congress Cataloging-in-Publication Data
Reeves, Amy Carol.
  Ripper / Amy Carol Reeves.—1st ed.
    p. cm.
  Summary: Sent to do volunteer work at the Whitechapel Hospital in the east end of London in 1888, seventeen-year-old Abbie discovers the identity of Jack the Ripper.
  ISBN 978-0-7387-3072-1
1. Jack, the Ripper—Juvenile fiction. [1. Jack, the Ripper—Fiction. 2. Murder—Fiction. 3. London (England)—History—19th century—Fiction. 4. Great Britain—History—19th century—Fiction.] I. Title.
  PZ7.R25578Rip 2012
  [Fic]—dc23

                                        2011041401

Flux
Llewellyn Worldwide Ltd.
2143 Wooddale Drive
Woodbury, MN 55125-2989
www.fluxnow.com

Acknowledgments

First and foremost, I would like to thank my incredible agent, Jessica Sinsheimer. If ever I'm trying to survive a sinking ship, I definitely want Jessica with me. And I owe so much gratitude to everyone at Flux: to my editor, Brian Farrey-Latz, for extensive help editing, to Sandy Sullivan for helping me tease through the final edits, and to my publicist, Courtney Colton.

I am greatly indebted to my writing mentors throughout the years. Specifically, I would like to thank my creative writing professor, Dr. Del Doughty, for telling me ten years ago that I should be a writer. I would also like to thank my sage dissertation director and friend, Dr. Paula Feldman, for urging me on as a writer. And I simply cannot repay Dr. Dianne Johnson for encouraging me as I began writing books for young adults.

I'd like to thank friend, fellow Anglophile, and writer Jamieson Ridenhour for reading part of an early draft and for giving advice. Jamie is awesome for knowing everything about London, vampires, werewolves, Aleister Crowley, and Ripper lore. A well of gratitude to my friend and fellow lover of Brontë novel hunks, Nicole Fisk; she sent me insightful and careful critiques for the rough draft of the novel and kept me sane and amused during this whole process.

And this book simply would not exist if it weren't for Team Reeves. My husband, Shawn Reeves, read draft after draft after draft of *Ripper* and provided honest and detailed feedback. Finally, I can't forget to thank my children, Atticus and Amelia, whose paper airplanes, sticky fingers, and fake vampire teeth kept me from taking myself too seriously.

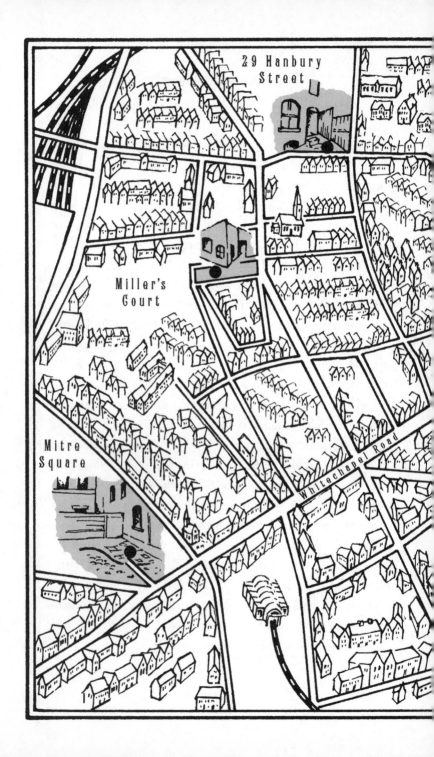

PART I

"I was weary of an existence all passive."

—*Jane Eyre*

One

D*amn.*"
If the pickpocket had taken anything other than *that,*
I could have let it go. But not Mother's brooch. I had to
keep that.

Grandmother, in front of me and already stepping into
the coach, heard the curse and clucked her tongue. Richard, her long-time servant, held the carriage door open for
me. His eyes widened in exasperation.

"Sorry, I'm so sorry," I gasped to him and to Grandmother before running after the soot-streaked boy. This
pickpocket was a slick one. Even as he ran from me, I saw
him snatch a pocket watch from an unwary gentleman. I
would not have noticed the thievery if it had not been for

my years in Ireland where I had learned to pay attention to any and every feather-brush from passersby. The brooch had been an easy catch, exposed as I clutched Grandmother's stack of new purchases—all the shiny boxes with hats and beaded gloves.

"Arabella! Arabella!"

Grandmother's voice rang out from the open window of her carriage. I would get a tongue-lashing from her later: *"Seventeen-years-old, Arabella! And running through the streets!"*

While I ran, I thought of the many times I had disappointed Grandmother since coming to live with her two months before. I thought of all the behaviors that she deemed necessary, of all the etiquette that she deemed proper. I had tried to comply, but most of her rules seemed nonsensical and as enticing as rotten fruit.

Focus, Abbie.

Running against the crush of late afternoon Knightsbridge shoppers, I was having difficulty keeping up with the boy. My heart pounded in my chest. He dashed across the Sloane Street intersection, and a carriage narrowly missed colliding with him.

"Stop, *please* stop!"

The boy continued, unhindered by my shouts, even quickening his pace. I ran faster, catching up with him a bit as we approached the corner of Hyde Park. I nearly overtook him there. But then I collided with a cluster of schoolchildren, and I lost sight of him.

Dizzied, I stopped and scanned the scene around me.

Like a bloom, evening's pink flush spread rapidly across the sky. Children and dogs ran within the park boundaries. Shop owners closed their doors. The cacophony of city shouts and street noises seemed to ring out louder just as church bells everywhere chimed the five o'clock hour. When I was about to give up, I saw the boy again, running fast past the Wellington Arch and straight into Green Park.

He continued east.

"Stop!"

Shouting was futile, and I paused, telling myself that this chase was foolhardy and useless.

But I knew I would keep going, even against my better judgment. The brooch was a material connection to Mother, one of the few items of hers that I had left.

I had to get it back.

The chase continued, and I dashed after him into the park.

The path was damp from a recent rain shower, and as we neared Buckingham Palace, the boy fell. I almost caught him, but he was up and running again just as I was about to grab his jacket collar.

As we ran along the Strand, I stumbled twice—splashing mud upon my skirt. We ran down several more streets and rather than tiring, I began to feel renewed energy. I bolted after him, nearly catching him once again as we passed St. Paul's Cathedral, but then, I almost lost him among the cheesemongers' stands within the Leadenhall Street Market.

With every passing block, we penetrated deeper into the East End.

I smelled the odor of the slaughterhouses. Crowds of barefoot children dashed in and out of workhouse alleys. Women, their mothers perhaps, positioned themselves under streetlamps for their nightly occupations.

At the base of a set of concrete steps, the boy suddenly stopped and turned around to face me. A large, worn brick building loomed behind him. A shiny, newly engraved sign that had been bolted neatly into the bricks caught my eye: *Whitechapel Hospital for Women. Est. 1883.*

I stopped, only a few yards away from the child.

"I have money for you," I said quickly, worried that he might take off. "Four crowns. You can have them. That brooch is worth nothing. I only want it back because it belonged to my mother. She's dead now."

The child cocked his head, very serious about our exchange. He studied me from under his cap, and then I saw his gaze focus greedily on the coins on my palm. He wanted and needed the money. Now that I stood closer to him, I saw clearly his dirty, broken fingernails, that his cheekbones were too prominent for a boy in good health. I wondered what else he needed.

"Are you hungry?"

No reply. He was resolved to remain mute.

The sky darkened, and I knew I had to return home. It was a long way to Grandmother's house in Kensington, and I worried that she might contact the police if she had not already.

"Here," I said, taking one cautious step closer to the boy. "Drop the brooch, and I'll toss the coins to you in this purse."

I dropped the coins inside the purse and tightened the drawstring.

"Deal?"

He remained silent, but I saw agreement in his eyes; he dropped the brooch when I tossed the purse to him. As I stepped forward and stooped to pick the brooch up, I expected him to bolt down the street. Instead, he stood still, facing me.

Suddenly, I felt sucked into another place.

The boy, the brick building, the street, everything before me melted away. It was as if I had been sucked into a black cloud. Then some of the darkness dissipated, swirled away a bit as I envisioned burning candles. Torches. Dusky-robed figures chanting something in a foreign tongue. I could see no faces, but I saw a chalice in the hands of one of the figures.

Then I found myself once again in the street facing the boy.

What had just happened?

The boy stood where he was, but a glassy, sharp look had taken over his eyes.

"Goodbye, dollygirl," he said before running away.

My heart pounded; I reeled and then steadied myself. The vision, the flash of change that had come over the boy, shook my core.

Shouts from a nearby pub and a mangy pack of dogs

running past reminded me that I had to return home, but I felt frightened and physically exhausted from the chase.

A very large wagon stacked with wooden boxes rode past me—west. I hopped onto the back end, my limbs still trembling violently from my experience.

Two

While walking up the front steps of Grandmother's grand house in Kensington, all of my alarm at the evening's events faded momentarily as I prepared to face her wrath.

I chewed my lip. Perhaps, like my mother, I could be a governess. After tonight, I could not imagine Grandmother allowing me to live with her any longer. She would almost certainly send me away. Light blazed from every window of her house, and I pictured the fury that seemed to burn Grandmother from the inside out whenever I embarrassed her. This evening would be the last straw.

Richard opened the door for me. Relief washed over his face, lightening briefly the deep folds upon his cheeks. "Miss Arabella is here, Madame!"

There came no reply from the parlor, where I knew Grandmother would be; instead, I heard only the cracking of the fire in that little room.

I smiled guiltily at Richard. He raised his graying eyebrows in an expression of amusement and chastisement and embarked upon a gentle tirade: "Miss Abbie, your grandmother is very … *put out.* She has been waiting for you in great anxiety for the past several hours. She already has the police out looking for you. And you are most fortunate that Ellen has the evening off. Otherwise, you *know* the uproar she might have made about this."

Ellen, Grandmother's other servant, had a little of the hysteric in her.

Richard helped remove my coat. "And you missed dinner. I will have to see about reheating some bread and pork. But that will be *after* I alert the police that you are home. Safe."

At that moment, I saw my reflection in the entrance hall mirror. Not only had mud splattered upon my dress, but it had somehow become streaked down my cheeks. My hair flared out in wild red coils. I looked insane, like a madwoman—a bustle-clad Medusa.

"Thank you, Richard. And I am very sorry for the trouble I have caused for you. Please tell Grandmother that I'm going to go upstairs to make myself a little more presentable."

"An *excellent* idea, Miss Abbie," Richard said sharply. However, just before I turned to walk up the stairs, he caught my wrist. I grinned and, opening my fingers, showed him the brooch in my palm.

"*Triumphant,*" I whispered.

Richard smiled and shook his head.

After placing the brooch on my bedroom dresser, I began washing my face in the porcelain washbasin. I splashed my cheeks with the icy water and then, on a split-second urge, plunged my entire head into the bowl. The rush of water into my eyes, my nose, brought no stinging relief to me. So I surfaced. I stared at the brooch as I dried my hair and wondered if I was sane. The chase into the East End tonight had been foolish, and then the vision, and the child's changed expression—that had seemed impossible. Perhaps I was losing my mind from my grief over Mother's recent death. Her illness had been brief and terrible. I stifled a sob. Memories of her loomed like a giant prism distorting, even occluding, my thoughts.

The clock over the fireplace in my bedroom struck nine o'clock, and I knew that I would have to meet with Grandmother soon.

After changing my clothes, I walked downstairs to face her.

Grandmother sat near the heat of the parlor fire. Her back remained ramrod-straight while she stroked the belly of her pug, Jupe. In her hand, she held a small copy of Tennyson's poems.

As she glared at me over her spectacles, I could see the proud forbearance that Mother must have endured before she eloped with my poor father. Grandmother wore her gray hair pulled into a perfect geometric knot at the back of her head. Her side hair swooped neatly over her ears, though not low enough to cover the dangling pearl-drop earrings.

"Sit down, Arabella." She gestured toward the cushioned chair facing her. She had lectured me many times in the past weeks. But this would be different. Something stony tinged her voice, and I knew that I would only have to wait a few minutes before hearing her banish me for good from her house.

She sat silently, laying her book in her lap beside Jupe and staring at me.

Overwhelmed by both shame and fury, I glanced sideways into the flames.

I half-hoped for Grandmother's dismissal; I had done nothing, *felt* nothing significant since coming here. It had all been hours of embroidering, card parties, and tea. And I knew that all of this life was purposed toward one point only—my eventual marriage. Then it would all be the same dance in a different household.

But instead of decreeing an instant dismissal, she said nothing. I waited. Then, after she picked up her teacup and took a deep swallow: "You know, Arabella, that in these past two months, I have been trying to *save* you."

"From what?"

"From *what?*" She set her teacup down with such force

that the tea splashed up, spilling over the rim and onto the side table. "From *yourself*, Arabella Sharp, from your own naïvety, and … from your past."

"Save me?"

I began to feel incredulous as I realized what drove all of this. Grandmother was seeking atonement for her own sins. She had banished Mother nearly twenty years ago for eloping with my father, Jacque Sharp. This was a ferocious haunt to her now.

No, I thought disappointedly. *She is not going to send me away.*

I remembered facing Mother's grave after her burial service, contemplating where I would go next. But then, in that Dublin graveyard, I had suddenly felt Grandmother's hand, clawlike, upon my shoulder. Though I had never met Lady Charlotte Westfield, I instantly surmised her identity even under her full-mourning attire. Her aquiline nose protruded from under the dark crêpe veil; her poise remained undaunted by the falling rains. This woman was the stepmother in all of the fairy tales Mother told to me, the Fury in every myth. And I left that very day with her, for my new life in London.

"Do you not understand the way things work?" Grandmother continued. "Your background is disgraceful. I have told everyone as little as possible about your mother's life since she left me. Do you think I can tell anyone that she could barely make ends meet as a governess and that, after your father died, she moved you from town to town, always looking for some well-to-do family to pay her to give lessons to their young brats?"

"But it was *you*, Grandmother, who refused to communicate with Mother anymore after she married my father. It was *you* who cut her off from ... "

"Enough!" Grandmother raised her hand to silence me. I saw that she trembled.

"I have *saved* you from a life of poverty. I have offered you a clean start, another chance. If we keep your background quiet, you might marry well, and you just might become respectable. But if you run through the streets as you did today, you will destroy everything that I am trying to do for you."

Ingratitude. That was the other element to this lecture.

"You, Arabella, are completely ignorant of the way you must act in London. I do not even *want* to know where you ran to this evening. In fact, never tell me. But it was *dangerous* not only to your life, but to your reputation— which you must work harder than most to solidify. If anyone saw you ... "

I began to feel suffocated, annoyed, and this did not go unmissed by Grandmother.

She glared at me pointedly, "I have been debating whether or not to allow you to do something. But I am convinced that your blatant ingratitude and your unwillingness to display the dignity of your class demands that I permit it."

Jupe leapt off her lap, running from the room and the rising tensions.

"A longtime acquaintance of our family and a well-respected physician and surgeon, Dr. Julian Bartlett, has offered to give you a *moral* education of sorts. He has proposed that you be allowed to work with him in the charity hospital he founded. It is a place of refuge for women in trouble. Whitechapel Hospital, I believe it is called."

My heart thumped louder—*the place where my chase with the boy had taken me!*

"Dr. Bartlett wrote to me a few weeks ago, offering the opportunity for you. At first, I thought it out of the question. That area is unredeemable. For you to be in that hospital, caring for *those* women … pitiful though they are."

"*Prostitutes*, you mean? Most of the patients are prostitutes."

Grandmother's face sharpened. "Yes, Arabella. Therefore, you understand why I was completely opposed to the idea. But then, earlier this week, he wrote again, and Dr. Bartlett can be extremely persuasive. Furthermore, Violet and Catherine, when I brought up the issue at tea the other day, thought I should consider the prospect. They said that it is quite vogue for young women to do some charitable service for a period—even in such a district. They thought that it would, in fact, be good for your character."

For once, I appreciated Grandmother's two Kensington neighbors. Lady Violet and Lady Catherine came to her house nearly every week for tea and cribbage. Their opinions weighed heavily with Grandmother, particularly their opinions regarding what was "vogue."

My heavy thoughts slid away a bit when I considered

the prospect of *doing* something. Ever since arriving at Grandmother's house, I had felt entrapped within a glass globe. Though I could see the world outside, I had been forbidden from venturing beyond the too-solid walls. The barefoot children I had seen today reminded me of the outer world, and a need surged inside me to become active.

"The work, of course, will be extraordinarily *distasteful*. In fact, the work will be quite foul."

"When am I to begin?"

"Dr. Bartlett wrote that you may begin whenever you wish." Her tone indicated to me that my reaction was not what she had desired. "I am requiring that you work there for one week. After that, you may decide whether you want to continue or not. My hope is that you will see how fortunate you are, and what I have saved you from—poverty, possible destitution. With me, you can have leisure and the opportunity to cultivate all the graces that will help you run your own household someday."

Grandmother stared at me, hawklike. I could already tell that she questioned whether this opportunity would have the desired effects upon my character.

"For once Arabella, you must follow my rules. You will not be allowed to enter or leave the hospital except in Dr. Bartlett's carriage—which he has assured me that he will provide for you. Please obey me. I insist upon it."

"Yes, Grandmother."

When it was time to go to bed, I kissed her forehead. As I bent over her, I smelled the lavender powder on her skin; her eyes hooked into my own, and I knew that I only poorly concealed my excitement about beginning work at the hospital.

Three

Only two days later, Dr. Bartlett's carriage delivered me to the steps of Whitechapel Hospital for my first day of work. The building itself was old, sprawling, and yet puzzlingly solid, seemingly uncorrupted by the surrounding factories and traffic, by the mid-morning shouts of vendors and drunken East Enders. It stood as a symbol of order amidst all the busy slapdash of the streets.

But there was nothing orderly in the immediate interior of the hospital. The moment I entered the front doors, I felt almost overwhelmed by a blanket of odors—feces, ammonia, urine, acidic smells I could not identify—that descended upon me. The enormous first floor ward was positioned only a few feet away from where I stood. Children, some mere toddlers, ran throughout the ward.

Pregnant women and women breastfeeding infants lay in beds only a few feet apart. Nurses, clothed in blue dresses and dirty pinafores, hurried about shouting at the children and attending to the women in the beds.

To my right, a narrow and grimy set of stairs twisted so sharply upward that I could not see the second floor landing. A stout nurse clothed like the others (with the exception that she wore an enormous crucifix around her neck) stormed down these stairs. She looked stressed, even angry, when she saw me.

"Miss Arabella Sharp?"

"Abbie, please."

I heard footsteps descending the stairs behind her.

"The Sharp girl is here, Dr. Bartlett!" the nurse shouted over her shoulder.

Dr. Julian Bartlett was like no one I had ever seen before. He had an expression of detached nobility, reminding me of the illustrations of antique busts in Mother's history books. With his white hair and trim beard, Dr. Bartlett could not have been less than sixty years of age, but his posture had no stoop, and his bearing was that of a much younger man. In one brief instant, he considered me with a blue-eyed gaze that was kind, cool, and penetrating all at once.

"Ah, Miss Sharp! It is wonderful that you have arrived."

His voice made me think of silk. Of pearls.

"Shall I find her something appropriate to wear?" The nurse stared rudely at the dark dress I wore, borrowed from Ellen that morning.

"Yes, of course, Sister Josephine."

When she left, Dr. Bartlett greeted me and inquired with perfect politeness about Grandmother's health and my adjustment to London.

"Let us walk up to my office. It is too difficult to talk amidst all this noise. I want to explain to you the business of the hospital, and, if you have no objections, I would like for you to shadow me today. Acceptable?"

"Perfectly." My chest tightened in both trepidation and excitement.

Dr. Bartlett led me up the stairs. Though not particularly tall, he possessed a towering poise, steely confidence, capability. I doubted that he faltered much in anything.

"On the first floor, we keep the pregnant and postpartum women. The delivery area and nursery are at the back of that ward. We have a delivery nearly every day here, several deliveries on most days."

"Where do the children on that floor stay?"

"Unfortunately, nowhere particular. At night, they sleep in their mothers' beds or on any makeshift beds the nurses can locate. This is, of course, not at all an ideal situation, but they do not have anywhere else to go while their mothers are under our care. I would like to build onto that ward, to create some sort of children's room, perhaps even a small school for them."

"When do you think that might be possible?"

We stepped aside for a nurse carrying a chamber pot down the stairs.

"I have not the faintest idea. Money is always an issue

here." Dr. Bartlett glanced sideways at me. "The Whitechapel district is not a great priority to many."

Mother, in all of her descriptions of London—of the museums, Buckingham Palace, the main parks—had not failed to tell me about the East End. "Forgotten," she had called it once, and I knew that her empathy for the district was more than the "vogue" and flighty sympathies endorsed by Grandmother and her friends.

When we reached the landing of the second floor, the atmosphere seemed quieter, not nearly as chaotic as the first floor ward. Dr. Bartlett explained that the women on the second and third floors were all patients admitted for reasons other than pregnancy care or childbirth. A middle-aged female patient reclining in a bed locked eyes with me as Dr. Bartlett and I continued up the steps. She wore a hospital gown, no better than a pinned sheet, and her gritty dark hair was pulled up on the top of her head and held in place by a broken tiara. I wondered what misfortunes had brought her here.

"Venereal diseases," Dr. Bartlett said quietly, as if he had read my mind. "On the second floor, most patients are being treated for venereal diseases and drinking ailments. Nearly every prostitute in this district is afflicted by both."

"So most on that floor are prostitutes?"

"Yes, entirely on that floor, and many, indeed most, in the first floor ward."

I appreciated his candor about the patients and their conditions, and I had a growing sense that Dr. Bartlett would treat me as a colleague. I had feared that, as the granddaughter of Lady Westfield, I would be shielded from the actualities of Whitechapel Hospital.

The fourth floor had no wards, only a laboratory and two offices: Dr. Bartlett's office, and the office of the other founder of Whitechapel Hospital, Dr. Robert Buck. According to Dr. Bartlett, Dr. Buck was more scientist than medical doctor and spent much of his time in the laboratory, pursuing his research alongside medical students and other physicians.

"So you have medical students here?" I asked him when we were seated in his office.

"Yes, a few." From behind his desk, Dr. Bartlett lit a pipe. The sweet smell soon filled the air. I had expected a grander place for him, but his office was cramped—a single bookcase covered almost an entire wall, and there was only one window. Perched on a small stand behind him was a human skull; pen scratches and notes had been drawn about the cranium.

Dr. Bartlett tapped some of his pipe ash into a little dish. "Most universities are still deficient in educating medical students on surgical procedures, emphasizing mainly theoretical knowledge. I like to provide medical students and new physicians with the opportunity to gain experience in surgeries and deliveries."

He eyed me curiously. "And there is no hierarchy between myself and the other physicians. Feel free to inquire of them if you have difficulties arise."

"Are you not here always?"

A foolish question—of course he would not spend all of

his hours at that hospital. But I felt a stupid panic at the thought of working alone with those angry, overworked nurses on the first floor.

"Mostly, but I do lecture some terms at Oxford. And there are always conferences."

"Of course."

As he continued smoking the pipe, he stared at me. It was a distracted stare, as if he did not see me at all, and yet I felt penetrated. I became transfixed, and the fibers of my muscles seemed to quiver a little. The sensation did not hurt, yet I felt a rising defensive urge to fight or to run. But I could name no real danger in Dr. Bartlett's office.

Sister Josephine's appearance in the doorway broke the spell. Agitated and flushed very red, she thrust a nurse's uniform into my arms without giving me a single glance.

"We are about to have a delivery," she snapped. "And it's a breech. Dr. Siddal is already there trying to turn the child."

Calmly, Dr. Bartlett set aside his pipe and stood, tall behind the desk. "I'll be there momentarily." He paused, "We'll try to turn the baby, but if I cannot...we might have to perform a caesarian."

Sister Josephine's forehead tensed.

"But..."

"It might be *necessary*. And best."

She said nothing more, but left, almost running down the hall.

Dr. Bartlett began rolling up his sleeves, revealing

surprisingly muscled arms for his age. "You are welcome to come, Abbie. Though I understand if you choose not to."

It seemed unthinkable to not attend the delivery.

"I'll be there."

The moment I had changed into the nurse's uniform, I returned to the first floor. I rushed toward Dr. Bartlett, who stood with Josephine at the back of the ward just outside the curtained area.

A scream sounded from behind the curtain as I approached. Dread rose within me.

My heart twisted upon itself when a young man stepped out from behind the curtain, nearly colliding with me. He was not any more than twenty-three or twenty-four, and remarkably handsome; his brown eyes shone shrewdly under his unruly dark hair. Something in his expression, a sort of craggy self-assurance, stirred and shocked me like a plunge into an icy pool of water. The shock was such that I gasped.

He locked eyes with me for a second. I felt a hot blush upon my cheeks and hoped that my rush of feelings had not been too transparent.

"Abbie, meet Dr. William Siddal," Dr. Bartlett said quickly. "William, Lady Westfield's granddaughter, Arabella Sharp."

William cast me a small nod, but otherwise barely

considered me. Like Dr. Bartlett, his sleeves were rolled to the elbows. Water soaked his shirt. Blood smudged his arms.

"Any progress, William?" Dr. Bartlett asked.

"None at all."

Nothing could have prepared me for the sight of the patient. She was young, no more than fifteen. Propped upward on the delivery table, her legs were spread wide underneath a sheet, her raggedy dress cut up to her chest. Water soaked the sheets. Her hair had been entirely slicked away from her forehead by sweat. The girl's face, disfigured by smallpox scars and impossibly pale, had an almost inhuman appearance.

She emitted only short sharp gasps now—gasps sounding more terrible than the earlier scream.

"She was brought in an hour ago, her water already broken," William explained, standing at the bottom of the bed. "I found immediately that it was a breech. I have not been able to turn the child, and a breech delivery is out of the question. Her pelvic bones are too narrow, I believe, to allow even a normal delivery."

Flushed and perspiring, William moved aside for Dr. Bartlett.

Dr. Bartlett's face remained marble-smooth as he bent to turn the girl's baby. Before reaching inside of her, he addressed her gently. "Sweet child." She rolled her eyeballs—red with broken vessels—downward toward him. The gasping ceased a little.

"You are going to be fine," he said to her. "You will have

a few minutes of discomfort, even some pain, but everything will be fine."

He turned to me. "Abbie, please sponge her forehead." He nodded toward a basin of water and a cloth nearby.

"William"—Dr. Bartlett's hand was still inside the girl as he spoke—"please try to manipulate the fetus from the outside."

She cried out in pain.

While I sponged the girl's forehead, Dr. Bartlett tried to turn the child. William pressed on various parts of the abdomen, all while observing Dr. Bartlett's movements.

The girl screamed again, this time even more piercingly.

I continued to sponge her face.

"I hope you're all right, Miss Sharp," William said irritably, mockingly, though he did not even glance at me. "You can leave at any time."

"I'm fine." I felt annoyed, viscerally annoyed— annoyed with him for his arrogance, annoyed with myself for finding him so handsome. And I felt guilty. My feelings of annoyance and attraction for him felt unorthodox in this moment where all of my energies should have been focused on the girl.

Dr. Bartlett's gaze remained focused. He seemed to have reached a decision. Calmly, he pulled his hand out of the girl and wiped it on a towel. "William, might I see you outside of the curtain for a moment?"

I was certain that the girl, nearly unconscious now from pain, could not hear them, but I could. They spoke in near whispers.

"We're going to have to do a caesarean, William."

"I agree."

"I am going to let you do it—the horizontal cut, *not* the vertical one, remember?"

Through the thin curtain, I could see their profiles. William shook his head vigorously.

"She's probably going to die. But if *I* do it, she'll certainly die. I have never done one before."

"You must try at some point. I'll guide you through it."

A long pause.

"All right, *all right.*"

I stared at the girl's face under my own. She trembled, and her eyes bulged before she resumed the violent gasping. I had never considered that she would die. I pitied her as I wondered what her story had been, who the father of her child was, how forsaken she was, and if anyone missed her now.

William stepped inside the curtain again. Josephine had left with Dr. Bartlett to find supplies and other attending nurses, and we were now alone with the girl.

With fearsome intensity, William ran his hand through his sweat-soaked curls and contemplated the girl. Then, in a single movement, he pulled the sheet that was across her legs away and cut off the rest of her dress.

At that point, Dr. Bartlett, Josephine, and two other nurses returned.

The nurses carried a tray upon which rested several instruments: scalpels, a small thin knife, scissors, many other instruments that I did not recognize, several lengths of dressing, large needles, heavy thread, and jars of liquid, including a jar of iodine and one of carbolic acid.

"We are going to have to cut your baby out," Dr. Bartlett said quietly to the girl. "My nurse will give you some medicine and you will not feel pain. Everything will be all right in the end."

He patted her shoulder.

At this point, even Dr. Bartlett could not calm her. In what was nothing less than a miraculous burst of energy, she began screaming, "I'm 'bout to die! I'm 'bout to die!" She grabbed at me violently.

"Hush! Hold her *still*!" William shouted to me and one of the attending nurses. I frowned at him, although he was too focused to notice. Such an explosion would only escalate the girl's hysteria.

After Josephine rushed forward to administer the ether, the girl fell asleep almost immediately.

William waited until a nurse had disinfected the girl's abdomen and then moved the scalpel lightly across her pelvic region, deciding the proper place to cut.

"That's fine," Dr. Bartlett whispered from where he stood behind William. "*There*." William had placed the scalpel on one section of the girl's lower pelvic region.

A thin red line of blood followed William's cut. I looked away then, not wanting to see the layers of fat and intestines that would be exposed.

After what seemed like several minutes, I heard a squeal.

"Perfect. A baby girl!" Dr. Bartlett exclaimed as William severed the umbilical cord.

Josephine efficiently whisked away the bloody, screaming infant.

I had never witnessed a birth and felt a little thrill at the delivery. Even William's mouth twitched a bit in the hint of a smile. I experienced a strange envy that he had been the one to bring that baby into the world.

But then his face darkened.

"*Damn!*" He stared at the girl's chalky face and then down at her incision.

I looked down and saw that the girl did not appear to be breathing.

"*Damn! Damn!*" William probed the incision wound with his finger.

"She's hemorrhaging," Dr. Bartlett responded quietly.

"From where?! Can we suture it?"

"By the time we find it, she will be gone." Dr. Bartlett felt the girl's pulse. "She's dying." He laid his hand on William's shoulder. "There is nothing that can be done."

I watched as life drained from the girl. Her breathing ceased, and then she became fearfully still.

William continued staring at the incision wound.

"This happens, William."

The girl had been a stranger to me, but I felt a little of the familiar, brutal emptiness I had experienced when I had watched Mother die.

"Go home, and take the rest of the day off," Dr. Bartlett

gently commanded William. "Sleep. And if it has stopped raining, take a long walk."

William did not say a word. Abruptly, he washed and dried his hands, snapped the curtain open, and stormed away from the delivery area.

Dr. Bartlett sighed, felt the girl's pulse again, and then shut her eyelids.

I felt frozen, unable to move. My throat burned painful and parched as I stood near her head, clutching the sponge in my hand.

"Abbie, why don't you go home, too? I am sorry that your first morning had to be so difficult. I understand if you do not wish to come back."

"I do. If it's all right, I would like to return tomorrow." After what I had just witnessed, my immediate answer sounded strange even to me. But I also felt that it was the only possible answer.

Dr. Bartlett glanced up from the corpse to look at me, his expression unreadable.

"Certainly. But do please go home now. You have done enough for today."

The nurses entered, and, after methodically covering the body with a sheet, they rolled away the bed.

The inside of the hospital had been so muggy that the autumn wind shocked me as I stepped out of the building to meet Dr. Bartlett's carriage, and I lost my footing.

In a single instant, I slipped, falling in three painful thuds down the nine wet concrete steps of Whitechapel Hospital for Women.

Four

My right foot, which had borne most of the burden of the fall, throbbed in pain. When I tried to stand, a firelike sensation shot up from my right ankle, bringing me to my knees. I looked up to see Dr. Bartlett's carriage approaching and tried to stand again. The pain in my foot was sharp, unbearable. My knees quaked violently.

I fell again.

This time someone caught me before I hit against the pavement.

My rear was only a few inches above the ground when he caught me; my legs had splayed awkwardly in front of me. The young man who held me was grasping me under the armpits, and when I looked upward, I saw the sun cracking through morning rainclouds and silhouetting his face. All of this only accentuated his striking, ethereal appearance—a pale complexion, blue eyes, and thick blond hair that framed his face like a halo.

"I think it is only sprained, but still, you had better not put your weight on it. Here, I'll carry you."

The carriage had just arrived.

"That is not necessary—my ride is here. I'm fine."

"Nonsense," he said. "You should not walk on the foot at all at the moment." Though tall and slender, he picked me up effortlessly, before I could say another word in protest.

"Where are you going?" he asked.

"Kensington."

"I can accompany you there."

Feeling a strange mix of irritation and gratitude for this stranger who was carrying me, I asked the glaring question.

"Who are you?"

"Simon St. John. I work here at the hospital. And you are?" His light blue eyes, kind and yet self-assured, cut into me. His voice was as soft and refined as gossamer threads.

Before I could answer, the driver dismounted to open the door for us. When I saw William departing from the hospital, I felt humiliated by my position; it was so very "damsel-in-distress."

Unfortunately, William saw us, and a great smile spread across his face while he approached. "How nice of you, Simon, to assist Dr. Bartlett's new young ward Miss Arabella Sharp, the granddaughter of *Lady* Charlotte Westfield."

I knew by the tension settling in the atmosphere that Simon and William were not fond of one another.

Simon ignored the sarcasm and carefully placed me on a seat in the carriage before turning to William. "She fell down the front steps leaving the hospital. I think it is merely a sprained ankle—badly sprained, but not broken. Still, I'm going to see her home."

"Yes, of course, this is no time to scrimp on chivalry."

Simon raised one eyebrow and kept his voice low and very level. "I'm going to accompany her home. In all seriousness, William, are the wards calm enough that I might be away for a bit? I will return as quickly as possible."

William glanced at me for the first time in the conversation, his eyes narrowed, but out of concern or just distracted interest, I could not tell. "Dr. Buck has just arrived, as well as a few medical students. So it should be safe for you to take her home. In fact, I am going home for the day."

"Fine," Simon said abruptly. After shutting the door behind us, he thumped on the carriage side and the vehicle lurched forward.

Through the window, I watched William walk away. His brows furrowed, and I guessed that he was thinking about the tragic delivery. His moody transparency captivated me to the point where I felt as if a cord connected us. I wanted to sever it, but I confess I continued to gawk until William crossed Whitechapel Road and was entirely out of my line of vision.

Simon, meanwhile, had knelt in front of me and gently

removed the boot on my right foot. His fingers felt cool and soothing, even through my thick stockings.

"You are a physician?"

Simon nodded, but said nothing as he examined my foot. All of his movements were quick and very graceful. I observed his sculpted profile and thought again that he possessed a decidedly celestial appearance, like a figure in a Blake painting.

"Does this hurt?" He bent my foot gently forward.

"Not much."

"And this?" He bent it slightly sideways.

I grimaced.

Gingerly, he put the boot back on my foot and sat on the seat across from me. "It is sprained, Miss Sharp, likely a torn ligament. It will probably swell and hurt very badly for the next day. But keep it elevated, wrapped in cold compresses, and it should feel better by Monday."

"Have you worked at the hospital long?" I desired to change the subject away from my injury.

"Only a few months—I passed my examinations in the spring."

"So you are finished with school?"

"With medical school, but I am not yet finished with seminary."

"Is not medical school difficult enough?"

He smiled. When he looked at me, I found his gaze to be irritatingly impenetrable—his eyes lovely pools that I could not quite see the bottom of.

"You are quite right Miss Sharp. But I feel that the

humanist responsibilities demanded of me by seminary make me more effective as a physician in this district."

He peered out the window as he spoke. "Reverend John Perkins, whom I studied under at Oxford, is the first to accumulate data from censuses in the area. The numbers of those in the East End who die from disease, alcoholism, starvation even, are startling. Most infants born in the district never live beyond their first year. I decided when I began my medical studies that I might be more effective as a Whitechapel physician if I cultivated a more holistic view of my patient. Seminary seemed logical."

I felt myself smile a bit at Simon's formality and zeal. "You believe that most physicians do *not* care about the patient in the holistic manner that you describe?"

"With the exception of Dr. Bartlett, I truly believe that most physicians at Whitechapel Hospital view the institution as a mere laboratory."

A shadow crossed his face, and I guessed that he was thinking of William.

"And you, why are you here?" he asked me, pointedly.

I sighed. The truth seemed best.

"I do nothing that matters in my life with Grandmother. I've lived with her for two months, and she is now requiring that I work at the hospital—punishment for my unrest. But it's not punishment at all. I've had very little exercise—mental or otherwise—since arriving at Kensington Court."

Simon smiled in cool amusement. "Did you know that I'm your neighbor?"

"Excuse me?" Simon did not seem like a typical Kensington resident.

"My mother, Elinor St. John, lives a mere block from Lady Westfield. She's a very good friend of your grandmother. In fact, we have known Lady Westfield since my childhood. You probably have not met my mother yet, as she is spending much of this year at our seaside residence."

I felt almost too astonished to speak. "I hope I did not offend..."

Simon waved his hand in gentle dismissal. "Not at all. You have no idea how alike we are in our sentiments."

The carriage stopped.

"Truly, I..."

"I insist." He lifted me into his arms.

I felt more humiliated now than when William had found me in such a position. If I returned to Grandmother, wounded on my first day of work, she would feel more than mildly vindicated.

Simon knocked, and the door swung open. I panicked when I saw that it was Ellen who had opened it.

Her freckled face puckered and her eyes bulged before the shrieking began: "*Lady Westfield! Lady Westfield! Dr. St. John is here with th' Miss Abbie! She's 'urt, she is! Dreadful 'urt!*"

She turned, running upstairs to fetch Grandmother.

Simon cast a wry smile down upon me, and I felt, in that moment, an affinity with him. He seemed to know Ellen's nature quite well. Unaffected by her hysterics, Simon stepped inside, still carrying me in his arms.

Richard arrived in the front entrance hall to attend to us as Ellen screamed from the second floor landing.

"Richard, would you be so good as to bring Miss Sharp some warm wine or brandy?" Simon asked as he carried me toward the parlor.

The moment Simon settled me onto the couch, Richard arrived with the brandy. As I sipped it, I saw that Grandmother had stepped into the parlor doorway. Her beaky face remained shadowed as the sun glared through a window behind her.

"It is merely a sprained ankle," Simon said, standing and turning to face her. "She fell down some steps today." He repeated to her the directions he had just given me regarding its care—rest, cool compresses.

Grandmother stepped a bit away from the glare. "Thank you, Simon. I will make certain that she rests over the next week."

"But that will not be necessary. I am returning to the hospital on Monday," I said, feeling already emboldened by the warm rush of brandy. I sat up straighter on the couch. "Dr. St. John said that I would be feeling better after the weekend, so I see no reason, if that is indeed the case, as to why I should not return to work on Monday."

Simon considered me coolly, and I saw the corner of his mouth curve—very slightly.

Grandmother glared at me and then turned her attention back to Simon. "That *cannot* be the case, Simon. I mean, she is not used to hard labor and must allow for recovery time from this injury. Am I not correct?"

Simon's eyes remained on me, "I see no reason why, if she is not in pain, that she should *not* return to work on Monday."

I smiled at him, grateful, and finished off the glass of brandy.

Grandmother exhaled in exasperation. "Fine, Simon."

She hated losing—even small battles.

"How is your mother?" she asked Simon suddenly. "When might I expect to see her again?"

"Mother plans to return sometime before Christmas." His reply came out kind, solicitous.

"We shall have dinner then. I have missed her during these months."

I could tell by Grandmother's demeanor that she respected Simon and seemed particularly fond of him.

"She would be delighted to see you again. She mentions you in many of her letters." Simon glanced at the clock over the mantelpiece. "You must excuse me, Lady Westfield. It is time that I return to work, and I am certain that Miss Sharp needs to rest."

"Yes, yes." Grandmother seemed almost irritated when he brought up my name.

"Goodbye." He bowed slightly to her and then to me.

The moment when Grandmother and I were alone, she came over to stand above me. I braced myself for one of her lectures, but she surprised me. She bent over me, and then lightly brushed my hair away from my forehead. Her touch was methodical, her expression one of concern. Then she sat on the edge of the couch, her hand swiping away another lock of hair. In an entirely rare moment of transparency, I saw her search my face, and I knew that she sought my mother. She was looking for shadows of Caroline—it was a faulty but sincere affection.

"You are pale, Arabella, even after the drink," she said finally, in her most guarded voice.

"It is only a sprained ankle. I have had sprained ankles before—it will be better in a few days."

She seemed to hear nothing that I said.

"You may spend the night here in the parlor, if you wish. You should not climb the stairs with your foot."

She felt awkward; in her awkwardness, she became efficient. Without another word, she swiftly closed the blinds, and, shutting the door behind her, left me alone in the parlor.

As the fire in the fireplace died down and evening set in, I thought of how this move to Kensington should not have jarred me so much—my previous life had been marked by near constant flux. After my father drowned in a swimming accident when I was still an infant, Mother and I had lived in Edinburgh, Sussex, and Dorchester while she worked as a governess. Our time in Dublin had been our longest stay in one place—seven years—as she tutored the children of the wealthy Edgeworth family. Each day, while Mother gave the children lessons, I completed my own studies in the cottage we shared behind the family's mansion.

If I finished early, I played outside the Edgeworth property's gates with some of the local children. During those times, I learned the hierarchies among Dublin street youth. If I wanted to play in certain circles, I had to learn some of the local activities, namely fighting. Sometimes the fighting was play, sometimes self-defense. But in seven years, I learned a great deal about it.

That life had been so textured compared to these past two months with Grandmother, which had made me listless and bored. I still ached for Mother, and fought feelings of guilt that I could do nothing for her when she fell ill. She had caught a violent case of dysentery that had been going around the city; it took her life within two days. Looking back, I wished that I had paid more attention to the increasing number of episodes or seizures she had had in the weeks before her death. But she had suffered from those my whole life.

Mother had an interest in art, and sometimes when she worked on a painting she would become lost to me, snap into a fixed stare. Sometimes she went months without having an episode, but they had intensified shortly before her death. Only two weeks before she died, we had been working in our small garden together and she fell back hard, her sunbonnet falling off her head. She stared at the sky for a full ten seconds as I called her name. I feared she was having a seizure. But she seemed to see something elsewhere; she seemed focused on something I could not see. Then, suddenly, she came out of the trance and returned to normal. Her explanation was that she had just become overheated. I thought that she might have had a touch of epilepsy, but now, ever since my bizarre encounter with the pickpocket, I was considering whether she might have had visions.

I shivered as I thought about the pickpocket; that experience had been a crack, a tear, in my reality. The robes, the chanting, the child's radically different expression—none of it made any sense. Nothing like that had ever happened to me, and I wondered, once again, if I was losing my mind. Yet whether Mother had had visions or not, I still wished that I could talk to her about what had happened to me, because I knew that she would understand.

As I became sleepier, my thoughts turned to my first day at the hospital. Dr. Bartlett's invitation seemed to be an open door to a place where I could be active again and move forward from my loss. He intrigued me. Our discussion about Whitechapel Hospital, the future possibility of building a school for children, of expanding the wards, all stirred within me a desire to be part of that establishment.

Eventually, the ticking clock and parlor shadows became increasingly lost to me, and I fell asleep. Like darting minnows, scenes from the day drifted in and out of my consciousness. William's focused expression as he performed the caesarean. Simon's face above my own when he caught me after my fall. Ellen's hysterical outburst upon my return. The girl's face as she died.

All of these memories blurred and faded until I found myself in a more solid dream facing the front doors of Whitechapel Hospital. The road was abandoned, the night cool and foggy. I could see my breath puffing out into the air surrounding me as I stared up at the building.

A window on the third floor opened. I felt my blood freeze as a man crawled headfirst down the brick front wall of the hospital. It was an impossible act, and, even in the darkness, I had to cover my mouth to keep from crying out in terror. I could not see his face; he wore black and his figure was shadowed. He turned his head slightly to his right toward me, and it was then that I knew he was aware of my presence. Whatever his purpose, my intuition told me that it was predatory. I tried to sink into the shadows of the hospital entrance, and I glanced toward the front doors, wondering if they were locked. When I looked back, he was gone. Vanished.

I felt hot breath on my neck, and, horrified, I knew that he stood behind me.

I awoke, choking on a scream. Chills shook my body, and yet sweat dripped down my brows.

The clock over the fireplace showed that it was three o'clock in the morning.

Five

The next morning, with great effort, I met Grandmother at the breakfast table. I felt exhausted, having
not slept well after the early morning nightmare—it had
seemed so vivid. Also, my foot was still swollen from the
day before, and it hurt quite a bit. It would be impossible
for me to return to the hospital before Monday. Nonetheless, I forced myself to walk on it. The more I walked, the
better it felt.

Grandmother sat across from me, reading a note from
Violet and barely looking up except to take a sip of tea.
On the east side of the dining room, immediately to my
left, Mother's portrait loomed against rose-patterned wallpaper. Sometimes I wondered why Grandmother kept the
portrait up in the room where we ate most of our meals.

Mother had been about my age when the portrait had been painted. She looked strikingly similar to me—except that she was beautiful. Her red hair escaped the confines of a ribbon, and I saw my dark eyes in hers. A chill swept through me as I remembered my dream, and I took a burning sip of coffee. She was rotting and wasted now. Nothing could change that.

Grandmother tapped her fork impatiently against her plate. When I glanced at her, I saw that she was not irritated with me; rather, she was staring through the dining room window at Ellen, who still clutched the milk bottles as she chattered ceaselessly with another maid. Their gossip must have been enticing, as Ellen kept clapping her hand over her mouth and shrieking in astonishment.

When Ellen finally ended her conversation to run inside, she burst through the front door.

"We're all going to be murdered in our beds! Richard! Lady Westfield! Miss Abbie!"

Grandmother almost dropped her teacup. Ellen, in her hysteria, *did* drop a milk bottle, shattering it on the floor. Jupe ran around the corner, lapping eagerly at the white puddle.

"Ellen!" Grandmother pressed her fingers to her temples, exasperated. "Must you affront us with this drama so early in the day?"

"I'm sorry, Ma'am. But a woman was *killed* last night, a 'hor it seems from the likes of her."

I saw Grandmother's shoulders straighten at Ellen's language. Ellen had only been in her employ since the time

I had arrived, and I did not anticipate that Grandmother would keep her for very long.

"'Er body was in the East End at Buck's Row, near the Whitechapel Hospital where Miss Arabella works."

Both Grandmother and I looked sharply at Ellen. The memory of the predator in my nightmare came back upon me full force.

Now that Ellen had our attention, her dramatics only intensified. "She had her stomach cut out, 'er throat slashed!" Ellen tried to reenact the murder by slicing at her own abdomen and neck with her finger in the air.

Richard had just entered the room. He began mopping up the spilled milk.

Grandmother turned to him. "Is this true, Richard?"

I flashed a look at Richard and barely shook my head. Apart from my own horror at the murder, I feared that Grandmother would forbid me from working at the hospital any longer.

Richard saw my look. "Yes, madam. But the lady, with her lifework…" He cleared his throat. "Death by murder is not an uncommon end for many of them."

Grandmother turned, staring at me in apprehension.

"Grandmother, I would like to continue working at Whitechapel Hospital. I've been planning to return on Monday. My first day was… enlightening."

"You nearly broke your ankle."

I had no plans to tell her about the caesarean and the death of the girl. The sprained ankle, as far as Grandmother knew, was the worst of my experiences.

After a moment of serious contemplation, she waved her hand a little. Her response shocked me. "Never mind, Arabella. Julian Bartlett is an old friend, and you may continue to work for him."

She cast a pained glance at the portrait of my mother. I knew that her relationship with me was based on a careful balance between directing my life in the way she would have it go and not driving me away.

"However, although you may continue to work there, you cannot neglect your current social obligations."

Grandmother took a sip of tea as Richard finished mopping up the floor. Ellen walked in with a vase of roses. She seemed calmer. A little. She dropped a pair of pruning scissors twice as she arranged the flowers in the vase on the sideboard.

Grandmother put on her spectacles as she peered more closely at the note she had been reading: "We have a dinner party at Violet's next Wednesday evening. I want you to meet a young man who will be there."

I narrowed my eyes at her. It was starting: her quest to find me a husband.

Dr. Bartlett met me in his carriage on Monday morning. Though he said nothing, I wondered if his presence meant that Grandmother had contacted him.

He inquired politely about my ankle, and we exchanged small talk as the carriage jolted its way through the early morning traffic. He opened the carriage window and as we turned onto Whitechapel Road, he lit a cigar. Before the smoke wafted about the carriage interior, I thought that he smelled pleasant—of candle smoke and tea leaves.

The story of the Buck's Row murder had been widely popular news, even in Kensington. Whitechapel Hospital worked so closely with such women, and the murder had taken place in the vicinity, so I wondered if the victim had ever been a patient. Unfortunately, I could not bring myself to broach the topic with Dr. Bartlett.

The moment Dr. Bartlett and I entered the hospital, two uniformed constables and a Scotland Yard Inspector greeted us.

Dr. Bartlett nodded politely at them as he helped to remove my coat.

"Abberline," the Inspector said as he shook Dr. Bartlett's hand. He was tall, stout, appeared to be in his mid-forties, and had a notepad tucked under his arm.

He acknowledged me with only a slight nod.

"Ah yes," Dr. Bartlett replied, "and Barry and John, your two excellent constables, who have proved quite helpful with our unruly patients."

John chucked. "A nice way of putting it, doc. I think you mean *drunk* patients."

Abberline cleared his throat, silencing his constable. He seemed stiff, overly professional as he removed a pencil from his pocket and began scratching notes on the pad with his thick fingers. "We have a few questions to ask you about Polly Nichols, murdered early on Friday morning."

Inspector Abberline seemed almost apologetic as he questioned Dr. Bartlett. "You are by no means a suspect. But it did come to our attention that Miss Nichols had been a patient here once."

"Yes. She had a severe problem with alcohol when she came into our care and, unfortunately, proved resistant to our rehabilitation practice. It is my policy to insist that patients cooperate with our methods. Miss Nichols did not, and she left our care twice to return to the streets."

A child began screaming in the nearby ward.

Abberline shuffled his feet awkwardly. "When did this happen?"

"The second time occurred the night before her murder, probably only hours before her death."

Abberline raised his bushy eyebrows as he continued to scratch notes into the pad.

"So your nurses might have been the last witnesses to see her alive before she met the murderer?"

"That's very likely."

"Might we see all medical records that you have on Polly Nichols?"

"Of course. They are in my office. Please follow me."

Before leaving, Dr. Bartlett gave me instructions to help Josephine in the newborn nursery.

As Dr. Bartlett and the constables turned to ascend the stairs, I saw Abberline pause to stare at me, penetratingly, as if I had suddenly become significant to him. He was too focused, an incarnate bloodhound caught up in a scent.

The scrutiny unnerved me, and before turning to pull an apron off a peg, I frowned at him.

As I struggled to tie the strings, I heard a voice near my ear.

"And Lady Westfield's granddaughter finds herself suddenly in the midst of a real-life penny dreadful novel: a patient in the hospital where she volunteers is murdered. Disemboweled instantly, throat sliced open to the spinal cord, the killer so quick in fact that Miss Polly Nichols did not even have time to scream."

I turned to find myself facing Dr. William Siddal.

"But what *will* young Abbie Sharp do? Is she safe? Will the killer come for *her*?"

I took a deep breath, gathering my mental weaponry. I needed to deal with William Siddal. Immediately.

"I have read many penny dreadfuls, William, but find most to be highly flawed."

I tried to pass him.

He blocked me.

I tried to get around him again, but he stepped to the other side and blocked me.

I felt my face redden.

He narrowed his eyes. "Don't lie, Miss Sharp, it's not becoming. My guess is that you do read many penny dreadfuls, but exclusively the ones written for *ladies*."

"Never."

"Vampires?" he asked skeptically.

"Always. Most recently, I've read John Polidori's *The*

Vampyre, and I'm getting ready to start another novel about a female vampire. *Carmilla*, I think it's called."

He smirked, still testing me. "So you like it when *women* bite?"

I leveled my gaze at him so that he would know I understood his insinuation exactly.

"Perhaps."

His eyes widened—a little wickedly, I thought.

"Now, will you excuse me?"

A small smile twisted upon his face, and he stepped aside.

I felt more than a little satisfaction when I walked away. After my terrible day last Thursday, my confidence was returning in small spurts.

When I reached the nursery, which was through the door behind the delivery area, I found Sister Josephine dressing the body of a dead baby. As she slipped the tiny white arms through a frock, she shook her head. "Mother died during the birth last night. The baby lived only for five hours afterward. Too small, born too early."

I felt a small shock when the always efficient Josephine kissed the infant's forehead before placing her in a small pine box.

But then Sister Josephine became herself again. As another worker took the box away, she turned and surveyed my dress critically.

"Your apron is clean."

"Yes."

She chuckled. "It won't be when you're finished here.

Select a bottle and let's get started. We have twenty to feed and change before noon."

The room surrounding us was full of squalling infants. Most were newborns, but the oldest looked to be around one year—almost at the age to walk. I picked up one of the milk-filled bottles—a glass bulb with a rubber tube extension. I would have to learn how to maneuver the contraption. All the infants screamed, and it was difficult to decide where to start.

"Where is the child of the girl who died after the caesarean last Thursday?"

"Right in front of you."

I looked down into the nearest crib at a red-faced and crying baby. Her wail rang out raspy, less strong than the others.

"*That* one had a name. Dr. Siddal named her before he left last Thursday—Lizzie is what he called her."

I found it mildly surprising that William would take the time to name an infant, but Lizzie seemed like a good name. I took her into my arms, and, sitting in one of the hard rocking chairs next to Josephine, I began trying to get her to suckle the bottle. But she pursed her mouth into a tiny "o" and grasped the air with her lips, not quite getting a tight-enough suck on the tube. She struggled and kicked her legs in frustration.

Josephine shook her head. "She was born too early. She'll suckle best from a breast. I'll try to find a wet nurse for her."

"What will happen to her?"

Josephine shrugged. "She needs to eat. I'll try her with the bottle when I'm done with this one, but, like I said, she's too young."

The baby in Josephine's arms had already gulped its entire bottle. She passed that infant to me and I gave her Lizzie. Sister Josephine had no better luck with Lizzie than I had. She finally gave up, saying that when we were finished she would set about trying to find one of the lactating mothers on the first floor to nurse the child.

When I emerged from the nursery in the afternoon, I felt exhausted. My shoulders reeked of spit-up, and my hands, though I had washed them several times, still seemed saturated by the smell of feces. A foul urine stain marked my apron, a souvenir from a baby boy I had bathed.

The ward of women and children seemed just as chaotic as the nursery. I saw William, with several other physicians or medical students, walking hurriedly in and out of the ward, inspecting patients and writing notes. Nurses chased children, changed bedsheets, and administered medicine. As I scanned the room, I saw in the bed farthest away from me, nearest to the front entrance, a woman holding a too-still infant. She seemed to be in despair.

Simon St. John sat in a chair by her bed.

I had not seen him since the day I fell. I remembered how kind and attentive he had been to me, and I watched him with interest. Though I could not hear what he said to the woman, I saw his long, graceful fingers smoothing the swaddling blanket of the dead infant she held. After a moment, he took the baby from her and began walking toward me.

"Abbie, I am glad to see you back at work. Your ankle is mostly healed?"

"Yes, it hurts very little now." I tried not to look at the dead baby in his arms.

"Would you mind sitting near Mrs. Rose Elliot?" He nodded back in the direction of the infant's mother. "She is heartbroken. This is her third stillborn child. And her marriage is truly terrible. Dr. Bartlett is trying to find a way to help her."

"Yes, certainly."

He took the baby back to the nursery area.

When I sat in the chair by Rose Elliot's bed, I did not say anything. She had begun sobbing again, and I did not see how any words of mine could help the situation. But I was there, and I hoped that my presence mattered.

She lifted one hand to wipe her eyes. It was then that I saw the bruises on her arm.

At almost the same time, the front hospital doors slammed open.

"You can't be in here, Mr. Elliot!" I heard a nurse shouting at the intruder as he pushed past her.

"Yes I can! You have my wife in here!"

The man spotted the woman in the bed beside me and began storming toward us. He was tall, burly, and sported a thick mustache.

"Get up! Get up, Rose!"

"No, Jess," Rose replied meekly.

I scanned the room. Dr. Bartlett was nowhere in sight, nor the constables who had accompanied him this morning. I saw several medical students in the far part of the ward, but they looked inadequate for a confrontation.

"Get up, Rose! Now!"

Then I saw William sprinting toward us.

As Jess lunged at Rose, William restrained him, pinning his arms behind his back. Jess cursed and shook him off.

Calmly, William spoke. "Sir, you have to leave. *Now.* She is under our protection."

"I will *not* leave! Rose, you can't just run away and think that I won't find you. Two days away is too much! Get up, now!"

He lunged at her again, this time to grab her out of the bed.

I stood.

William once again tried to pull Jess away from us, but the big man swung at William, who ducked instantly, barely avoiding the blow.

"Get out of my way!" I felt spittle hit my face when Jess shouted at me.

"No."

"Abbie!" William hissed from behind the enraged man. Then, through clenched teeth, he mouthed, *"Don't be foolish."*

Jess swung at me, and I ducked. Before he could swing

again, I sent the heel of my hand into his lower jaw. The jaw cracked and he fell backwards onto the floor.

Constables Barry and John had finally arrived, rushing forward to arrest him, but then they saw that he was unconscious.

Everyone in the scene around us moved quickly—the nurses attended to Rose, and another young physician tried to revive Jess. He would need medical attention before he could be arrested. Curious children crowded close to see the excitement.

Only William stood frozen, staring at me—a delighted bewilderment marked his expression.

"*Where* did you learn that?"

"Dublin."

I had made an impression upon William, and, strangely, I did not care. It was time to leave. I took off my apron and placed it on a nearby peg.

Six

As I stepped outside the hospital, I saw Dr. Bartlett's carriage approaching from far down Whitechapel Road. My heart still beat wildly from my confrontation with Jess, and I could not stand still. I decided to walk down the street to meet the carriage.

I walked rapidly, stepping over puddles of water, broken glass. Remembering my chase with the pickpocket, I clutched my bag close to me.

Although I tried to stay focused upon my surroundings, I also thought about my nightmare. I had dreamt it early in the hours of Friday morning—the same time that the murder had happened. It had been vivid, lacking the fuzziness of other dreams. I had smelled and felt everything around me so clearly. Though the crawling man's face had been hidden in the shadows, I remember hearing his fingernails scrape on the gritty bricked front of the hospital. I had felt his breath on my neck. Even now I shivered thinking of it, and I clung to the hope that the timing of my nightmare had been mere coincidence.

Remembering Mother's episodes, those moments when she seemed trancelike, I wondered again whether she had seen visions. I had never been superstitious, and now I felt odd even considering the possibility that she might have had the "third eye," as I had heard some call it in Dublin. The vision I had experienced with the pickpocket, of the strange ritual, had jolted me, but the nightmare—the coincidental timing of this dream with the murder—frightened me into thinking that perhaps my visions might be rooted in real happenings.

Someone slammed into me so hard that I almost fell into the busy street.

"Get out of my shop, girl!" a grocer shouted at a young woman. He had just shoved her out of his shop into the street. "I *will* call the police if I catch you in here again!"

"Sorry, miss." As the girl apologized to me, she brushed some dirt off her skirt. I saw lumpy, heavy objects in her pockets—apples or plums. Her eyes narrowed at me when she saw that I had noticed her loot.

"Yes, I did just steal. But don't judge me. I haven't eaten in three days and that grocer and his porky wife can spare a few apples."

"I'm not judging you." I turned to resume my walk.

I heard her sniff. "Whatever."

I stopped as my own stomach growled. The girl seemed like a caustic tart, but I could not help feeling badly for her. Finding food was not a problem for me.

"Here." I turned back around toward her and dug in my bag for money.

"Don't take charity."

"But you'll steal?"

Her eyes burned in fury. I could see that she was torn between her own pride and her very real need for the money.

I shrugged and started to put the coins back in my purse.

"All right! I'll take them. But I'll find you, and I'll pay you back."

As she took the money, I noticed the raggedy state of her shawl and the sharp, thin nature of her features. Her accent was Irish, and I wondered how long she had been in the city.

A young man with a cap ran up to her, caught her elbow. "*There* you are, Mary! I got the job at the docks!" He picked her up and swung her around in the air three times. "We aren't goin' to starve."

He also had an Irish accent. Recent immigrants, I assumed. I wondered how long they had been here. Finding a job was certainly something to celebrate.

I had finally reached Dr. Bartlett's carriage. I waved at the driver and he stopped for me. Quickly I stepped into the carriage, so as to not interrupt the happy scene.

Once inside the carriage, my mind plunged back into thoughts of my mother and the visions. I was hungry and exhausted, but everything in me recoiled from going to Kensington at the moment. It was Monday afternoon, which meant that Violet and Catherine would be at the house for tea and cribbage. I would be expected to visit with them, at least for a little while. Even five minutes seemed like too much.

But where to go?

I needed to be alone with my own thoughts for a little while. As the carriage progressed, I knew I had to make a decision. Highgate Cemetery, one of the quietest places in London, instantly came to mind. Without thinking any further, I called out to the driver, telling him I had plans to meet Lady Westfield in the Highgate area that afternoon. I felt relief when he asked no questions.

I entered the open front gates of the west part of the cemetery. The place was heavily shrouded in trees, encircled by a wrought-iron fence and thick shrubbery. The busy noise of the streets disappeared as I stepped inside.

I began wandering along the first path in front of me and observed the haunting, quirky beauty of the cemetery. I stood within a plethora of chalky, looming, unusually shaped tombstones. Gingerly, I touched a giant grave marker shaped like a lion before I spotted another one shaped like a dog. I had seen the place once before, immediately after arriving in the city with Grandmother. Even then, I had felt an immediate attraction to Highgate Cemetery; it had a strange aura about it, as if it channeled the cryptic, the unbidden.

I took side paths that meandered haphazardly, and, as I pushed away branches and brambles, I only vaguely worried about becoming lost. I saw and heard no one. After so much time in the city, where even the parks seemed crowded, I embraced the solitude.

Mother had mentioned Highgate Cemetery a few times. The tomb architecture had intrigued her, and she had shown me some of her sketches of the place. I felt her haunt me now, felt deeply the void she had left for me. I knew I was enough like Mother that I could not calmly accept the path in life that Grandmother would have for me: the upcoming dinner party, the person she wanted me to meet. I saw my life before me, flimsy and uncertain as a house of cards, and I knew that it was up to me to fight for what I wanted for my future. Mother had been an artist. I was not inclined in that direction, but I knew that I needed responsibilities and activities that stretched beyond running a household. I had only worked at Whitechapel Hospital for two days, but I felt excited about the challenges there and wondered about the possibility of working in a hospital for my vocation.

Many of the side paths I took led to isolated clusters of graves, lone family plots, or single mausoleums. These hidden graves were less attended to; some had even toppled. Yet these ruinous family plots particularly fascinated me.

Just as I pushed through a particularly brambly side path, emerging into a tiny clearing, I froze, mortified.

William Siddal crouched near me, pulling weeds away from the base of a tall headstone.

I tried to back away, back onto the path from whence I came before he saw me, but it was too late. He whirled around. Startled amusement spread across his face.

We said nothing as he stood abruptly, wiping some dirt off his hands with his shirttail.

"I … I was just leaving." I blushed and turned to return to the path.

"No, please don't go."

"How did you arrive here so quickly?" It was a stupid question. He must have come directly from the hospital; I could smell upon him acidic hospital odors—ammonia, chloroform. But I had *not* expected to find him here.

"Carriage," he smirked. "Same as you."

Even now I felt taken by his handsomeness. In spite of his stained and smelly clothing and his mildly disheveled appearance, William Siddal might have been a portrait model. I felt myself hold my breath at his approach. He made me self-conscious now in a way that I had never felt before.

Then William's arch expression reminded me that I would have to stay focused.

He reached his arm out toward my ear.

I bit my lip to keep from trembling, and I felt my cheeks burn as if they were on fire. I had never felt such a powerful attraction to anyone. My body's reaction to

William was even more disturbing given that I did not fully trust him.

Or even *like* him.

"A leaf."

He withdrew a crisp oak leaf from my hair, and when I saw his dark eyes shine a little, I felt horrified that he might have suspected my thoughts.

I took another step back, away from him.

I suddenly felt foolish. In my desire for solitude, I had arrived here, so many blocks away from Kensington, and the long quest had been futile. I had stupidly catapulted myself into an awkward encounter with William Siddal.

I moved to leave again, but he gently caught my elbow.

"Don't go. This is actually a pleasant surprise. You left the hospital too quickly, and I have felt ignited with curiosity about how you acquired, in *Dublin*, such a skilled knowledge of fighting. What you did today was superb."

I stared at him, trying to discern his tone—I thought I sensed a tinge of openness, perhaps even some friendliness.

"Come on, Abbie. Calm down a bit. You can talk with me while I finish pulling away these weeds from my father's lover's grave. The bloody workers never seem to make it back here."

I decided that nothing could be hurt by talking to William for a little while. I leaned against a nearby tomb, watching him pull weeds.

"Your father's lover?" I felt my interest piqued.

He didn't even look up. "Dublin *first*, Abbie."

"Friends in Dublin taught me to fight. We have dodgy streets there, just like any city."

"What kind of *friends* did you mingle with there?"

I chuckled a bit, but my memories of Dublin were still too weighted by Mother's death. I felt my eyeballs sting, and I swallowed. I could not cry in front of him.

William had taken a rag from his pocket to begin wiping away bird droppings and dirt from some of the writing on the grave marker. I could make out, over his shoulder, the name *Elizabeth Eleanor*. Then I saw the name *Rossetti* on the marker, as well as on other surrounding stones. My heart skipped a beat as I wondered if William had any connection to the Rossetti family, well-known for its writers and painters. It was not a common name.

But before I could ask anything, William continued with his questions.

"And why were you in Dublin?"

"I lived there for seven years."

"Why?"

I wished he would stop. "My mother was a governess for a family in that area."

"Lady Westfield's *daughter* had to find governess work in Ireland?"

"Enough."

He stood up, finished with the grave. As he examined my face, I saw perplexity cross his features. Then his expression turned slightly apologetic. I felt softened toward him, a little regretful for being so clipped.

"Your turn." I nodded toward the grave marker. "Who is she?"

He smiled roguishly before looking upward toward the sky.

"It is nearly five o'clock. Where does Grandmother Westfield live?"

"Kensington."

"That's what I thought. You have come a long way to find solitude, Abbie Sharp. Can I tell you the story on the way home?"

"I already know that you like to read, but do you enjoy twisted love stories?" William asked me.

We had just reached Swain's Lane, immediately outside the cemetery gates.

"Particularly."

We crossed the street into busier traffic, and William signaled a hansom cab for us. "My father was the writer and painter Dante Gabriel Rossetti—one of the founders of the Pre-Raphaelite group. Are you familiar with them or their work?"

My heart thumped loudly. "I adore Pre-Raphaelite art, both the paintings and the writings, although unfortunately I have not seen any of the actual paintings—only copies in books—but my mother taught me about their work. I love the paintings based on myths and stories, particularly the paintings of Ophelia and of Pandora opening the box."

William looked sideways at me. "So you know about the Pre-Raphaelites' shocking use of colors. You know of the accusations against them for heresy and eroticism in their portraits."

"Oh yes, of course."

Mother had been vehemently against any censorship in art; I remembered her eyes flashing when she spoke of the controversy surrounding Pre-Raphaelite art. She defended them, calling them "innovative" and "truthful."

"The model for many of the paintings was my father's lover and then wife, Elizabeth Siddal. She was the model for the Ophelia painting you mentioned. Her grave was among those that I attended back there."

"So she was your mother?"

"No, I never met Elizabeth—Lizzie, as he called her. She died a few years before my birth. In fact, Gabriel was not even my actual father. I have no idea who my parents were. He found me alone in the streets, an orphan of about four years old. He was already a widower then and very lonely."

"Your name is Siddal . . . he gave you Elizabeth's maiden name rather than his surname?"

"Precisely."

We were passing the park now. Night stars and swirled cloud-shadows speckled the late afternoon sky.

"My father had loved his wife, Elizabeth, intensely, even obsessively. Besides modeling for the group's portraits, she also painted and wrote along with them. My father loved her, but he struggled with monogamy, and had affairs with several of his models. He felt great guilt over this, particularly when Elizabeth learned of the affairs. She miscarried his child, and her health declined. She became depressed and ceased writing her own poetry. She soon died from an accidental overdose of laudanum."

The cab took a hard right and I held on to my seat.

"My father never fully recovered from Elizabeth's death. He felt guilty for cheating on her and responsible for the death of the baby. He began drinking too much and overdosing on chloroform. As you pointed out, he gave me her last name. I was always grateful to Gabriel for giving me a home. But my growing up was rather haphazard. While many my age attended boarding schools, my father taught me himself. I was present at all of his dinners with his artist friends and his mistresses; he had bizarre pets—a pair of wombats that he would dress up for fun. My father was interesting, but I felt a little suffocated by his fixation on the dead Elizabeth. She was this ghost in our household that would never leave his shoulder. His obsession deteriorated him, and he died a few years ago."

We approached the Kensington neighborhood. I knew that my time with William was about to end, but I still had more questions.

"So, if you were raised in this family of artists, how did you choose to become a physician?"

"We have very few members of our family who have chosen the medical profession, but an artist's life wasn't for me. And Gabriel always encouraged me in my pursuit of becoming a doctor. He provided for me in his will with some money that remained from his book royalties. It was enough to cover my expenses at Oxford. And now I have a nice living arrangement with my father's sister, my aunt Christina."

"That is extraordinary! You *live* with Christina Rossetti. I love her poetry. Is she still writing?"

"A little. But now she dedicates her life to helping prostitutes find more wholesome professions. Quite literally, she has opened her home to them. Instead of paying her for my room and board, I work in her house as a sort of live-in physician. Though most of the women she houses are much more stable than the women you see in our second floor ward at the hospital, they still have their lingering medical and mental issues. I live upstairs, making myself available for assistance whenever I am at home."

"So you never have any free time. Even when you go home at night, you might have to work."

"I don't mind. Christina is reasonable. And she works all the time herself. Her dedication to the women who come to her is limitless."

"Does Dr. Bartlett know about her work?"

"He does. Indeed, often he sends our more hopeful and stronger patients to her when they are stable enough to leave the hospital. She has had much success in placing them in millinery or seamstress work—housing them until they can support themselves."

As William helped me out of the cab, I saw light

through the parlor window. Grandmother would be in there by now. And she would be angry. I had not only missed tea and cribbage, but also dinner.

Then I saw Ellen's beady eyes peering around one of the curtains.

My mind raced. I had been so absorbed by William's story that I had not thought how I would explain my absence; and now, I would have to explain who I had been *with*.

As if reading my thought, William said, "I should probably leave now. Am I not correct?"

"I am afraid that you are." My reply tasted sheepish, and I cringed inside.

William bowed slightly and departed.

I ascended the front steps, summoning a plausible, acceptable story: I had been walking in the park. I had stayed too late and had by chance met a physician who worked at the hospital. He had offered to escort me home. This had seemed prudent.

Grandmother would rant, lecture, and threaten.

Still, I knew that in the end, nothing would change for me.

Seven

I think they're doing nothing except making everyone nervous. The women, the children in the main ward, they can hardly feel comfortable with these uniformed constables and inspectors circulating everywhere."

Sister Josephine had just left the nursery, and I finally had an opportunity to vent to Simon about the situation. It was Wednesday, and Scotland Yard had maintained a sporadic and yet oppressive presence at the hospital since Monday.

Simon's mouth curved into a smile as he examined a newborn baby boy's eyes using a small instrument with a concave mirror. An "ophthalmoscope," he had called it.

"You know, the theory is that the murderer might possibly be a physician or medical student," he said. "But I have also heard that the police have been questioning butchers and other workers in the area. Try not to take it too personally."

"Still, I wished they would ask their questions and leave. They could at least take suspects to the station to question them. Have they questioned you?"

"Twice, actually. They interviewed me in Dr. Bartlett's office on Monday, then again yesterday. They have spoken to all of the male workers here. I think there are no leads, and I am inclined, like you, to think that they should move on, or at least maintain a more discrete presence."

I watched Simon as he turned to examine another baby. He possessed a cool handsomeness, his forehead marble-smooth, uncreased even when he concentrated. Since yesterday, besides working alongside of him, I had assisted him in three deliveries, and his perpetual control even in stressful moments impressed me. He seemed dedicated and kind, spending more time with patients than most of the physicians did. Perhaps because of his kindness, or perhaps due to our bond from the morning when he returned with me to Kensington, I felt more comfortable with Simon than I did with William. And yet oddly, in spite of all this, there was an enigmatic strain to him, a veil in Simon beyond which I could not see.

The baby Lizzie, when we reached her, concerned us both. She had continued to lose weight, even just since Monday.

"Has Josephine found a wet nurse for her?" I asked, after Simon had listened to her chest with a stethoscope.

"I do not believe so."

"Rose Elliot? Is she still here? She just had a child, perhaps she still has milk. I know she needs to rest, but after losing her own child it might help her to care for Lizzie."

Simon straightened, paused. A flicker crossed his gaze momentarily.

"An excellent idea, Abbie."

Later that same day, I assisted Dr. Bartlett during a surgery on the third floor.

He had congratulated me, the day before, on my triumph over Rose Elliot's husband. That incident, to my relief, had gone mostly unnoticed—I think due to the overall chaos in the ward and also the general preoccupation of staff members with the Polly Nichols murder.

The particular patient Dr. Bartlett was operating on was a middle-aged woman, an alcoholic, who was one of the second floor patients. She was anesthetized with chloroform. I stood beside Dr. Bartlett at the operating table and gazed into the woman's open abdomen.

"Here is the mass, Abbie," he said, removing a lumpy substance from the woman's liver. After placing it in a metal pan held by one of the attending nurses, he explained to me that the woman suffered from tumor growths in the liver. Although he had removed this one, the tumors would probably continue to return more aggressively until she succumbed to the disease.

I listened intently as Dr. Bartlett explained the surgery. He was an expert in surgeries and conventional deliveries, and he was not afraid to attempt new surgical practices. At one point the previous day, Simon had explained that Dr. Bartlett not only taught at various universities but also traveled a great deal; according to Simon, the horizontal-cut caesarean I had seen the previous week was not practiced widely in Europe. Dr. Bartlett had learned the practice from African midwives, and believed that it caused less blood loss and abdominal trauma in an already dangerous procedure.

I watched as Dr. Bartlett stitched up the liver and then slowly, carefully, stitched up the woman's abdomen. Many of the attending nurses had left for their other tasks. Our conversation moved away from the details of the surgery to more personal matters. He asked after my grandmother and how she was doing.

"Quite well."

His eyes met mine very quickly before refocusing on his continued stitching, the long needle moving in and out of the skin tissues.

"You look remarkably like Caroline, Abbie."

I had forgotten that one of the reasons I was here was because Dr. Bartlett was a family friend. I swallowed, suppressing the lump of grief that began to swell in my throat. I knew very little about Mother's life in London before she eloped and gave birth to me. Even Grandmother rarely talked about her.

"How well did you know my family?"

Dr. Bartlett did not take his eyes off his work as he spoke. "Decently well. Your grandmother for years has donated generously to various charities. In fact, she was one of our main financial supporters when I began this hospital."

I sniffed in spite of myself. Giving to charities, for Grandmother, was quite "vogue."

He had finished the stitches and, after laying aside the needle and thread, he began wiping blood away from the wound.

"I dined with her and with Caroline a few times. Caroline, as part of her artistic pursuits, attended a few of my surgeries in the operating theatre at Oxford."

"Operating theatre?" I asked.

"Essentially a place exactly like this surgery room, except that the surgery is conducted on a sort of stage surrounded by an auditorium where medical students and physicians might observe the surgery. Once in a while, artists attended my lectures—to learn more about the anatomy and structure of the body as they painted. Your mother was one of those artists."

He turned to wash his hands in a nearby basin.

"Lady Westfield and I have corresponded through the years, but unfortunately I lost touch with Caroline once she moved away from London."

The air became heavy with the unspoken. I felt sure Dr. Bartlett was aware that the reason I had returned to London was Mother's death.

Gracefully, he changed the subject.

"Abbie, on Friday evening, would you join me and some of the other physicians at my home? We meet frequently for socializing purposes, though we also review scholarly topics and medical ethics issues together. I value their input as I develop this hospital, and I would very much like you to be included in these meetings."

"I would love to attend!"

"Wonderful." He moved to leave the room. "I cannot accompany you, but I will send my carriage. About seven o'clock?"

"Yes, that will work well."

As I left the operating room to assist William in the second floor ward, I felt a flurry of excitement. Through allowing me to attend the surgery and now in this invitation to his house, Dr. Bartlett was treating me with the same respect he gave the younger physicians who worked with him. I had not said anything to him about possibly pursuing a career as a physician, but I felt encouraged, now, that he would not make any issue of my gender. I made a mental note to ask him about medical school.

I had not seen William since Monday when he escorted me back to Kensington; however, the second floor ward was so busy that I scarcely had a chance to talk to him. Almost every bed along the wall was filled. For three hours, I did nothing but change sheets and chamber pots, and help some of the nurses give medicine doses to patients.

Shortly before it was time for me to leave, I found myself in a side room of the second floor, a sort of laundry room, folding towels and bedsheets. My feet and back ached and I wanted nothing more than to sleep.

"I see you survived Lady Westfield's wrath the other evening."

William stood in the doorway. His stance was awkward, unusual for him.

"Yes, I'm still here."

I felt myself flush against my will. The story of William's bohemian upbringing had intrigued me, and I wanted to know more of him. Also, as always, his presence could be so disorienting. I felt my heart thud repeatedly inside my chest.

There was a strange pause in the air. I steadied my breathing and placed another folded towel in a basket.

"I heard that Dr. Bartlett invited you to his house."

"Yes. Are you going to be there?"

"No. Christina will be volunteering at New Hospital—it's another hospital for low-income women, actually quite similar to Whitechapel Hospital. She will be there late on Friday and wants me to stay at the house with her 'friends,' as she calls the women who live with her."

His eyes flashed, a little mischievously—as if he were about to tell me some gossip. He lowered his voice and stepped closer to me.

"Dr. Bartlett lives in a huge house at the end of Montgomery Street. His house is quite posh, but the street is rather—transitional. He does not live alone; for years, he has lived with three other men. None of them have families of their own, and all are dedicated whole-heartedly to their work. The only time they live apart is when one or more of them lectures for a term at Oxford or travels abroad for study or research purposes."

"Are the others physicians as well?" I asked.

"No. That is the interesting part. Each has his own profession that he excels at. Marcus Brown is an accomplished scholar of philosophy and history. John Perkins is a devoted theologian. And then there is Robert Buck. Although he occasionally helps treat patients, he truly is more of a biologist than a physician. I'm sure you know that he has an office here and specializes in botany, zoology, and herbology. He has collected plants, fish, and animals from all over the world. No home has ever contained so much talent and intellect within its walls as the Montgomery Street house—it could be a university or even a museum. It's sprawling and fascinating. There is one particular gallery on the second floor, near the top of the stairs … "

"Dr. Siddal!" Josephine's voice rang out on the stairs. "We have a delivery!"

William lingered near me for two more seconds, as if he wanted to say something else.

"Dr. Siddal!"

He exhaled loudly, flashed me a brilliant smile, and then hurried from the room.

The moment I finished the laundry, I felt I could leave. A quick peek out of the laundry room window showed me the bleak dusk settling upon Whitechapel. Wind whipped across the street, scattering trash and bottles. The heaviness of the atmosphere had a pre-storm appearance, and I involuntarily clutched my arms as goose bumps broke out across my skin. The carriage already waited for me in front of the steps, and I rushed from the room hoping that the driver had not been there too very long.

In my hurry, I collided with a man who had just stepped onto the landing from the stairs. If he had not caught my arms at the elbows, steadying me, I would have plunged straight past him down the stairs.

"I'm sorry," I stuttered, feeling foolish and embarrassed. Then I glanced up at him.

He was well-built, with startlingly green eyes and curly dark hair. I had not yet seen him around the hospital. He was perhaps in his mid-thirties, and might have been one of the hospital's young physicians. His eyes arrested me, and for a split second I could not look away.

"Are you all right?" he asked. He smiled, and yet his eyes sparked more rogue than kind.

"Yes, quite. Thank you."

I continued quickly down the stairs, feeling his eyes upon my back.

Eight

"Arabella, you smell." Grandmother wrinkled her nose. "You smell like infant vomit."

The carriage ride to Lady Catherine's house for dinner was tense. I had arrived home later than Grandmother had expected, and I had only a few minutes to get ready for the dinner. I had washed, but apparently not well enough.

"I'm sorry. I did wash. The hospital odors can be so strong."

Grandmother sighed loudly and looked out the carriage window. Still without looking at me, she said, "Please make an attempt not to embarrass me tonight. Lady Catherine has arranged this for *your* benefit."

"What do you mean, for *my* benefit?"

"Cecil Clairmont, a barrister, will be there, as will his

fiancée, Mariah Crawley. She is Violet's ward. She is your age and a trifle libertine, but otherwise…" Grandmother's voice trailed off a bit. "The point is, as I told you last week, there *is* someone at the party whom Catherine and I very much wish for you to meet: Chester Clairmont. He is Cecil's nephew. He is a student of the law, not much older than you, and the Clairmonts are an excellent family."

We had stopped. The carriage ride only lasted a few blocks, given that Catherine also lived in Kensington; it was quite ridiculous that we took a carriage at all.

The driver stepped down to open Grandmother's door.

"If Chester is not much older than me, how old is Mr. Clairmont?" I asked. I was perplexed at the thought of Cecil Clairmont marrying a girl my age.

Instead of answering me, Grandmother merely turned as she stepped out of the carriage, her eagle eyes sharp on my face. She clenched her teeth a bit.

"I know you were raised among the Irish, Arabella, but, once again, do *not* embarrass me tonight."

She smiled daggers.

The party proved to be as dull as I had expected. It was suffocatingly small, with only Lady Catherine, Lady Violet, Mariah, Cecil, and Chester in attendance.

Cecil was in fact old, at least fifty. Chester was twenty-one and the spitting younger image of his uncle. As I had expected, Catherine seated me next to him at the table.

Despite being young, Chester had terrible allergies and was already balding. He talked the entire meal about himself, about his law studies and travels. I tried to be polite, but he bored me out of my mind.

Mariah, across the table next to Cecil, appeared much more interesting.

Tall. Elegant. With her black curly hair piled high on her head, Mariah might have been a model for the sketches in the magazines I browsed. But she looked even lovelier than the magazine illustrations due to her bold and distinct aura. She talked very little during the dinner conversation, and yet her sharp eyes did not miss anything. Once she caught my eye and smiled.

Mariah's demeanor intrigued me, particularly as, in spite of her well-dressed appearance, she seemed a misfit here at the Kensington dinner. I wanted to speak to her, but it was difficult to escape Chester. Finally, when she left the table to refill her glass, I drained my own, excused myself from Chester, and followed her.

While we stood near the punch bowl, she took a nearby plate of gooseberry pie and, without even bothering with utensils, began to eat it, staining her fingers sticky red in the process. She did not seem to care about the stains, and after licking her fingers a bit, she wiped them clean with a napkin.

Catherine had already introduced us earlier, and now, to make conversation, I congratulated her on her engagement.

She lowered her voice, even though we were well out of earshot of the rest of the dinner party.

"Thank you, but you should know that the wedding is never going to happen."

"Excuse me?" I nearly choked on my drink.

"The date is set for early January, but of course I'm not marrying him. Just look at him. Can you imagine what a dull life that would be?"

As discretely as possible, I glanced at the table. Catherine, Violet, and Grandmother continued to chatter; Chester Clairmont watched Mariah and me and looked about ready to refill his drink, too. Cecil Clairmont had already fallen asleep at his seat and was beginning to snore.

"All right. You're absolutely correct," I said quickly. Chester rose from the table. Mariah and I didn't have much time. "So why are you engaged to him?"

"Makes things a bit more fun, doesn't it?" She winked. "I have a lover, and we're planning to run off the night before the wedding. The whole thing will make a splash. It will be quite scandalous. In fact, I doubt Lady Westfield will want you to be my friend anymore."

She smiled warmly. Briefly, I wondered if she was making this up, joshing with me a bit. I could not believe that within minutes of knowing me, she would confide all this. But something in her eyes told me it was true.

Chester had almost reached us.

"Why are you telling me all of this?" I whispered.

Her reply came instantly. "Because you look like you would understand. *And* because you look like you won't tell a soul," she added as she gave me a quick peck on the cheek and departed. She left a faint scent of honeysuckle behind. Chester had just arrived at the punch bowl.

As Chester rambled on, I watched Mariah walk back to the dinner table. She was correct. I would not tell a soul. Grandmother had called her a libertine; I found her intriguing compared to my monotonous Kensington life, and I saw the possibility of a new friendship.

Two workdays passed quickly, and on Friday evening I arrived at Dr. Bartlett's enormous white gabled home. William had been correct about the street seeming transitional. Though the outside of Dr. Bartlett's house was quite well-kept, most of the houses on the street were much more worn and seemed abandoned. I also saw gutted workhouses and factory buildings. The street was mostly dark, as there were no working streetlamps.

As I stepped out of his carriage, I felt curious and excited about the impending evening. I anticipated that this would be very different from my evening at Lady Catherine's.

"Welcome!" Dr. Bartlett exclaimed as he opened the door for me and took my coat.

He led me to an enormous drawing room immediately to the left of the front entranceway. The room had dark green patterned wallpaper and long narrow windows heavily curtained in sage velvet drapes; it had a grand, earthy feel. Giant potted plants abounded along the walls and in every corner of the room. I saw at least three large fish bowls; one, under a gaslight in the center of the room, was huge, globelike. This globe aquarium absorbed and reflected prisms of light above it into every angle of the room. Unlike the two smaller aquariums, this aquarium contained jellyfish. They were tiny and silver—each a pulsating thimble with long tentacles floating behind like hair. Part of Dr. Buck's collection, undoubtedly.

Across the room, past the fish bowl, several young men, many of whom I recognized as physicians or medical students from the hospital, sat around smoking cigars, small glasses of gin or sherry in their hands. The conversation lulled a bit when they saw me, and I saw glimmers of disappointment in the gazes that flashed toward me. Undoubtedly they thought that a woman would cramp and exasperate their conversation. The only warm gaze came from Simon. He drank only wine.

Several men, whom I took to be Dr. Bartlett's housemates, sat beside the large bookcases near where we stood. Like Dr. Bartlett, the housemates appeared to be middle-aged or late middle-aged—except for one.

I stifled a small gasp when I recognized the youngest man as the one I had slammed into when leaving the hospital. He stared at me now with his leopard green eyes and cast me a nod. My curiosity rose regarding his identity. I had thought he was possibly a physician at the hospital, but he lounged on an ottoman near the others in a manner that seemed far too familiar for a subordinate physician.

He stayed where he was while the others rose to meet me.

Dr. Bartlett began introducing them at once.

"Abbie, this is Reverend John Perkins."

Reverend Perkins stepped forward and took my hand. Dressed all in black, he wore a clergyman's collar; however, unlike many of the pleasant, powder-haired clergymen in England, he exuded shrewdness. More lion than lamb, I concluded. Tall, and sporting a long pepper-colored beard, Reverend Perkins—though polite—had an imposing and formal appearance.

Dr. Marcus Brown, meanwhile, was of average height, had short brown hair, and seemed much friendlier. He stepped forward to shake my hand and we exchanged pleasantries. *The scholar*, I remembered William saying as he introduced himself to me.

"Do you teach at Oxford occasionally?" I asked.

"Yes." He chuckled lightly. "But not medicine. My mind is not inclined anywhere in *that* direction of study. I lecture for the history and philosophy departments at Kings College. Robert here," he said, patting the man next to him, who I assumed was Dr. Buck, on the back, "is our scientist—both botanist and zoologist, specifically. You can find him lurking around the laboratory upstairs at Whitechapel Hospital, though he has his own laboratory here that he shares with Julian."

Dr. Buck, tall and spectacled, seemed almost as formidable as Reverend Perkins. He stepped forward, giving me by far the firmest handshake of the group.

After meeting them, I wondered when the younger man would arise to greet me, but when I looked toward the ottoman again, he was gone. Discretely, I glanced across the room to where the small group of guests sat.

He was not there, either.

Dr. Brown placed a drink in my hand.

"Is Scotch all right?"

"Perfect, thank you."

I had never had a Scotch. I rarely drank anything stronger than wine, but having noticed that most of the others drank hard liquor, I did not want to seem weak.

For the first time, I noticed that Dr. Bartlett and his housemates had no servants. They served the drinks, closed the drapes as the evening progressed, and turned the lamps on and off.

Two hours passed; my head began to swirl after I unwisely drank a second Scotch. I became hesitant to talk too much for fear that anything I said at that moment might sound foolish. Then, perhaps because of the alcohol, I felt a wave of nausea.

"Are you quite all right?" Simon whispered from where he sat beside me.

"Yes, quite. I'm just going to find the water closet."

"It's upstairs. Do you need me to … "

"No, no. I can find it myself."

I focused on walking steadily as I crossed the drawing

room. I paused at the jellyfish aquarium when another small wave of nausea swept over me. Stepping closer to the glass, I waited for the bout to pass. The talk and laughter from the other part of the room funneled away, and I became completely absorbed in the swimming creatures. I had only seen sketches of jellyfish in books, and they had seemed much larger than these. Also, no sketch could ever do justice to their gossamer loveliness.

"Lovely, aren't they? But deadly. This type will kill within minutes, often within three minutes."

Blood roared in my ears and I felt a scalding flush spread across my cheeks. The man I had encountered at the hospital now stood quite close beside me, staring into the glass and smoking a cigar. I had not heard him approach; neither had I smelled the sweet cigar smoke, which in my less-than-sober state dizzied me a bit.

He glanced down at me. In the light from the aquarium, he was darkly handsome, and his eyes arrested me. He averted his face, blew the smoke away, and refocused again on the aquarium.

"Dr. Buck discovered them in the waters around Indonesia last year. They are, as yet, unclassified as a species."

He looked back down at me. My spine prickled and I straightened, not wanting to succumb to his spell.

"I remember you from the hospital, but I don't believe we've met. I'm Abbie Sharp." I put my hand out.

He hesitated for a moment, looked down at my extended hand, something of amusement upon his face.

His expression seemed uncomfortably intimate, as if a handshake between us was foolishness.

But after a second, he took my hand and squeezed it firmly. "Max Bartlett, Julian's nephew."

"Are you a physician?'

He chuckled and did not answer. He stared listlessly at the jellyfish, then back at me.

The chuckle puzzled me. Was I *supposed* to know who he was? I wondered if he was perhaps offended that I did not know of him.

But he did not appear offended as he continued to stare at me. He took another lingering draw upon the cigar. "*Au revoir*, Miss Abbie Sharp."

With that he walked away, past the loudly conversing guests and through a set of French doors. All I saw beyond the doors was greenery and shadows.

Odd, I thought, as I finally left the drawing room.

Once I was in the entranceway again, I ascended the stairs and found the water closet. Splashing water on my face from the washbasin made me feel a bit more sober. When I emerged, I noticed an open door across the hallway. A soft glow emanated from the room. I remembered that William had mentioned some sort of gallery near the stairs in the Montgomery Street house, but I had not yet asked him what he meant.

As I stepped through the doorway, my surroundings suddenly disappeared. Vaguely, I felt my body tremble, and I panicked as I plunged into blackness. I did not like this loss of control, and I fought hysteria as I felt another vision coming on.

The darkness dissipated a bit, and I saw a silver chalice—there was some sort of inscription on the side, in Latin, but it wasn't clear enough to read. Feeling a magnetic draw toward the cup, I reached for it, to take it as I would kneeling at a Sunday church service.

The vision evaporated and I was once again in darkness. My body fell, hitting a hard floor, and, distantly, I felt pain.

Then I found myself standing in a dead-end alley at nighttime. I smelled rotting meat—some type of spoiled beef and fish from the cluttered trash piles of the alleyway. A cat leaped from one of the piles, sending an ale bottle rolling loudly across the flagstone ground.

That's when I heard the scraping noise, from high on the wall at the end of the alley. I looked upward and saw a shadow moving through the darkness. I felt rising terror; I could not move.

The figure of a man crawled down the bricked wall. His movements were unhurried, even-paced—the scraping noise I had heard was his fingernails and boots upon the bricked surface. With each crouching movement, he came closer to the ground. I tried to run, but the rotting meat smell became overwhelming. Then nausea and fear overwhelmed me and I felt paralyzed.

His head was almost to the ground when he looked up at me, and though I could see very little in the darkness, I saw the flash of a smile and a knife blade clenched between his teeth. There was something serpentine about his movements as he crawled downward, defying gravity, and yet I knew that he was a real human being closing in for a kill.

"Abbie. *Abbie.*" I felt Simon's cool hands gently shaking my shoulders. And then I saw Simon's face in front of my own.

Somehow I had fallen onto the floor of the gallery. I refocused my eyes. A new panic rose inside me. I could not tell Simon about the vision. As understanding as Simon seemed, if I told him I was having visions, he might think me insane; it might mean an end to my work at the hospital.

"What are you doing here?" I asked him.

"You looked unwell when you left the drawing room. I thought I would make certain that you were all right. I found you in here, collapsed."

Slightly annoyed by his chivalry—this was the second time Simon had caught me falling—I stood up abruptly, smoothing my skirts.

"Thank you. I think I just had a bit too much to drink."

A single lamp shone behind us, and Simon peered at me in the semi-darkness. His eyes dropped to my hands, which I felt trembling.

Damn. He doesn't miss a thing, I thought.

"Where are we?" I asked suddenly as I scanned the gallery, which although not particularly large, was long and lined with glass cases. I saw a closed door at the other end of the room.

Simon remained silent, and I felt his eyes still upon

me as I began examining the gallery. Each case contained various archeological and anthropological displays. The one nearest to me contained coins—medieval coins. They were neatly aligned in rows, arranged, I assumed, by the time period from which they came. Then I noticed a case at the far end of the room lined with bones—human skulls, finger bones, human hair. I found the case both morbid and intriguing, and I wondered where the remains had come from—undoubtedly they were collected by Dr. Bartlett and Dr. Buck in the course of their medical and scientific researches.

Many of the other displays, such as the one with the coins, contained items that had nothing to do with medicine. I noticed one filled with ancient and medieval weaponry. Another contained various styles of pistols. Some cases contained more recent weapons. I even recognized a famed bowie knife from America, sturdy and slightly curved for frontier hunting.

"It's like a museum."

"It *is* a museum." Simon seemed to relax a bit and walked to where I stood in front of the bones case. "It's a private museum. Very extraordinary. It's actually connected to another gallery," he said, nodding toward the other door. "But I have not been in that one."

"The house must be absolutely sprawling," I said, peering into one of the cases. "These bones ... where are they from?"

Simon shrugged, standing beside me, staring at the case's contents.

"Do they bother you?" he asked.

"No. Just a bit macabre."

"Yes, I understand." In the darkness of the room, his angelic face seemed luminous. I felt a rising curiosity about him. Ever since our brief discussion that morning in the carriage, I had wondered why he had chosen this profession, *why* he would be drawn to the East End. Most often, Kensington produced Chester Clairmonts.

"You grew up in Kensington. How did you become a physician—in Whitechapel of all places?"

"My work is more selfish than you might think, Abbie."

"I am not understanding you."

That smile again. "It's my search for God."

"But you're a seminary student. Wouldn't your theology studies give you those answers?"

His mouth curved into a smile as an answer, but his eyes took on that distant look.

A throat cleared loudly from the door.

I whipped around. Reverend Perkins stood in the doorway. His expression was unfriendly, and I wondered how long he had been watching us.

"Miss Sharp, the carriage is ready. It is late, and I'm certain Lady Westfield would want you home at a decent hour."

There was something condescendingly sharp in his voice, and I picked up an accusatory undertone. I blushed at the thought that perhaps he thought it was forward of me to be alone in this upstairs room with a young man.

Either way, I took my leave immediately.

Nine

I sensed a heavy atmosphere at the hospital when I arrived for work on Monday morning. The clusters of children in the first floor ward played more quietly; the nurses went about their work with strained, preoccupied faces. Mothers spoke in hushed voices from their beds. I passed two constables leaving as I entered the front doors.

"What has *happened*?" I asked Josephine as she rushed past me.

Her small brown eyes flashed. I could see that she debated within herself whether or not to tell me something.

She pulled me toward the side. "There's been another murder."

I saw Abberline's broad back following Dr. Bartlett up the stairs.

"One of our patients?"

Josephine nodded. "Annie Chapman. We think she was killed within a few hours of being discharged from here—sometime in the early hours on Saturday morning." She lowered her voice to a barely audible whisper. "The killer mutilated the body in the manner of Polly Nichols."

My mind flew back to the vision I had had on Friday evening—of the man in the alley.

With a wave of dizziness, I tried to pinpoint the time that I'd had the vision: I had left Dr. Bartlett's home late, around eleven o'clock—only a few hours before Saturday morning. I pushed away my persistent memories of my mother's episodes. The inexplicable was too much for me to deal with at that moment.

Josephine informed me that I was needed on the second floor that day, and then rushed back to the nursery.

When I arrived in the second floor ward, I found Simon sitting beside the bed of a patient, reading to her from a volume of *Great Expectations*. His voice reminded me slightly of Dr. Bartlett's—soothing, hypnotic. I knew that Simon St. John was the only physician—in fact the only staff member anywhere in the hospital—who would take a few moments to read to a patient.

The woman pouted as he closed the book. "Wish you didn't hav' to stop readin' it, doctor." She was sharply thin, with brown hair and light blue eyes. I guessed her to be somewhere in her forties. I heard in her voice the hint of a Scandinavian, possibly Swedish, accent.

"I have other patients, Miss Stride. But I'll return later."

Simon ushered me into a side room to show me the schedule for the day.

"I know, Simon," I whispered. "Josephine told me of the murder."

"What did she tell you?" His ice-blue eyes remained expressionless.

"The truth. That Annie Chapman was discharged in the early hours of Saturday morning and that she was found not too long afterward, dead and mutilated."

He remained quiet.

"You don't have to protect me from this information. I am working here. I need to know. Why was she discharged then?"

Simon remained collected. "As you know, I was not here Friday night. Neither was Josephine, nor most of the other physicians. Nurse Nancy, perhaps unwisely, allowed Miss Chapman to leave when she became argumentative. Like many others here, Miss Chapman was a severe alcoholic, and she probably left to find drink. The hour was late, but Inspector Abberline has maintained increasingly vigilant patrols in the area due to the extraordinary brutality of Polly Nichols's murder. No one expected it to happen again."

"Josephine said she was eviscerated. It's probably the same killer," I said, almost to myself.

And I've seen him.

I wanted to tell Simon, anyone, about the visions. But I feared his reaction.

"So what are we going to do about nightly discharges?" I asked quickly.

"Unfortunately, patients are legally free to leave anytime they wish. But we're still going to have to be more careful. Abberline has promised even more patrolling in this area."

I began to wonder if the killer was specifically targeting Whitechapel Hospital patients, but there had only been two murders; it seemed futile to speculate too much at this point. The day had just begun, and I had too many tasks awaiting me.

When we returned to the main part of the second floor ward, I found that one of my first challenges was just learning patients' names. Many did not go by the official name they were admitted under. Nicknames abounded. Liz Stride was "Long Liz." Maudie Brooks was known as "Mad Mother Maudie." "Sister Dotty," whose actual name was Dorothea Brighton, was a prostitute, *not* a nun. But she had earned her title among the patients due to her fondness for loosely quoting from the Bible whenever convenient. When I brought her water that morning, she said, "She who gives the whore some water will receive her reward in heaven."

Sister Dotty's bed was at the far end of the second floor ward. Like Long Liz, who according to Simon suffered from syphilis, Sister Dotty also was afflicted by the disease.

But Dotty was also in the final stages of liver failure. Simon later told me that she would likely die within a month.

After giving her the water, I began stripping the two empty beds next to her. They were the last beds at the end of the room, immediately beside Dotty's bed.

"You know that was *her* bed. She was next to me, she was." Sister Dotty grabbed my hand and nodded toward the bed closest to her.

"Who?"

"You know, Annie Chapman, the latest one the killer caught."

Although I had not met either of the victims, Chapman's empty bed caused a small knot to form in my stomach. I wondered if she had a family, and if they knew about her death yet.

"I'll be back in two hours with your medicine," I said.

I bundled up the dirty sheets and turned to leave.

"Don't you want to ask me about the *other* bed?"

I stopped.

"On the other side of Annie, *that* bed belonged to Polly. He's goin' down the row, he is."

"Dotty…"

"Don't hush me. He's after us."

She let go of my hand and settled back on her pillow. She stared ahead, up to the ceiling.

"Don't matter much if he gets me." She closed her eyes. "I'm not leaving 'ere alive. Whether he gets me or the disease gets me. As the Bible states, 'There is a time to *die*.'"

"Miss Sharp, Miss Abbie Sharp!" someone shouted.

I looked up, recognizing instantly the girl I had given money to outside the grocer's. She was calling out to me from the entrance of the second floor ward. Simon stood beside her, slight amusement on his face. Clutching the bundle of dirty bedsheets to myself, I hurried away from Dotty's bed to meet them.

"Miss Mary Kelly here says she has repayment for you." Simon's mouth twitched.

"I'm sorry, I saw you go into the hospital earlier," Mary said, slightly out of breath as if she had been running. "I went through the first floor looking for you. A nurse—large, big-boned lady, dressed like you but she had a cross around her neck..." Mary had to pause to take a few breaths. "She confronted me and said the *prostitutes* were on the second floor."

Sister Josephine. I suppressed a laugh. Simon's lovely long mouth broke out into a smile.

Mary's nose wrinkled in irritation. "Prostitute! I couldn't believe it. Anyway, I told the lady that I had borrowed money from a young woman who I had seen walk in here, and that I had to find her. She told me to get out. I started to run up the stairs, seeing that you weren't on the first floor and this kind gentleman here... Doctor...?"

"Simon."

"*Simon.*" She turned back to me. "He listened to me when I described you and said he thought Abbie Sharp might be the one who I was looking for. So—" She held out her hand with a few coins. "Here is your money back."

Then, proudly, "I told you I would repay you."

"Thank you." I could tell by her expression that refusing the money would do no good.

With a hurried stride, Dr. Bartlett and Dr. Buck entered the second floor ward. Dr. Bartlett possessed his usual poise, but his expression seemed troubled. I noticed Abberline's hulking form shadowing the doorway.

Dr. Bartlett spoke to me quietly. "I am afraid, Abbie, that I am going to have to take Dr. St. John away from you. I have no concerns; you will be quite capable here on your own for the time being. If you need any help, Sister Josephine is downstairs, and Dr. Siddal should arrive at any time."

I felt Abberline's unnerving gaze upon me and tried to suppress my unrest.

"Simon," Dr. Bartlett continued, "I would like you to accompany Dr. Buck and myself to St. George's Mortuary. The district surgeon has some ideas, and I would very much like to hear your opinion."

"Most certainly. If Abbie feels comfortable by herself here?"

"Quite. I'll summon Josephine for assistance if I must."

Mary stood by us, wide-eyed, taking in the whole conversation with curiosity. I wondered if she knew about the murders.

As Dr. Bartlett, Dr. Buck, and Simon left the ward, I stared around at the many patients.

"Do you have a job?" I asked Mary.

"No."

"Do you want one?"

"Yes... very much."

I was certain that I was breaking the rules, but it was an unusual day. And I knew that Dr. Bartlett would pay her for her work.

I extracted an apron from a nearby supply closet and thrust it into her arms.

"You're employed."

Mary provided invaluable help on the second floor. She proved to be both efficient and stern with the patients. When Sue refused to take her medicine, Mary raised her voice to such a shrill pitch that I heard her from the other side of the ward. "Fine. Then I won't empty your chamber pot. Sit in your piss all day. See if I care."

Sue promptly relented and drank the medicine.

I felt curious about Mary's story. She appeared desperate for money, but I did not think she was a prostitute—she had taken such genuine offense at Josephine's words. Yet I heard her gossiping a bit with the patient Cate Eddows, and she seemed somewhat familiar with East End life.

We conversed briefly while stacking some folded sheets in the closet.

"How long have you been here?" I asked. "Your accent's Irish."

"Is that a problem?" Mary's expression hardened.

"It was just a question. I lived in Dublin for seven years."

She sniffed. "Two months. I've been here two months."

"Me too, actually."

I saw her glance at me sideways and relax her expression a bit.

"Your friend the other day—the one who found the job," I continued. "Did he come over with you?"

"Aye, my friend Scribby and his sister Liliana both came with me. There wasn't much for us in our village in Ireland; we thought we needed a change of scenery. London seemed exciting. Liliana found a job right away working at the Ten Bells pub on Commercial Street. Scribby and I have had a bit of a harder time. But now that we're both employed, we might be able to make a go of it here. Liliana lives with me, and she has barely been able to make our rent."

"Where do you live?"

"Miller's Court." She shot me another look and I said nothing. Several of our patients lived in that area near Dorset Street—a particularly dodgy district. If Mary had trouble paying rent in *that* area, she must be hurting for money. I decided to speak to Dr. Bartlett about making her position permanent.

I worked nonstop alongside Mary until early afternoon, when things slowed a bit and I checked the supply closet. We were completely out of one of our most necessary antiseptics: carbolic acid. Simon had told me earlier that the largest supply closet in the hospital—actually, more of a small room that also served as the hospital's pharmacy—was on the fourth floor, attached to the laboratory.

The fourth floor seemed quiet except for some whispers coming from an office on the right side of the hall, not far from the stair landing. I saw the large open doors to the laboratory at the end of the hall, near Dr. Bartlett's office.

As I started toward them, the voices from the open office seemed harsh and excited, as if the speakers were arguing. I realized that part of the reason I could not understand the conversation was because it was not spoken in English. I paused, listening.

German. My knowledge of German was extremely poor.

One voice belonged to Dr. Buck. He must have returned already from the mortuary.

I could not recognize the other voice.

Suddenly, the voices broke off. I froze. They must have heard my footsteps.

Max Bartlett suddenly stepped out of the office, an annoyed expression on his face. Then he saw me, standing only a few feet away, and the look immediately dissolved. He smiled.

He shouted something in German back to Dr. Buck before descending the stairs.

As I walked past the office doorway, I saw Dr. Buck

sitting behind a desk, bent over several books laid out in front of him. "Hello, Miss Sharp."

He awkwardly adjusted his spectacles and seemed uncomfortable. A great taxidermied horned owl, perched on a nest on the short bookshelf behind him, caught my eye.

"I hope that your work on the second floor is going well, Miss Sharp."

"Yes, quite. I have help now."

"Excellent. Let me know if I can do anything."

"Thank you."

As I proceeded toward the laboratory, I wondered about what I had overheard. Neither Dr. Buck nor Max had any hint of a German accent. Why were they speaking in a foreign language?

The laboratory was larger and more interesting than I had imagined. Shelves lined with glass tubes, bottles of colorful fluids, and odd-looking instruments covered every inch of the walls. I saw dozens of labeled glass jars containing what looked like organs—though from humans or animals, I could not determine. One long shelf displayed jars of various fish specimens, such as shark and stingray fetuses, each organism suspended in blue liquid. Formaldehyde. The odor permeated the room.

My eyes stopped at a giant, slablike table, on which a woman's naked white corpse lay. Her hair was shaved off and her chest cavity opened. A stack of notes and a journal lay on the counter behind the table.

I felt my body stiffen as an image of another corpse flashed through my mind. The vision lasted only a few seconds—I saw a woman's naked, pale corpse floating in a large metal tub. The water surrounding her rippled red. Crude dark stitches stretched across her lower belly, along various places on her chest, and across her throat, and her graying brown hair billowed out like gritty tentacles from her face. Blurred figures shuffled around the body.

The vision faded as I clutched the slab table and refocused on the corpse before me. I knew intuitively that in the vision, I was seeing one of the victims. Perhaps Annie Chapman, moments after her autopsy.

Still shaking, not having had time to process too much of what I had seen, I heard water running loudly from a side room.

William stepped out. He seemed surprised to see me. "If it were any woman up here other than Abbie Sharp, I'd be worried about her fainting," he said.

"*As* a woman, I take issue with that compliment," I replied lightly, taking a deep breath and forcing myself to stop trembling.

William returned to examining the chest cavity, alternating between looking at the open chest, checking his lightly bloodstained notes, and scribbling more notes into the journal.

Something in the corpse's left lung area interested William. He peered closer. "Interesting. This is what killed her. She has a blackening tumor in the lung. Small but *quite* malignant."

He wrote some notes.

"Who is she?"

William shrugged. "A corpse, donated to science. Family gave her to the medical school, so now she's part of my own anatomy studies."

He moved across the table to where I stood. "Excuse me. I need to have a look at the right lung."

He bent over the corpse. I tried to ignore the cracking sound as he began breaking each rib with his hands. William turned around once again, his mouth twisted in amusement.

Although I had seen plenty of blood and organs in Whitechapel Hospital, I could not feel unaffected by the sound of the breaking ribs, and this did not go unnoticed by William.

"Don't worry. When you become a surgeon, you'll get used to it."

I thought that conversing might make me less queasy, but as I stared at the body, my mind had a difficult time getting away from the grotesque. I swallowed. "Dr. Bartlett and Dr. Buck took Simon to the mortuary to look at the latest victim. Dr. Buck is already back—I just saw him in his office. Do you know why Abberline would want them with him at the morgue?"

William went back to writing notes.

"Yes." He peered again into the lung, and then began sketching a section of the lung into his notes. "Bagster Phillips, the district surgeon, seems to think that the murderer is a physician, or at least someone with anatomical knowledge." Without looking up, absorbed with his sketch, he continued. "The speed at which the killer struck both victims was incredible, and he knew the exact locations of the organs he mutilated, particularly when he killed Annie Chapman. He removed her uterus, cutting it cleanly away from her abdominal cavity. Also, Dr. Phillips is nearly certain that a surgical knife was the murder weapon, similar to the one I am using here."

I stared at the sharp surgical blade laid on the table beside the corpse. A shudder swept through me as I recalled my vision of the victim, the long, stitched slashes across her body.

"So why would Abberline bring Dr. Bartlett and Dr. Buck and Simon to the mortuary? Is he questioning Simon again? Does he consider Dr. Bartlett a suspect?"

William clucked his tongue and lowered his voice before casting a glance toward the door. "No, no. Dr. Bartlett and Dr. Buck are above reproach. Abberline wanted them to view the body merely to confirm Phillips' suspicions. I think that Abberline trusts Dr. Bartlett so much that he is confiding in him at every turn of the investigation. If anything, Dr. Bartlett has become an unofficial medical consultant."

"But why bring Simon?"

William put down his notes, picked up the knife, and began slicing a small piece away from inside the lung tissue. "One of the reasons Dr. Bartlett *is* so respected, so admired as a physician, surgeon, and medical lecturer, is his unique relationship with his novice physicians. As you're aware, he treats us, particularly his favorites, as colleagues rather than the subordinates that we are. He believes that he learns from us as much as we learn from him. I imagine that when Abberline asked Dr. Bartlett and Dr. Buck to accompany him, Dr. Bartlett insisted on including the fresh, unbiased eyes of one of his young physicians."

"Doesn't that get a bit dicey, considering that Abberline has been questioning all of the physicians and medical students here?"

"Probably," William said, digging at something again in the lung tissue.

"Dr. Bartlett is confiding in students...so I assume he does not suspect any of his own physicians in these murders?"

"Exactly. He confides in all of us too much. That's why I know all that I do about the murders. And *I* don't think the murderer is anyone here, either."

Finally, William looked up from the corpse. "No one here is that interesting, strong, or clever." He smiled at me. "Except perhaps *you*."

I heard a throat clear in the doorway.

William's eyes narrowed. "Why hello, Simon."

I turned to see Simon's long figure in the doorway. I had never seen him cross. Mary stood beside him, equally angry. Staring from me to William, and then back again to me, she snapped, "I couldn't find you anywhere."

Simon finally spoke. "William, don't you think it's completely unnecessary to dissect a corpse in front of Miss Sharp? None of our female staff would welcome this scene."

I spoke up in William's defense. "I came here on my

own accord, to get some supplies. The corpse really doesn't bother me."

"Still," Simon said, continuing to glare at William, whose hands and forearms were now very bloody as he probed deeper into the corpse's lung. "You might have ceased your anatomical studies with Miss Sharp up here. Have a *little* decency."

Crack!

Without breaking his gaze from Simon's, William flashed a large smile as he cracked the last rib of the corpse.

I suppressed a laugh with such difficulty, my chest ached.

Simon merely turned to me. "Abbie, would you mind coming with me? We have a delivery downstairs."

After bringing the infant that Simon had delivered into the nursery, I stopped to check on Lizzie. Her crib lay in a stream of sunlight, and she was kicking her feet weakly.

"How is she doing?" I asked Josephine.

She came to stand beside me in the front of the crib. "She is not feeding well. Rose Elliot's milk has dried up. Also, particularly at night, we are short-staffed and cannot give her all the special care that she needs."

My heart sank.

Then a reckless plan entered my mind.

Ten

That night, after Richard, Ellen, and Grandmother had gone to bed, I slipped out of the house. Near the Thames, I hopped onto the back of a carriage heading east and reached the hospital before too very long. Although I saw constables patrolling sporadically along Whitechapel Road and Commercial Street, no one questioned me about being out at night. I cynically observed that Scotland Yard seemed more interested in catching the murderer than in making sure women were safe from him.

When I entered the hospital, patients slept soundly, and I did not run into a single nurse. Some light streamed down the stairs. Perhaps the few night nurses were busy up there. Either way, I made my way to the nursery, took a bottle, and fed Lizzie until about four o'clock in the morning, when I made my way home.

The next morning, I could barely keep my head up at breakfast. I needed to find more time to sleep. Perhaps, after these nights that I worked at the hospital, I could leave a little earlier in the afternoons. Dr. Bartlett's carriage would soon arrive for me and I felt as if I had already worked a full day.

"Arabella? Are you unwell? Did you hear me?"

I was so tired, I think I might have fallen asleep briefly at the breakfast table.

"I asked you how you have liked your work at the hospital." Grandmother's thin lips pursed. After a quick look at my face, she put her morning spectacles on and resumed reading her morning mail.

"You look awful, Arabella," she added. "Absolutely *awful.* I only required that you work at the hospital for one week."

"I'm going to continue."

The eagle-eyed gaze and pursed lips again. "Very well. I'll have my carriage bring you home at one o'clock today."

"Why?"

"My official answer is that we are invited to tea at Lady Violet's house."

"And the unofficial answer?"

A great pause, as Grandmother put down her mail and

took off her spectacles. She glanced toward the doorway and lowered her voice.

"Lady Violet's ward, Mariah, has been quite restless as her wedding approaches. When Mariah is restless, she … misbehaves."

I raised my eyebrows.

"Don't let your imagination run too wild, Arabella. Violet is just concerned. That is all."

I assured her I would be ready for the carriage by one o'clock, and that yes, I would have plenty of time to wash before we left for Violet's house. This would be easy, as Violet lived even closer to us than Catherine did—on our street, in fact.

As I resumed eating my scrambled eggs, I privately wondered if Violet suspected anything about Mariah's planned elopement. Although Mariah had confided in me, the whole affair was none of my business. I had no plans to interfere—either to expose Mariah or to cover for her, should she choose to involve me.

Our time at Lady Violet's proved to be more interesting than I had thought it would be. Instead of taking tea inside, Mariah and I drank elderberry cordials outside as we played archery in the small, walled courtyard behind Violet's house. Grandmother and Violet remained indoors, protesting that it was too cold for us to be outdoors, but after being inside the stuffy hospital all morning, the cool air felt wonderful.

Unfortunately, I had never played archery in my life.

"Your aim is terrible, Abbie," Mariah said as she shot a perfect bull's-eye.

I shot my arrow again; this time it didn't hit anywhere near the target. It merely clattered against the high stone wall behind the targets.

"Didn't you *ever* play sports?" she asked.

In Dublin, I had been quite active in fighting sports and knife-throwing competitions, where we took aim at wooden targets. By sixteen, after much practice, I had become a bit of a champion in the neighborhood, winning several of our organized street competitions. I had thought that archery could not be much different from knife throwing; I had been very wrong.

"I *have* played sports in the past," I responded, missing the target again. "Just not archery."

Mariah shot an almost-bull's-eye, rubbed her arm, and took a long sip of cordial. Our breath puffed out in the cold air.

"So," she began in a low voice, "as I told you the other evening, I'm going to run away from here, elope. I write, and I'm going to be a writer somewhere, *anywhere* but here. How are *you* going to escape?"

I smiled as I adjusted my bracer, loaded my bow, and prepared to take aim again. *That* is why I felt so drawn to Mariah. Although this was only my second time speaking with her, she represented a break from the ridiculous rules and rituals of Kensington. We were sudden allies in our desperate attempts to live a bigger life.

"Education," I said. "I'm thinking about going to medical school."

I had not yet told anyone about my possible plan, and it felt wonderful to finally say it out loud. Mariah smiled widely as a light wind pulled at her curls and small flecks of rain began to fall on us. She looked gorgeous in the cloudy late afternoon.

"I'm finding you more and more interesting, Abbie Sharp."

"So, are you going to tell me about this lover?" I asked, pulling my arm back and squinting—I felt determined to at least hit the target this time. I released the arrow.

"Perhaps another time…" Mariah's voice trailed off in horror as the arrow sailed over the wall.

I heard a screech, followed by two seconds of silence. Then came a bloodcurdling scream.

"Oh God, I've killed someone," I murmured.

Mariah grabbed her skirts up and ran from the court-yard toward the front of the house. I ran after her. She saw my victim before I did, and an expression of horror and amusement spread across her face.

"Bloody hell, Abbie," she said.

"*What?*"

"You've shot your grandmother's dog."

Mary was in a foul mood on Wednesday morning as we began working in the second floor ward. I had hoped for a little more gratitude from her, particularly since, to my relief, Dr. Bartlett had agreed to allow her to continue working at the hospital.

I knew that even with this job, Mary still had money troubles, but I hoped she could believe that life wasn't exactly rosy for me that morning either. Jupe had, fortunately, survived the hit. Grandmother had just stepped outside with him when the arrow sailed down, grazing his back. However, the wound bled profusely and Grandmother summoned Simon, who had recently arrived home from the hospital. After he assured Grandmother that Jupe would live and bandaged the pug until it looked like a pet mummy, Grandmother shrieked at and lectured me for no less than two hours—after which she settled into an angry silence. I had received the cold shoulder at breakfast and had wanted nothing more than to get to the hospital today.

William entered the ward.

"Oh … it's *you*," Mary grunted. She hadn't much taken to William, describing him to me as "bossy and arrogant."

William looked serious and a little tired. He ignored Mary. "Abbie, Dr. Bartlett wants to see you in his office." He seemed preoccupied and spoke very little as we walked up the stairs.

Then he cast a sideways glance at me. "You look weary."

"I've had a difficult morning."

"Wha—"

"Nothing," I said, cutting him off. "It's a long story."

I would have felt like a fool telling William that I had almost killed my grandmother's dog. Before he could press me further, I changed the subject. "Should I be nervous? Maybe Dr. Bartlett thinks it's too dangerous for me to work here after the murders."

"No... I doubt that. You're too valuable here."

William had none of the flatterer in him, so I took his compliment to heart.

As we approached the fourth floor, William's mood lighted a bit. "My aunt wants to meet you."

"She does?" I felt a little thrill at the idea of meeting Christina Rossetti.

"Yes. I promised her that I would bring you to her soon. I hope you don't mind."

"No, I would love to meet her."

We had just reached Dr. Bartlett's closed office door.

"Well, I'll leave you here. Christina needs my help this afternoon."

After bidding me goodbye, he left.

I knocked, and then opened the door quietly when Dr. Bartlett called for me to come in.

He stood behind his desk, staring out the window. His thoughts seemed far away too, and I wondered if his mind was on the murders—perhaps dwelling upon a recent interaction with Abberline or Bagster Phillips. But almost immediately, he became attentive.

"Abbie, do please sit down." He nodded toward a leather chair in front of his desk, then sat down behind the desk and removed a cigar from a small top drawer.

"Lady Westfield only required that you work here one

week—but I see that you are back," he began. He lit the cigar. "I know, I'm a physician, but please pardon my vice."

"Yes, of course." I felt myself smile. Dr. Bartlett could be enigmatic and yet, frequently, he put me at ease.

"So," he said, blowing the smoke away. "Why are you continuing to work here?"

"Because I love the work." I thought this might be as good a time as any to bring up the subject of medical school. "Actually, since I'm in your office, I wanted to tell you that I've been considering medical school. But I haven't the first idea of where to start."

A glint sparked in Dr. Bartlett's eyes, and he tapped some of the ash from the cigar into a nearby dish. "You, Abbie, have read my mind. Your future is exactly why I called you in here to this meeting. You have remarkable control during surgeries and difficult births, and I have heard from Dr. St. John that you are both caring and creative when it comes to patient care."

I knew that Simon must have told Dr. Bartlett about my suggestion that Rose Elliot nurse Lizzie. My heart sank a bit as I thought of how little good had come from my idea. I still planned on returning to the hospital some nights.

Dr. Bartlett leaned back in his chair a bit. "The field is still extraordinarily resistant to women. Oxford and Cambridge are both closed to giving women medical degrees." He emitted a disgusted chuckle. "Of course, they're closed to giving women *any* degrees at all. However, there is a women's medical college, recently started here in London.

I know the founder, Dr. Elizabeth Garrett Anderson. She is excellent, and a highly dedicated physician. You can attain a medical degree through that college, and I would be happy to help you along the way if that would be something you would like to consider."

"Of course." The news of the women's medical college excited me.

"Continue to work with me here now, gaining experience. Then I would like to introduce you to Dr. Anderson, and perhaps you could go ahead and apply to her school."

I had so many more questions, but at that moment, Dr. Buck stepped into the office.

"Inspector Abberline is here again to see you, Julian. He is waiting downstairs."

Dr. Bartlett sighed and threw away the end of the cigar. "I'll be there in one minute."

The moment Dr. Buck left, Dr. Bartlett stood up from his desk. "I expect I'll be at the mortuary for a few hours. The inquest was on Monday and everyone's pressed for time, as the body must be buried soon."

"Inspector Abberline is no closer to solving the crimes?" I asked.

"I'm afraid not. Such murders are not incredibly uncommon in the East End, but there are some perplexing elements to these two. Because of this, journalists are already picking up on the story, and I am certain that if yet *another* patient of ours is murdered, the papers will be covering the story in even more detail. Three Whitechapel Hospital patients killed in this horrific way would seem to be beyond coincidence. We will have..." Dr. Bartlett raised a graying eyebrow. "Unwanted publicity."

"Do you think there is *going* to be another murder?"

Dr. Bartlett looked at me, distracted once again, his thoughts seemingly elsewhere.

"No."

But his tone was far from convincing.

PART II

"Women are supposed to be very calm generally; but women feel just as men feel; they need exercise for their faculties and a field for their efforts as much as their brothers do; they suffer from too rigid a restraint, too absolute a stagnation, precisely as men would suffer; and it is narrow-minded... to say that they ought to confine themselves to making puddings and knitting stockings, to playing on the piano and embroidering bags."

—Jane Eyre

Eleven

The moment I entered her home after work the next afternoon, Grandmother called me into the parlor with her.

A still-bandaged Jupe lay across her lap and her cup of tea steamed from the tray on the sideboard beside her. Before even greeting me, she thrust the *Times* into my hands.

I had assisted in three deliveries and then helped staff the nursery that day. I felt particularly tired because I had not slept the night before while secretly attending to Lizzie.

However, I skimmed the several newspaper articles discussing the recent murders. When I reached the editorial section, a specific letter caught my eye.

If anything beneficial is to emerge from these recent
Whitechapel murders, it will be to expose the
rampart poverty of those forgotten in the East End:
men who work seventeen hours at a time to bring
a little bread and fish to the table, children who
die before the age of five from starvation, cold, and
disease, women, forced to abandon virtue to buy
food. These are the forgotten, the sad, the lonely.
Fiend though he may be, this murderer has brutally
slashed open the already dying and destitute souls in
Whitechapel, for all of London to see. No longer will
they be ignored.

—Reverend John Perkins

I stared hard at Perkins's name.

Dr. Bartlett's prediction—that a journalistic frenzy might occur—seemed to be coming true. At first, I felt some bewilderment as to why Perkins, as Dr. Bartlett's friend, would publish such a letter, but then I realized that it was probably the right thing for him to do, considering his profession as a clergyman. He should pull the focus away from the sensational factor a bit and draw attention to the area's poverty. My dislike of Perkins's manner was clearly prejudicing me.

Grandmother snatched the newspaper back, placed her spectacles above her nose, and skimmed the upper section again. "One of these articles describes *both* victims as being Whitechapel Hospital patients. *I* did not know about this fact."

"A coincidence, Grandmother. I would very much like to continue working there." My heart quickened for fear that she might not let me return.

Her eyes darted in the direction of the dining room, where Mother's portrait hung. This quick glance settled my fears a bit. She did not want the break with me that she had had with her daughter, and I knew she feared losing me more than anything.

"You always take Dr. Bartlett's carriage to and from the hospital?"

"Yes," I lied. I hated lying.

"Still, I might speak to Dr. Bartlett about the matter, just to make certain that you are safe. He has excellent judgment." Her expression relaxed. A little. "I have known Julian Bartlett on and off for about twenty years—mostly through donation dinners," she added.

I sighed inwardly; it appeared that Grandmother wanted to talk. In spite of my exhaustion, I felt as if I should converse with her for a few minutes. I assumed an interested expression.

"When I met him, he had just returned from the Continent—Germany, Vienna, or somewhere—and had decided to stay in London permanently."

"The Continent?" I remembered hearing Max Bartlett conversing in German with Dr. Buck.

Grandmother's face darkened a bit, irritated that I would interrupt her remembrances. "You know, Arabella, how fond he is of travel. He lived the first part of his life in

England, but then he spent several decades abroad. He is *highly* respected in the best social circles."

Jupe woke himself with a startled bark and promptly fell off Grandmother's lap.

She emitted a small shriek and picked him up. The conversation was over at that point, as Grandmother fussed about the little dog.

Yet now I wished that she would keep talking—not about her past with Dr. Bartlett, but about my mother. I wanted to hear more of what Mother was like before her "ruinous" elopement with my father. What she was like as a child, as a young woman like me. When she became interested in painting. I paused, briefly wondering if I should bring it up. But then, considering Grandmother's fears about the recent murders, I decided against it.

Once again, I slipped out that night to go to the hospital. As before, I did not see any nurses in the first floor ward.

Almost immediately, however, upon my settling in a rocker to feed Lizzie, the nursery door opened noiselessly.

It was Simon.

"Abbie, how did you come here?" His voice was quiet. Reproachful.

I felt like a naughty child. *Caught*.

"I walked."

"Why? Do you know how dangerous it is walking

through this district at *any* time? And it seems sheer madness to do it at this time, with the murderer still loose."

I had no defense.

"Lizzie was weakening—not getting enough milk from Rose. I wanted to give her the care she deserves. She needs to be bottle fed at night as well as during the day."

"*I* am here on many nights."

"Yes, but I know that you're busy."

Simon gave up, dropping his reprimand for a moment. Empathy for the baby won out. Gently, he took Lizzie from me for a minute. "She *is* looking better. I noticed that earlier today." He hesitated for a second, his ice-blue eyes assessing me with a bit of mirth. "You are welcome to work here at night."

I had indeed hoped that Simon, the persistent humanitarian, would not argue about me working at all times if I wished.

"But you *must not* walk here alone," he added.

An infant fussed as Simon quietly unlocked a small cabinet to retrieve a bottle of iodine. Before leaving, he turned back to me. "I'm assisting in a surgery on the third floor. We will be finished soon. Why don't you come upstairs when you want a break and we can discuss safer means of transportation?"

He cast me a small smile and left.

I thought that two o'clock in the morning was an odd hour to be conducting a surgery. I hoped that it was not an emergency surgery.

Lizzie made greedy sucking noises on the bottle. My

concern about her immediate survival had eased a little. Nonetheless, I worried about her future. She would probably go to an orphanage like so many others.

After a bit, when she finished the bottle, I laid her in her cradle and walked out of the nursery, in the direction of the stairs. Light streamed down from the third floor. I wondered if the surgery was still in progress.

I had not spent much time on the third floor. Although there were some patients there, the floor was mostly reserved for surgeries and post-surgical care. Two large doors stood open immediately to my right. A nurse hurried away from the doors with a chamber pot. She looked a bit startled to see me but nodded politely before descending the stairs.

When I entered the large room, I saw a single patient, Liz Stride. She lay in a bed, still asleep from the surgery.

Simon and Dr. Bartlett stood by her bedside, speaking in low voices before they noticed me.

"Abbie! Excellent timing," Dr. Bartlett exclaimed. "We have just finished surgery. Dr. St. John has informed me of your nightly ventures to the East End. Your actions were nothing short of foolhardy."

I felt my face redden even though his reprimand seemed oddly mixed with compliment.

"You are welcome to come here anytime you wish, but I am going to require that you ride here by carriage. Dr. St. John is willing to send his family's carriage at night."

I winced a little. With a late carriage arriving, I would

have to inform Grandmother that I would be working at night.

"Do you usually perform surgeries this late?" I asked, trying to change the subject.

Before Simon spoke, I caught the brief glance he cast Dr. Bartlett. "Only some surgeries."

I left shortly thereafter with Simon, in his carriage.

During the ride home, I noticed that although Simon had been up all night, he seemed wide awake, completely alert. I could barely keep my head up. I watched him through drowsy eyelids, his pale face angelic in the dark carriage.

"How is Jupe?" Simon asked, amused.

I felt myself blush deeply. "Better. He's walking about the house like a little wretched mummy."

"Has Lady Westfield forgiven you?"

"Mostly. Although I am banned from playing archery for my whole life."

At some point along the way, the jolting of the carriage put me to sleep. "You are home, Abbie," I heard him say quietly. I had not even noticed when the carriage stopped in front of Grandmother's home.

I quietly opened the front door.

Richard sat on a bench in the entranceway, immediately in front of me.

I could not speak.

"Do you realize what your grandmother would say if she knew about *this*? An hour ago, Jupe opened your door and when Ellen went into your room to retrieve him before he could wake you, she saw that you were gone. Vanished."

Damn. I must have forgotten to shut my bedroom door completely.

"I *lied* for you, telling Ellen that I had seen you downstairs drinking a glass of water. She went to bed. But since then, I've been sitting here debating whether or not to call Scotland Yard. I know that you can usually take care of yourself, and I had a feeling that your absence had something to do with your work. But Abbie, you typically have more *sense* than leaving the house like this at night! *Why* did you leave?" His eyes blazed in an unusual display of emotion. "Am I correct? Does this have something to do with your work at the hospital?"

"Yes." I could not lie to Richard. "I must work some nights now."

Richard tilted his chin a bit. Exasperated.

"It won't be all the time, just sometimes," I said quickly.

Richard remained silent for a few moments.

I thought some truth and humor might lighten the moment. "Richard, I'm rather fierce. Did I ever tell you about my knife-throwing days in Dublin?"

His forehead tensed momentarily as he considered a negotiation to present to me. "Whatever your hours might be at the hospital, I *do* require that you tell your grandmother about this. As soon as possible." He stood to leave. "At breakfast, in fact."

"I will."

Richard looked at the grandfather clock in the entranceway. "You had better go to bed. You only have two hours before Ellen wakes you."

Before leaving, he turned around. "Knife-throwing?"

"Yes. I was a bit of a local champion."

Richard smiled, scratched his chin, and left.

"Nights *too!*"

Grandmother's voice might have broken glass.

"Just *some* nights. And I'll come and go with Simon in the St. Johns' carriage. He lives near us. He said it would be no inconvenience to escort me when I leave."

"I suppose I am simply going to have to be all right with you running back and forth from the East End! Day *or* night."

She began slicing at her egg ferociously. I felt confident that Grandmother would let me work, although she would rage on for a good while.

I heard Dr. Bartlett's carriage approaching.

"I should have *known* that this would happen!" Grandmother was saying. "I am only trying to protect you." She slammed her cup of tea down on the table. "Not that *I* have any say in the matter."

As I left, Richard stood in the hallway facing me, his back against the wall. He looked highly amused. I smiled at him and glanced back toward the dining room, where Grandmother rattled the marmalade jar in her fury.

That morning at the hospital, I assisted in the curtained delivery area with Dr. Bartlett. During a particularly stressful delivery, he helped Simon perform a caesarian. The woman lived through this one, but Dr. Bartlett asked me to bring some dried ginger root from the pharmacy to ward off infection—a very real threat.

I had not familiarized myself enough with the pharmacy contents, particularly the herbal medicines and their Latin labels, and as I scanned the shelves for the bottle of ginger, I knocked a bottle of ammonia onto the floor.

I cursed.

As the strong smell of the solution permeated the pharmacy, making my eyes water, I ran back through the laboratory toward the small utility room. Hoping that it contained not only a sink, but also a mop and bucket, I swung open the door.

I gasped, and my blood ran cold.

The room did in fact contain a large, tublike sink, a broom, a bucket, and a mop. But it was the wall that caught my eye. It had a single decoration—a small, dingy painting. It looked old, the canvas buckled a bit against the rotting wood frame.

The painting featured a silver chalice with a single Latin phrase engraved across the side: *A Posse Ad Esse.*

I felt my world spin a bit; this chalice was identical to the chalice in my visions.

But why? Why would I see it here?

I stayed frozen where I was, processing what was before me, until I heard footsteps, and then William cursing loudly as he discovered the spilled ammonia.

I recovered my senses a bit. Although my throat felt parched, dry from the shock, I had to act normally.

"Guilty," I said as William stormed into the utility room. His angry expression softened when he saw me. I took this as a good sign.

"I knocked it over as I tried to find the ginger root, and was just in here to get a mop." Then, nodding my head toward the picture, I asked casually, "What is that?"

"That?" William responded, distracted as he filled the bucket with water in the sink. "It's just an ugly portrait of a communion cup or the Holy Grail or something. It's always been in here."

"But the inscription? The Latin words. From possibility..." My brain fumbled through my poor knowledge of Latin.

"I never noticed the inscription." He peered at it a little closer. "From possibility to actuality."

He hauled the bucket out of the sink and I quickly grabbed the mop. It would seem odd if I focused on the old painting too much. But I was certain that it depicted the chalice from my visions.

William finished mopping up the ammonia, and I finally located the bottle of ground ginger root on the second shelf. William stood up awkwardly as I began to leave. His voice came out a bit abruptly. "So, I thought that today might be a great day for you to come to our house and meet Christina."

I panicked. So far, although I felt attracted to William, he intimidated me, and I had managed to keep him at a safe distance. His famous writer aunt also seemed a bit daunting to me. Meeting Christina Rossetti, being in their home, both excited me and made me anxious. I felt even more flustered as I looked down at the blood, amniotic fluid, iodine stains, and splashed ammonia on my dress and apron.

"I need to change first."

"Christina will think none the less of you."

"I do need to tell Grandmother also."

"Go home, clean up, and inform Lady Westfield that you have dinner plans with the Rossettis. Unless I hear otherwise, I'll assume that you're joining us for dinner."

Grandmother seemed in a good mood when I arrived home—far from the rage she had been in that morning. She looked quite nice in a plum-colored dress with pearl earbobs. I assumed she had spent the day with Lady Violet. She sat at her desk in the parlor humming to herself while she wrote a thank you note. I felt a sense of relief that she seemed to have lost some of her anger from the morning.

"Hello, Arabella. You are home early today."

"Yes." I swallowed. "Grandmother, your dress is lovely."

She turned around in her chair, staring at me suspiciously, quill pen still in hand.

I took a deep breath. "Would it be all right if I dined this evening with Dr. William Siddal and his aunt?"

Her eyes narrowed. "Is he the physician who kept you so late, the evening you became lost on your walk?"

"Yes."

"And his aunt is going to be there?" The edge in her voice must have made the still-bandaged Jupe nervous. He rolled off her lap and ran stiffly from the room. "Who is she?"

"Christina Rossetti."

Grandmother's eyes blazed. I had given her the wrong information.

She stood up. "William Siddal is a relation to the *Rossettis?*"

I heard a sharp, suppressed laugh from the hallway. *Richard!* I was glad that the situation amused him.

"Yes. William is Gabriel Rossetti's adopted son."

"Not *only* are you spending days and nights at the East End hospital, but now you are cavorting with the *Rossettis*. Do you know about their family?"

"I know that Christina Rossetti has been a very dedicated and devout woman to the poor ... "

"They are *poets*." She spit the word out as one would say *thief* or *whore*. "Arabella, Dante Gabriel Rossetti was a classic hedonist, a womanizer, and a drug user. His models—well, he had affairs with *all* of them. He had countless mistresses."

She did know about the Rossetti family.

"I like William."

She paused. Horror crossed her face. With a tremulous hand, she dropped her quill.

I knew that Grandmother was fighting with all of her might not to forbid me from accepting the dinner invitation. As she almost always did, she cast her eyes in the direction of the dining room. She knew I was too much like my mother. Blinking back angry tears, she took a deep breath and struggled against her own will.

There was nothing to say, so I bowed slightly and left.

Twelve

I had never met anyone as socially conscious as Christina Rossetti. An advocate for animal welfare, she never ate meat. She never drank alcohol. And, as William had previously told me, she did allow a limited number of former prostitutes to live in her house, referring to them as her "friends."

According to William, the seven or eight residents who lived with Christina at any time had to have impeccable recommendations from their physicians and demonstrate much promise in terms of seeking and keeping respectable employment. Christina treated them with dignity, allowing each woman to have her own bedroom, and even encouraging them to attend church with her on Sundays. As long as they worked and refrained from alcohol, Christina housed them until they could afford to rent their own rooms. It was a remarkable system, and beyond various physical ailments, which William attended to, she had never had any severe problems—she had established too excellent a system of mutual respect with her friends.

Furthermore, Christina charitably employed an eighty-year-old former prostitute, Perdita, to work as her maid. On the carriage ride, William told me that the old woman, blind and nearly deaf, was incapable of doing much real work.

Christina herself was pale and fragile in appearance, with beautiful, orblike dark eyes. Though in her fifties, she had the energy of a much younger woman. Furthermore, in spite of her tiny figure and short stature, she carried a giant stewpot to the table with ease, and I could see how she managed, on top of her other responsibilities, to volunteer at New Hospital.

Her house was dark inside, the walls painted in dark greens and browns. In spite of this, the dwelling was by no means inhospitable. Books lined nearly every inch of the walls, even one wall in the dining room. Glancing over the titles, I observed an eclectic and broad range of topics. Devotional and religious books stood beside art books and anthologies of fairy tales and myths. Sketches, charcoal skeletons of more famous paintings, hung upon many of the walls. A polished cross hung on the left wall of the dining room, across from the books. But apart from the cross, Christina maintained a relaxed atmosphere at the table. William's Great Dane, Hugo, sat at his feet, and Christina's beloved parrot flew about the room, finally perching on my shoulder as I sat down for dinner.

"Toby likes you," Christina said as she sat near me.

I didn't mind the bird much—except for when he beat my face with his feathers.

As the meal progressed, Christina's hospitality made me feel at home. I found William more at ease around his aunt, less intense than he was at work. Christina was very kind to me, and I could tell that she was quite fond of William. I noticed her peering at me occasionally in a manner that I found a bit unsettling. She asked me several questions about my growing up and I told her a bit about my years in Dublin, sans stories of the knife throwing.

Around seven thirty, Christina began watching the clock. "Some of my friends are supposed to return a little after eight. These recent Whitechapel murders have made me nervous for them."

"Dr. Bartlett thinks that the murders are over," I offered, curious about William's opinion.

"That's not likely," William said.

"You think there will be more?" I felt a bit surprised at the tone of William's voice. He had spoken with certainty.

"I do. These murders are far too planned, too methodical. The murderer is sending a message. He is not finished yet."

Christina's eyes seemed liquid as she pondered this for a second. "Please explain, William."

"I *saw* the body of the first victim, the Nichols woman, at the mortuary. My reaction was that the murder was *not* a random violent act against a prostitute. Every injury on her body seemed intentional. With Annie Chapman's body, even more so. Each cut seemed part of a larger message for London. He is carving out some sort of code. More is to come. Unfortunately."

"If you are correct, William, I wonder if the 'message' might be against Whitechapel Hospital. Don't forget that both victims were also your patients," Christina said.

I picked up on a tension in the air, like an electric current.

"*He's goin' down the row, he is,*" Dotty had said.

Christina looked as if she wanted to say something else, but refrained.

"Why might someone want to do that?" I asked.

"The hospital has provoked some criticism from more judgmental Londoners. Dr. Bartlett has been accused of fostering too much compassion for prostitutes and not putting enough emphasis on religious conversion," William responded.

The atmosphere became a bit sober, and Christina quickly veered the conversation to a lighter subject.

Soon dinner ended and Christina called for Perdita to clear the dishes away. No response came from the old woman's bedroom quarters, located just beyond the dining room.

"Did you forget, Aunt, that Perdita naps between the hours of nine o'clock in the morning and nine o'clock at night?" William asked. "Unfortunately, straight through two of our meal times."

"She is old, Will. I'll do it myself in a few minutes." Christina stood and exchanged an odd glance with her nephew. "William, why don't you take Abbie to the parlor? I'll be there in a minute."

I glanced at William, but his expression was unreadable.

The parlor was small, cozier than Grandmother's parlor. A roaring fire in the fireplace drew my eyes to the portrait above it. The portrait depicted a young man, very handsome, with dark curly hair and an intense look on his face. He did not look unlike William.

"Who is he?" I asked, walking toward the fireplace.

Hugo padded into the room and began sniffing me, probably smelling Jupe's scent on my skirt. I patted his head; the dog was about the size of a small horse.

"That is Christina's uncle, my great uncle, John Polidori."

"John Polidori, the author of *The Vampyre,* is your relation?" I remembered our conversation about vampire literature. He had said nothing at that time. "Why didn't you tell me before? Did Christina know him well?"

William just laughed a bit and came to stand beside me at the fireplace. I only vaguely felt the heat of the flames on my skirts.

"He was not only a writer, but a physician. He was actually the poet Lord Byron's physician for a while in the Alps. And to answer your question, Christina never knew him. Polidori had several spoiled love affairs, an overreliance on laudanum, and loads of gambling debts. He died quite young of an overdose of prussic acid. Whether the overdose was accidental or suicide has always been a family debate."

William's expression seemed far away for an instant. Lost in a sea of memory. Then he snapped back to the present and chuckled. "Because everyone in my family seems to be so *literary*, I've always felt a connection with my great uncle, the physician."

"But he was also a *writer*. You might write also if you wish."

"If you are wondering why I haven't tried my hand at writing or painting, I simply haven't the skill. But being a physician *is* a creative act. At least I think so."

I understood the line of thinking. Perfectly.

"Are you telling Abbie about our sordid family history?" Christina entered the parlor with a tray of steaming cups of tea. As we seated ourselves, she met William's eyes again.

There was an awkward pause before Christina spoke. "Abbie, William and I not only wanted to visit with you tonight, but we wanted to tell you something. We both wanted to wait until after dinner, so as not to shock you with too much information at once. But the fact is, after your first day at work, when William explained to me that you were Lady Charlotte Westfield's granddaughter, returned to London, I knew immediately that you were Caroline's daughter."

My heart quickened, and I set my tea down, afraid and excited about what was to come.

"Your mother was a friend of my brother, Gabriel. She was part of his Pre-Raphaelite artist circle."

I felt speechless and did not know what to say. My mother had not merely painted—she had known the Rossettis. She had painted and worked *with* them. This was extraordinary, and I wondered why she had never told me. My emotion in that moment was a little overwhelming.

"You knew her?" I asked.

Christina smiled. "I didn't know her as well as Gabriel did."

Dear God. I remembered what Grandmother had said about Gabriel's many mistresses. I remembered Christina's eyes on me throughout the evening. A cascade of questions formed in my mind. Was my mother one of his mistresses? When exactly had she known him? I felt it would be indecent to ask these questions at that moment, but they burned in my mind. I recalled Grandmother's visceral reaction to my friendship with a Rossetti relation; perhaps Mother's elopement was not the only reason Grandmother had severed ties with her.

A tear slid down my cheek, and, after rapidly wiping it away, I felt my face burn with embarrassment. I hated appearing so vulnerable—particularly in front of William.

"It's all right, Abbie," Christina said quickly. "I just wanted you to know."

I took a quick breath to regain composure.

"She not only painted, but also did a bit of modeling for Gabriel," Christina added.

I met her eyes. *Model.* Rossetti had likely been my

mother's lover. The timeline of Mother's relationship with Jacque Sharp in relation to my birth had never added up; it was always as if she was keeping something from me about my father. Could Dante Gabriel Rossetti have been my father?

The question burned on my lips, but once again, it seemed too bold to ask. I had only known Christina for a few hours.

"For which paintings did she model?" I asked quickly.

"There was just one. It's missing now. I never saw it," William said, a bit gruffly. I feared that my show of emotion might have made him uncomfortable.

"I've seen it," Christina said.

We heard voices coming down the street outside. Christina's friends were returning from their jobs. She glanced at the window and stood. "Gabriel frequently liked mythological subjects. Your mother posed for a portrait of a lamia—the part-serpent, part-female monster. If I remember correctly, Caroline dictated to him much of the portrait style and her position in it, as well as what colors to use. The portrait was really quite stunning, and was in his studio. Then, around the time of his death, it disappeared. Either someone took it or it was lost as we cleared out the room."

I couldn't speak. Somewhere, there was a lost Rossetti portrait featuring my mother.

"If I ever locate it, or if it is returned, I will give it to you, Abbie. It should be yours."

There was a knock on the front door.

As Christina left the parlor to let her friends in, I found myself alone with William.

I bent over, rubbing Hugo's ears as he lay at my feet in an effort to hide my emotions. I felt angry at my mother for all of her secrets, for not telling me about her past. I had now been thrust into her London life with very little knowledge of who she had been, whom she had loved. Furthermore, if she had had visions—as I suspected she had—she should have discussed them with me. Now that *I* had them, the question of where they came from and how to process them frightened me. With my mother dead, I was left to navigate them on my own. I also felt a renewed anger at Grandmother. She had participated in concealing Mother's past from me.

After a full two minutes of silence, having regained my composure, I finally looked up at William as he sat in a chair near me.

The expression on his face made something flicker inside me, and I gasped. He was staring straight at me, and it was not the William I knew. The cynical expression was gone, and I saw, very clearly, something like affection in his eyes. We both knew that we shared a bit of history, through my mother's relationship with his adoptive father.

Then it hit me. William had been a small child during the years Mother spent with the Pre-Raphaelites.

"Do you remember her?" I whispered.

"I wish I did. My father had many women in and out of his house and studio." His look still lingered on me.

At that point, voices from Christina's friends in the dining room broke a bit of the spell between us.

"It's getting late," I said. "I should leave soon."

I bid Christina good night. I wanted to talk with William during the carriage ride back to Kensington, but I had too much to process. Facing Grandmother—after learning what I had—would be difficult. Many emotions were bubbling inside me, and I knew a confrontation would be unavoidable.

Thirteen

Grandmother," I asked as I nonchalantly buttered a roll at breakfast the next morning, "why did you not tell me that my mother associated with the Pre-Raphaelites?"

Her fork clattered to the floor. She stared at me, unbelieving. After summoning Richard to bring her another fork, she flicked her eyes once again at Mother's portrait above us. Her eyes returned to me, and she said nothing.

Now I felt angered. I deserved the truth.

"Your estrangement from my mother was not only about her elopement with my father, was it?"

Richard returned with the fork.

"Thank you, Richard. Would you shut the door please?"

As soon as Richard left, Grandmother turned to me. I

could tell that she was deciding how much to tell me. But then her eyes flashed angrily.

"I *knew* this would happen. I feared it. But I hoped that Rossetti woman would not know you were Caroline's daughter, or that she would have the good sense not to bring up Caroline's *brief* connections with them." Her face quivered with rage. "Your mother's interest in painting became particularly serious when she connected to that Pre-Raphaelite circle. It was a wild phase, one that I am convinced led her to her hasty elopement with that *Frenchman*, an amateur poet in the group."

"You mean my father."

At least, I had *thought* he was my father.

"Yes." If her anger toward my mother had softened over the years, I could tell that Grandmother still bitterly hated my father. She was silent for another minute before continuing. Her eyes were glazed with tears.

"Abbie, you have *no* idea how tolerant I tried to be. I tolerated so much, until ... "

Her voice cracked and she paused.

"Until she eloped," I said.

"No. Until I heard from a reliable source that she had modeled for a Rossetti painting."

She had known! Grandmother was no fool; she would know that this implied a love affair between Mother and Gabriel.

"When I heard from my London circle that she had done this, you can imagine my horror and embarrassment. We argued late into the night. Your mother had never been so angry at me. *I* had never been so angry at her." Grandmother paused, her thoughts elsewhere. "The next morning, Caroline had run away with Jacque Sharp."

"Did she ever write to you after that?"

Grandmother said nothing.

"She did," I said angrily. "She *did*. But you never wrote back until Sir Edgeworth sent you that note informing you that she was dying. She had disgraced you too much!"

When I saw the way Grandmother's face contorted into grief, the venom of my words caused me to recoil. She had never looked so vulnerable. She was like a wounded animal.

I might as well have struck her in the face.

"Do you think I'm not paying for that?" she said, so softly I could barely hear her. "I see her every time I look at you."

"But you still try to force me to live like you."

"I have given you liberties, Arabella." Here she wagged her finger at me. "Although I dislike it, I have allowed you to see this William Siddal, to go to the Rossetti house, and to work in that East End hospital, excessively and at strange and even obscene hours. I wish that you might see how difficult all of this is for me, after what I went through with your mother."

Full tears fell from her eyes at that moment.

She stood up and took a few breaths to regain composure. She wiped her eyes with a handkerchief, left abruptly, and went upstairs.

It was Saturday, so I was not scheduled to work at the hospital that day.

Simon stopped by briefly in the late afternoon to take tea with me and to examine Jupe. Rain poured outside, pelting against the windows and the guttering. I had still not seen Grandmother since that morning. I felt bitterly angry toward her, but I also felt guilty for hurting her so badly. I had not expected her to cry. If she did not make an appearance at dinner, I would try to talk to her.

After tea, Ellen brought Jupe downstairs to the parlor. Simon cut away most of the bandages and pronounced the dog better, prescribing only plenty of rest.

"Although finding time to rest should not be a problem for Sir Jupe." He smiled.

I smiled too, weakly. It was difficult to summon humor in that moment.

Simon had so far gracefully tried to ignore my glumness and Lady Westfield's absence. But now he met my eyes. "Lady Westfield ... " he murmured.

"She is unwell." I spoke too quickly, and I saw that Simon knew there was more to it.

We briefly discussed some hospital business. My spirits rose a little when he told me that he had weighed Lizzie that morning and that she had put on sufficient weight. He said that her survival was likely and that he did not think the nightly feedings were necessary any longer. Regarding other news, the victim Annie Chapman had been buried the day before. Simon had attended the small funeral and said that both Dr. Bartlett and Dr. Buck were there and were very gracious to her family.

Through the parlor window, I watched carriages slosh through great muddy puddles. Recalling my vision of Chapman's naked body, I thought of all the surgeons who had been poking, prodding, and cutting at her during the post-mortem examinations.

"I'm glad that she's finally buried, that she's at peace now," I said out loud, still watching the carriages.

"Yes, finally," Simon said, his voice cool as running water. Although he was reserved at times, Simon's friendship meant a great deal to me, and his demeanor was always calming even at the worst of times. I felt grateful for him now.

Grandmother did come down to dinner. She asked me about Jupe and wanted to know everything Simon had said about the little dog's health, but she said nothing about what had happened between us that morning. During dinner, she talked as if everything was normal, and I said nothing about our confrontation. In spite of my anger, which I still felt was justified, I decided it would be best to follow her lead.

That night as I slept, I dreamt of Mother. I was a child again, and we were on an outing near a beach. The sun burned hot on my face, and the ocean roared in the distance. Mother stood on top a large dune, her face shaded by an enormous hat, and she smiled, beckoned for me to come to her. I climbed, but the sand kept slipping out from under my feet and fingers. After grabbing onto roots and snatches of grass, I finally made it to the top of the dune.

"Mother!" I called.

But she had disappeared, and although I scanned the horizon, I could not see her anywhere.

When I awoke, it was the early hours of the morning, and my face was wet with tears.

On a Thursday almost two weeks later, as I stepped out of the carriage to walk up the steps of Whitechapel Hospital, I noticed that the air seemed strangely muggy for a fall day. The sky that morning was bright pink streaked with dark clouds, dark like liver spots on aged skin.

The *Times* and other newspapers had been trying to maintain public interest in the recent murders; some journalists even claimed to have received letters and bloody souvenirs from the murderer. Furthermore, the papers went so far as to name the killer—Jack the Ripper. But there had been no more murders, and, because of this, I had only vaguely followed these stories. I thought that most were probably sensationalized, trumped up by journalists to sell papers. Even though the Ripper still lingered for many as a public menace, at least at Whitechapel Hospital the general environment in the wards seemed more relaxed.

I had continued to assist Dr. Bartlett in delivery and surgeries, taking in all the information that I could about organs, illnesses, and procedures. That particular morning,

I attended a surgery of one of the second floor patients who had been afflicted by upper abdominal pain and fevers. She had been in a carriage accident shortly before coming to us, and William feared that she might have an undiagnosed broken or cracked rib that had possibly poked or punctured an organ, causing pain and infection.

William was the operating physician in this case, and, as in many surgeries, Dr. Bartlett stood nearby, saying very little but making himself available if William needed assistance. He also explained to me what was happening as William went along. Except for two assisting nurses, I was the only other person in the operating room.

"Nothing. Absolutely nothing," William said, frustrated when the rib proved to be merely cracked from the accident trauma.

I saw Dr. Bartlett watching William carefully from across the patient's body. "Nothing, William?"

William stared into the woman's open abdomen. I had watched him in many surgeries, and although skilled, sometimes he became flustered, missing something directly under his nose.

Fever. An infection must be going on. She had been in an accident, had experienced trauma. Upper abdominal pain. My mind ached as I sorted through all the information I could remember about her.

"Spleen," I said quickly. "Have you checked her spleen? A ruptured spleen from the accident might have brought on bleeding and asplenia."

Dr. Bartlett caught my eye across the bed and gave a small nod. "Check it, William."

William probed a bit in the opening. "Ah-*ha!* Congratulations, Abbie Sharp. There is a small splenic rupture. Not serious, but the rupture might compromise her ability to fight infection, and there is a bit of bleeding. Here it is, Abbie, look. I don't think we should take the spleen out..."

William glanced up at Dr. Bartlett, who nodded in confirmation

"Will she be all right?" I asked.

William nodded as he prepared to close the abdominal opening. "If she can beat this infection. Taking out the spleen entirely seems excessive given the small size of the rupture, which is already healing. This bit of bleeding should cease and reabsorb soon, as long as she stays off her feet for a while. The pain should go away at that point, too."

As William stitched the patient up, I saw Dr. Bartlett's eyes settle upon me. The look was layered, undecipherable.

Fourteen

Immediately following the surgery, as he washed blood off his hands, William thanked me for bringing the spleen to his attention. He showed no sign of wounded pride for missing it. William had so many sides—he could be sardonic and easily flustered, yet display these shining moments of kindness.

Just before we left the operating room to go about our other work, he caught my arm. "Christina wants you to come over again. And frankly, so do I."

I felt a rush of warmth and worry. Well aware of my attraction to William, I feared that I was plunging down a path from which I could not return. I had never experienced such feelings for anyone, and I felt split between trusting my desires and halting everything.

In that instant, at least, I sided with my desires. "I would love to visit—with both of you again."

William seemed pleased, and we both returned to our more mundane work for the afternoon.

The second floor remained quiet that day, so I joined Mary in the laundry room. Laundry at Whitechapel Hospital was a task never fully conquered. With all the dirtied sheets, clothes, and beddings, the baskets in the tiny room seemed always full. I often spent an hour or two every day folding laundry, but *washing* days were unchallenging, tedious days spent scrubbing foul rags, towels, and nightgowns against a metal washboard. At the end of every washing day, I spent the evening trying to hide my raw and bloodied fingers from Grandmother. I feared the rest of this day would be devoted to washing.

Mary was scrubbing the laundry with speed and ferocity against the washboard. Soapy bubbles spilled over onto the floor. Then I noticed what seemed like small hailstones striking the window pane.

"Mary, Mary!" The shouts came from the street, two stories below.

Mary continued washing the laundry, ignoring both the shouter and the pebbles.

"I think someone is trying to get your attention," I said.

"That would be Scribby. I haven't talked to him for two days."

I peered out the window to see the same young man I

had seen with Mary on the street that very first day I met her, enthusiastic about his new job.

"Argument?" I asked.

"Yes. And I thought I might see him today, Thursdays being his day off."

"What did you argue about?" I asked. Perhaps it was a nosy question, but I was a bit curious. Mary didn't wear a wedding ring and she lived with Liliana, not with Scribby, so I assumed they weren't married. Nonetheless, I guessed the relationship was amorous in some way.

My nosiness must have annoyed her; Mary paused in her washing just long enough to flash me a look of fire.

I peered out the window once again. Scribby looked like a nice fellow, possibly one who didn't deserve Mary's foul treatment.

"Mary!" he called again.

Her mood was getting under my skin a bit, and I felt a little mischievous.

"Hello!" I yelled, prying open the window. Dried paint had sealed the lower part of the sill.

I ducked a little as a stone narrowly missed my head, bouncing to the floor behind me.

"Oh … sorry, miss!"

"Can I help you?" I shouted.

"Tell Mary … "

Before he could finish, a constable shouted from down the street, "You! *You*! Stop there!"

In a sudden, stupid panic, Scribby ran.

"Scribby!" Mary shouted, suddenly beside me, leaning

out the window. She had transformed from indifferent to concerned.

"He wasn't bothering us!" I shouted. But it did not matter. The constable seemed intent on picking on someone that day.

Scribby ran, narrowly dodging carriages as he raced down Whitechapel Road. The constable had a hard time keeping up.

"He'll get away," I said to Mary as I began to shut the window.

But then I saw a small child, no more than seven, look up from playing on the side of the street. With a fiendish smile, he shouted, "Hey! *Hey*! He's chasin' the Ripper! He's chasin' the *Riiiipper*!"

Two women, sweeping out the guttering in front of a shop, shrieked. One shouted, "The Ripper! It's the Ripper!"

A burly man, unloading produce in front of a store, dropped his boxes and joined the chase, shouting to others that the constable had the Ripper in sight. He began running after the constable, who was still in hot pursuit of Scribby.

I could not believe how quickly mass chaos ensued on an otherwise ordinary Thursday afternoon.

Faces leaned out of windows. A few people, and then many, began flocking out of shops, workhouses, and even carriages—all intent on catching the Ripper. Whistles sounded as I saw police making their way through the growing crowd, trying to restore order. But the police force seemed too small in contrast to the enraged crowd at that point. By the time Scribby disappeared from my view, a full-blown mob was chasing him. I watched the scene unfold, unbelieving.

"*No! No!*" Mary shouted, pushing past me to get to the stairs. "We have to help him! They're going to kill him."

Nurses and even some patients ran down the stairs with us, slowing our pace. Sister Josephine, William, Simon, and several other hospital workers blocked the front doors, barring anyone from leaving.

I heard shouts and cries grow louder from the streets.

"Let me *through*," Mary screamed, elbowing her way through the small indoor crowd. William remained her final obstacle. He stood his ground, his back firmly against the doors. "No one can leave, Mary. The crowd out there is too dangerous."

"He's her friend," I said, pushing my way toward them. "William, *please*, Mary and I can take care of ourselves," I added calmly.

"Abbie." William pulled me aside, all while maintaining his vice grip on Mary. Josephine's sharp voice rang out behind us in an attempt at restoring order. A few curious nurses still loitered near the front doors, hoping to get a glimpse of the excitement outside. "For once, Abbie, *listen* to me. It would be madness to go out there. No good can come of it."

The shouting continued in the streets. I heard glass shatter somewhere. I had no idea how we could help him, but Mary and I could not just stay in here, leaving him alone to the mercy of that mob.

William's brow arched as he studied my expression. He knew he had not convinced me. Was he relenting, I wondered, or was he just rethinking his tactics?

"Mary, I want to help you." He still held her firmly around the shoulders. I noticed Mary relax a little. At the same time, William placed his hand on my back reassuringly. "Let's step over here and talk rationally."

Rationally? I prickled at the word. My neck grew hot. I felt a small fury toward William that I had not felt since my first day in the hospital. He led us a few steps away from the entrance, toward a side hall.

When he turned me toward him in the narrow hall, I felt a quiver in my stomach and a bloodrush in my cheeks, despite my anger.

"I'm sorry," he said. "I *cannot* let you go out there."

Instantly, he opened a door and shoved Mary and me through it.

I heard a lock bolt us in.

"No!" I screamed.

Mary cursed, kicking at the door. "If we could just get *outside*!" she screamed. "I think I might know where Scribby is heading. He works at the docks. He was running in that direction. There's a warehouse there that he might be in . . . " She continued to kick.

Frantically, I looked around, trying with much difficulty to put a lid upon my angry feelings toward William. I needed to focus on escaping. I saw buckets, bedsheets, and boxes stacked along the wall and then along shelves on the other wall. The room was tiny, about the same size if not smaller than the laundry room upstairs. Though it was mostly dark, light seemed to be coming from somewhere in the closet other than from the crack under the door.

It seemed the light was streaming down from above the shelves.

Mary continued to kick the door, cursing William to hell in the process.

"Mary! *Stop*! I think there's a window."

She hoisted me up, and when I reached the top shelves, I saw a giant box blocking a small window. With much effort I tried to move it, but then just pushed against it.

"Watch out!" I yelled as the box crashed to the floor.

The window was small and narrow, but I thought we could fit through.

Mary had already climbed to the top shelf and crouched beside me.

"Kick it!" she said.

I did, and shattered the glass with surprising ease. We slid out, one at a time, into the alley beside the hospital.

The riot sounds continued, though they had moved away from the hospital.

"I know a back way to the docks!" Mary shouted as we ran out of the alley. "I'm nearly certain that Scribby is heading for that warehouse. It's huge, five floors at least, most of them empty. But there are plenty of places to hide from the police and the others."

Mary led me away from the crowd's shouts. "We'll figure out how to smuggle him away when we get there," she yelled back at me.

"*Abbie! Abbie!*" I heard William's enraged voice shouting from the front steps.

"*Hurry!*" Mary shouted. "Don't let him catch up with us."

We cut through alleyways, jumped over steps, and climbed over alley gates. I had no idea where we were, but I trusted that Mary knew the route. She was fast and light-footed.

Suddenly, after going through many narrow alleyways, we emerged into an enormous, dirt-packed lot. Shouts roared, though I did not see the crowd. The warehouse, gigantic and seemingly abandoned, loomed ahead of us. We appeared to be at the back of the building. It was then that I understood Mary's plan. The crowd had just reached the front of the building. Giant wooden fences flanked both sides of the warehouse, connecting to the sides of nearby buildings; and, at least for the time being, effectively sealing the crowd away from the back lot in which we stood.

All the back windows were either broken or boarded up. Padlocks on the two visible back doors had been snapped.

"I was right. He's in here," Mary said, running toward one of the broken but unboarded windows. "The crowd is in front, so he *must* have gotten in somehow."

We crawled through the open window. A musty smell assaulted my nose. Cat-sized rats scurried along the base of the walls. Water dripped from large cracks in the first floor ceiling.

Luck seemed to be a bit on our side. Every one of the front-facing windows on the first story had been boarded up tightly. If the windows had had only glass as a barrier, the crowd would have already been in the warehouse. Still, the sturdy boards could be broken down with moderate effort. We had to hurry; I knew it was only a matter of time before the crowd either broke in through the front or breached the high side fences.

"Over here," Mary said. "He'll be upstairs."

On the far side of the room, a steep iron staircase twisted upward into the ceiling. We ran toward it.

"*Scribby!*" Mary shouted. "Scribby! I'm here."

"Abbie!" I heard a shout from somewhere behind us, on the first floor, after we had ascended.

William!

"Scribby! Where are you?" Mary shouted.

Several open rooms lined the damp, darkened hallway of the second floor.

"Here!" Scribby shouted from the room immediately to our left.

He was crouched underneath a large wooden table. He had lost his hat and his clothes had been torn, his right pant leg tattered and blood-soaked. Blood streamed from his temple.

"Scribby, Scribby," Mary whispered in a soft voice. "We're here now. It's going to be all right. I know a way out."

He nodded at me: "I'm so sorry for getting the both of you into this mess. You didn't have to follow me here."

He sucked in his breath from the pain. "I can't run. I think there's something broken in my leg. I barely made it here, Mary. They got me for a moment. Thought I was going to die then. A big guy took a hammer to my leg. But I broke away—got in here through a side crawlspace."

"*Abbie!* Mary!" William ran into the room, his face scarlet. He looked angry. Terribly angry.

Ignoring William, I peeked through a crack in the boards across a nearby window. The crowd below was enormous now. Several policemen blew whistles and lined up against the front of the warehouse, attempting to block the crowd. Still, it could break through. We did not have much time.

"William, you need to do something for his leg!" I yelled.

"I *cannot*," William said in quiet anger as his eyes cut into me. He crouched down by Scribby, who winced as William examined the bloody part of his leg. "It's fractured—maybe broken clear through. It must be set, but I don't have any medical equipment here, obviously."

He sighed loudly and stood up. "This was a foolish and futile endeavor, Abbie. I tried to prevent you from doing this."

Mary glared at William. "You locked us in a *closet*."

Gunfire erupted outdoors.

William and I ran to the crack in the boarded-up window. Police reinforcements had arrived. Scotland Yard carriages lined the street. Inspector Abberline stood amidst the crowd, his gun raised to the sky.

"Everybody leave now! Stop this nonsense!" his voice boomed out. "We are pursuing a petty criminal, *not the Ripper murderer.* I repeat: *Not the Ripper murderer! Leave!* All of you leave at once!"

The portly but sturdy inspector made his way through the crowd to the padlocked doors. Gunfire erupted again as he shot off the locks. Much of the crowd scattered.

"Open this door!" Abberline shouted to the constables beside him. Then, turning to the crowd again: "If anyone, *anyone* other than one of my designated constables follows me in here, he *will* be arrested."

Many, who seemed disappointed that no Ripper had been caught, hanged, or torn apart, left. Still, several of the most angry onlookers remained, eager to get a glimpse of their object of hatred.

"Come out at once!" Abberline shouted up the stairs from the first floor. "You have caused *more* than enough trouble today. We will escort you safely out now, but you must surrender. *Now!*"

A rusty tin basin in the corner of the room quivered with the vibrations caused by Abberline's voice.

"He needs to surrender. He'll have a safe escort now," William said quietly.

"But he'll be arrested," Mary snapped.

"He can't escape, Mary," William replied irritably. "As I said before, his *leg is fractured.* If he hides, or waits until the police leave, he might be *dead.* Some of those still down there will want a shot at him. Furthermore, in case none of you have noticed, the police have guns downstairs.

There is nothing to keep them from storming up here and shooting us all to high heaven."

"He's right," Scribby said. "I'll go. They can't book me too long for breaching the peace. And"—Scribby struggled as he stood up, leaning against the table—"I'll go first. It's my fault that we're all here anyway. I should never have run away in the first place."

"We'll *all* go," Mary said. "You need my help to get down there, anyway."

Leaning awkwardly against Mary while standing protectively in front of her, Scribby led the way down the stairs. William and I followed.

"Keep your hands *up*! Hands on the back of your head!" Abberline yelled from below as Scribby, with Mary's help, began descending the stairs.

William smirked sideways at me as we put our hands on the backs of our heads. "Congratulations, Arabella Sharp. You just got us arrested by Scotland Yard."

"I can't *believe* that you locked us in that closet."

"*What the . . .*" I heard a constable shout below.

The scene below became visible to us as we descended the stairs. At least thirty cops stood in the large, dripping, rat-infested first floor, their guns pointed straight at us.

"He's got others with him!" another cop shouted.

Abberline stood in front of all of them, his gun still pointed at us, but his face was flushed in confusion. They had been chasing *one* criminal and now there were four. "Lower your guns," he said evenly to the cops behind him. The inspector's bulgy, shrewd eyes landed on my face, and

I saw that he remembered me from the hospital. *Did he remember William also?* But his gaze remained on me, calculating. Something bothered me about his expression.

"We were trying to protect him!" Mary yelled at every constable in the room. "It's not like you all were doing a good job. He's got a broken leg."

"*Silence! Everyone!*" Abberline shouted. He had made a decision. "Handcuff *all* of them and take them *all* to the station!"

I felt humiliated as several cops raced over and pulled me away from William, put my arms behind me, and clicked the metal cuffs into place.

"Your grandmother is not going to be very happy about this," William said under his breath as we sat with Mary, still handcuffed, in Abberline's office.

I desperately hoped that she wouldn't find out; fortunately, everything had happened too quickly for the journalists to arrive. Grandmother would disown me if a photograph of me handcuffed appeared on the front page of the *Times*.

The office was surprisingly small for a Chief Inspector's office. It had the oppressive atmosphere of being the den of someone who worked hard for long hours at a time. A stack of papers towered on one side of the desk, while dirty, half-empty teacups were piled on the other side. A bookshelf with more stacks of papers and only a few books flanked the left wall. A water-stained map of London, with different districts highlighted, was precariously pinned to the wall behind the desk. The only personal, non-work-related item in the entire office was a small watercolor painting propped up near the pyramid of half-drained tea-cups. The little portrait portrayed a woman, middle-aged like Abberline himself, with the name "Emma" scripted in charcoal directly under her face.

Detective Inspector Frederick Abberline, as his name-plate proclaimed, walked heavily into the office with a steaming cup of tea. He sighed as he sat down and rubbed his calves as if they ached.

"Uncuff them," he said to a nearby constable. "You can let Dr. Siddal and Miss Kelly go."

"Where is Scribby?" Mary asked.

"In the London Hospital. I went ahead and released him from our custody. I apologize. He should not have been throwing stones, but my constable was over-vigilant when he pursued your friend for disturbing the peace." Abberline raised his eyebrows. "You must understand, my men have been a bit on edge since the Ripper murders commenced."

"So, I can leave now?" Mary asked pertly.

"Yes."

"And Miss Sharp?" William asked as he stood to leave.

"She'll be out in a little while. There is no need to wait for her. I'll have a police escort take her back to Kensington."

William paused, casting me a glance. I nodded a little

to let him know that Abberline's proposal was fine with me. He left.

"Miss Sharp." Abberline leaned back a bit and took a long sip of tea.

As I smelled the tea steam—orange, with a hint of mint—I became uneasy. From the moment I had met Inspector Abberline, after the Polly Nichols murder, I had felt that he was watching me intently. I couldn't imagine what possible role I might play in his investigation, but it seemed as if he wanted something from me. I had an intuitive notion that this day had unfolded conveniently for him—he finally had an opportunity to corner me.

Trying a bit too hard to sound casual, he said, "This Jack the Ripper case is becoming the most aggravating case in my career. Extraordinarily baffling."

He paused. Looked at me.

"Do you like your work at Whitechapel Hospital?"

"Yes."

He waved his hand as if we had an established, unspoken contract between us. "There is no need for Lady Westfield to know about this. I have emphasized the necessity for *discretion* to my constables."

"Thank you." I felt closed. Guarded.

He waved his hand again, signaling that the gratitude was unnecessary.

I knew this must be part of his professional tactics. He had emphasized to Mary that Scribby was free and safely in the hospital—he maintained the perfect balance of sternness and politeness, so that he always remained in control.

"Do you know, Miss Sharp, that Whitechapel Hospital is a key point of interest in this case?"

I said nothing.

"*Both* victims had recently left the hospital. The murders are unlike anything I have ever seen in nearly twenty-five years of work."

I wondered what else he had seen. Then I focused again; he was trying to pry information from me.

"Do you mind?" Abberline had removed a pipe from a hidden drawer.

"No."

He lit the pipe.

I said nothing and instead focused on keeping my breaths even. I knew as much from Dr. Bartlett, William, and Simon, but why was Abberline telling me about the investigation? Did he suspect William? Simon? Anyone *specifically* among the physicians?

"Julian Bartlett—and I know that you will keep this conversation confidential from him—has been most helpful as a medical consultant. He is brilliant. Experienced. But he is more trusting toward humanity than I am inclined to be. He refuses, absolutely refuses, to consider any of his physicians as suspects. He has made it quite clear to me that he will consider them nothing short of *co-consultants* when it comes to the investigation. This has become frustrating lately, and I am finding myself confiding in him less and less."

I decided to confront the inspector head-on.

"What do you want from me?"

He gave the slightest cough before regaining his composure. Then he leaned forward, so far across the desk that I could see the small red veins in his eyeballs.

"I want *several* things, Miss Sharp. I want to know *why* our Ripper seems so intent on murdering Whitechapel Hospital patients. What is his purpose in targeting them? And yes, I do believe he *has* a purpose. I want to know why a physician, or someone with anatomical knowledge, would do this. I want to know why, but, more importantly, I need to know *who*. Because he will strike again, Miss Sharp. We are not dealing with an ordinary killer. The character is a psychopath, pulling me into a puzzle that I have yet to solve."

He leaned back in his chair again. "What do I want *from you*? I want you to cooperate, to inform us. I have watched you, Miss Sharp. You are shrewder than most ladies your age; most ladies of any age, for that matter. But I do hope that you will not allow yourself to be blinded."

I cocked my head. "What do you mean?"

"Overly trusting of anyone. Confiding too much in anyone. *Loveswept.*"

I exhaled in exasperation and began to stand, intent on leaving. I felt offended at what he was trying to imply.

Abberline coughed, choking a little on the pipe smoke, and sat up straighter. He was irritated and flustered.

"Miss Sharp, *sit*. Hear me out."

I sat. Part of me felt as if I *should* hear him out.

"I am so bold for a few reasons. First, this is a polite, professional warning—if anything should happen to Lady

Westfield's granddaughter, I will have more, much more trouble to deal with than the riot in the East End that you witnessed today. Actually, it would be much easier on myself, must less of a risk to this investigation, if I had a discussion with Lady Westfield herself and put an end to any and all of your work at the hospital."

My blood stopped flowing. *If Grandmother knew about my arrest and if Abberline told her anything regarding the details of the case, my time at the hospital, and my work, would certainly be ended.*

"However, my first loyalty is to the city of London, to fulfill my duty to uphold dignity and order, as much as possible, on the streets. To this end, I *must* find Jack the Ripper. If you might reveal to us *anything* said, or done, that even *seems* suspicious, among any of the workers at Whitechapel Hospital, it would be most beneficial. This is not common knowledge, but we're finding very few leads in this case. I think you can help me. You are perceptive, intelligent, and if I might say so, attractive. You, I believe, can be the most helpful when it comes to probing the secrets of that hospital."

He wanted me to be an *informant.* A *spy* among my co-workers. I felt an awful astonishment. Such a role was beneath me. He wanted me to use my education, my gender, and my position to deceive my friends. If I agreed to what he wanted, I would have a double agenda in all my work and work relationships.

I knew my answer.

"I can't." I stood again. "I must leave now."

"*Arabella Sharp*." It was the first time that Abberline had used my first name, and a distinct thread of anger infiltrated his words.

Would he talk to Grandmother? I felt slightly panicked. No, Abberline was above using blackmail to get what he wanted.

He stood. "I do not think you fully know what a dangerous game you are caught up in. You have no idea that you work within a *hotbed* of suspects. You have no idea how sick this game is turning!"

I had never seen Abberline discomposed, and my feelings of unease rose.

"There is something I want to show you before you leave," he said. "I think, when I show this to you, you will see how wise it would be to cooperate with me."

I followed him out of his office and down several halls. The must and gloom of Scotland Yard felt overwhelming. Small offices, similar to Abberline's, lined many of the hallways we walked through. At the end of a particularly dark and narrow turn, we came to a large, locked room. Abberline took a key from his pocket and unlocked the door to reveal a large room containing numerous shelves, on which sat hundreds of boxes and stacks and stacks of paper.

Evidence? Open cases? Cold cases?

He led me down several aisles toward the back. He stopped at a shelf against the back wall, very near an enormous, mold-stained desk, and pulled down a huge box. Dozens of letters and envelopes filled it.

"Miss Sharp, in case you're not certain yet about what

a smash this Ripper is among the London public, all of these letters are either from concerned citizens, believing they have information on the Ripper, or from people actually claiming to *be* the Ripper."

I felt astonishment at his last statement. "What do you mean? I can't believe that anyone would claim to be the Ripper."

"Believe it." Abberline began taking out whole handfuls of letters and tossing them onto the nearby desk. "I have everyday lunatics, fame-seeking journalists, and the delusional, all of whom would like nothing more than to be Jack the Ripper. We've had several confessions from blokes almost daily here at the station. They are willing even to die in a public hanging if it means that they can claim the glory of going down in history as the Ripper."

"You don't think any of these confessions are real?"

"All of them are nonsense. Garbage. Trash." Abberline began tossing some of the letters one by one back into the box. "I have had my best detectives and handwriting experts go through each and every one of these, and all of them believe the citizens' information to be worthless, and each and every confession nothing more than a hoax. However ... *this*"—Abberline reached for an unmarked box on the very top shelf—"is what I wanted you to see."

His red-veined eyes bulged again. "Needless to say, *no one* must know of this. By divulging the contents of this box, I am showing you how much I need and trust you. But more importantly, I'm showing you the cat-and-mouse element of this case."

The box, when he opened it, contained a letter. Abberline unfolded it carefully on the desk. Evening had begun to close in, and the room had darkened. He moved a candle closer so that I might read the letter. It had been addressed to Abberline, with the return address referenced merely as *FROM HELL*.

In the shadows of the box, I saw a jar of liquid. Abberline saw my glance at the jar. "Do first read the letter, Miss Sharp."

In the light of the candle, I read, feeling Abberline's intense gaze on me.

Sir, I send you half the kidney I took from one woman and preserved it for you. The other piece I fried and ate. It was very nice. I may send you the bloody knife that took it out if you only wait a little longer.

> *—Catch me when you can Inspector.*

My head swam and an acidic taste rose in my mouth. "You think this is real?" I asked.

"Oh, yes. This one is. No one except the Ripper would have known that Annie Chapman's right kidney was missing. This was not information shared with the public. Dr. Bartlett, of course, knows nothing about this. But one of our other forensic consultants has affirmed with near certainty that it matches the victim's other kidney. Chapman's left kidney manifested Bright's disease—the kidney half the Ripper sent me shows signs of the disease, in the same state of progression as the other one was at the time of Chapman's death."

"You have the part of the right kidney that he sent?"

Abberline reached into the depth of the box, toward the jar. It was then that I noticed a small blob, jellied, dark, floating in the liquid.

"No, I don't need to see it."

Abberline nodded. He lowered his voice and leaned toward me. "You see, this *is* a game, Miss Sharp. He is taunting us, mocking us, cannibalizing for pleasure to show us that he has no moral boundaries."

My stomach turned.

"You are already in the middle of this, Arabella. And I will be your friend throughout, but you would be smart to cooperate."

"I must leave." I averted my gaze, not able to look at his penetrating expression. I walked away. Without looking back, I said, "My answer to your proposal is unequivocally *no*. I am a worker at Whitechapel Hospital. Nothing more."

Then I stopped and turned to face him, quickly, hoping that he could not see the nausea I felt to my core. "And you needn't worry, Inspector, about me sharing any information you've discussed or *shown* me tonight, with anyone."

"I know," Abberline replied quietly. In the darkness, I could no longer see his expression. "You know where to find me if you change your mind."

He began sealing the box and its contents. "Your escort home will be at the front door."

I focused on making it out the front doors of Scotland Yard before vomiting. The heaving, the purging, brought me some relief from the thoughts I could not face.

Fifteen

The next morning at the hospital, I tried to push the meeting with Abberline out of my mind—that image of the floating kidney—and focus instead on my tasks. But that letter, and the writer's claim that he had eaten half of the kidney, saving and mailing it . . . I shuddered every time I thought of it. The killer was certainly more than a lunatic to be able to murder, escape the police this easily, and then taunt them as he was. Abberline was probably right that the killer was a psychopath, someone shrewd, cunning, and methodical.

But I didn't understand why Abberline was so convinced that the Ripper worked at Whitechapel Hospital. Like William, I did not believe that anyone I worked with was the Ripper. I didn't want to be stupidly naïve; if the

Ripper was as much of a mastermind as Abberline supposed him to be, he *would* blend in—he *would* be able to charm. To amuse. But at Whitechapel Hospital, we were all too busy to plan and carry out such a game. Furthermore, everyone had such excellent rapport with Dr. Bartlett and Dr. Buck—why would someone who worked there want to soil the hospital's reputation by killing its patients?

I wondered why Abberline felt so adamantly that the Ripper worked in Whitechapel Hospital specifically. London had other hospitals, and dozens of medical students and physicians. Certainly Abberline, with all of his years of detective experience, must have thought of this. Perhaps he had withheld something from me, some further proof that the murderer worked at the hospital.

I did not trust him. Inspector Abberline had said that he would be my "friend" if I worked with him. But after leaving Scotland Yard, I didn't regret for an instant my refusal to work with him. His first and foremost concern was not me, and certainly not Whitechapel Hospital. What he wanted most was to catch the killer.

Although there had not been any more killings, Scotland Yard police were still patrolling in and around the hospital. I vowed to avoid Inspector Abberline whenever he appeared there. I understood that he was interested in me because I was involved with the staff, patients, and happenings at Whitechapel Hospital at a level that he could not be. Nonetheless, I still did not want to involve myself.

Ironically, publicity from the killings was bringing us more volunteers. We had more nurses now than before.

Several volunteers came from local parish churches. The newspaper stories and letters to the editor, such as Perkins's, were raising awareness of life in the East End. This had not only inspired the extra volunteers, but we were also receiving significant money and supply donations. Even New Hospital was sympathetic, sending us a large shipment of medical supplies. I hoped rather than believed that this outpouring of generosity would continue even after the papers finally grew tired of covering Whitechapel stories.

That morning, I finally got a chance to confront William about his behavior prior to our arrest with Scribby. I found him seated by a bed, pulling bloody bandages off a female patient who had come in with an abscess on her arm. Before he saw me approaching, I studied his profile. He looked even more weary than he had previously; his expression seemed troubled, strained.

I brought him a bucket for the bandages, half-filled with soapy water. I dropped it heavily on the wooden floor at his feet.

"Did you have a nice chat with the Inspector?" William did not look up from his work.

"That's *none* of your business." The patient was sleeping, but I spoke in a whisper. "We have not yet addressed how you locked Mary and me in the closet downstairs. Bad form, William."

He smirked. "Yes. It was. But I wanted to save your life. I knew you wouldn't listen to me." He looked up at me for the first time in the conversation, dropping the bloody cloths into the bucket. "And you *did not* listen. By running out in the middle of that riot, *your* leg, instead of Scribby's, might have been broken. Or worse."

"You know I can take care of myself. For goodness sake, William, you have seen it."

"I do, Abbie. But you should know your limitations. There is a difference between bravery and the conceited independence you seem to enjoy—walking through the East End at night, running outside amidst a rioting crowd. All of this *will* get you killed someday."

Perhaps it was the stress. Perhaps it was the pressure of the hospital work. It might have been the tension broiling around the wards ever since the murders began. But I could no longer ignore that cord between William and myself. I was angry, and I wanted to test its strength.

"And why would you care?"

William remained silent as he finished removing the last of the bandages. Then he stood and pushed his chair back, skidding it hard into the wall.

I jumped back a bit. Like a startled rabbit.

"I'll take *this*." William snapped up the bucket of bloody, wet bandages.

He left the ward, and I did not see him for the remainder of the day.

That evening I arrived at Dr. Bartlett's house for a dinner party.

I had been invited along with a few other physicians—only his favorites, William had told me. There were less than six of us. Since this would be a bit more formal than the first time I was at his house, I wanted to wear something nicer than usual. On a whim, I had chosen one of Mother's more formal dresses, a lavender gown that bustled in the back. The bodice fit tightly, providing a dramatic contrast to the bell sleeves; cream-colored lace framed the inside of the sleeves and the neckline of the bodice. I had also found the faux-diamond headband Mother had worn with the dress—it was in decent shape except for one gem gone, like a missing tooth.

When Dr. Bartlett opened the front door, he looked a bit startled, which was odd for him. But he regained his typical demeanor within seconds. "You look lovely." He cleared his throat. "I'm sorry. So much like Caroline."

His eyes lingered on me for a second before he looked away. Mother and I did have the same coloring and height, but in that moment I felt insecure, as if wearing the dress had been a mistake. I was a duller, less attractive version of her.

The Montgomery Street house looked more resplendent than I remembered it. The globelike aquarium cast so many prisms of light around the drawing room that it gave the illusion of the room being underwater—the shadows of jellyfish glided along every inch of the green walls. The potted foliage seemed even more lush and abundant than before.

Dr. Buck nodded at me from behind Dr. Bartlett. He looked as stiff and bookish as ever.

"John, Marcus," Dr. Bartlett called, waving his cigar toward the other men who stood near the bookcases. "You remember Miss Arabella Sharp? She has become my prize student, and, I believe, a future physician."

Reverend Perkins put a glass of wine in my hand. Although polite, he still had not thawed toward me. I had seen him once or twice in recent weeks, in his clergy collar visiting patients at the hospital. Each time, he had barely acknowledged me.

"Thank you," I said as I took the glass, unnerved by his demeanor.

Dr. Marcus Brown was all politeness and kindness. He immediately put me at ease, lamenting cheerfully that I was choosing the medical profession as opposed to his area of study, history and philosophy.

"But I do love to read," I said. "Particularly the Brontë sisters' works. *Jane Eyre* and *Wuthering Heights* are my favorites."

"Ahhh … the Brontës!" Dr. Brown clapped his hands together. "Quite ahead of their time, actually! So perceptive about the situation of women, about the blindnesses that still exist in our patriarchal society."

He flashed a look at Reverend Perkins and I instantly realized that he was not talking about the Brontë sisters' fiction, but rather was making some other point entirely to Reverend Perkins.

"Let us not keep Abbie from the other guests," Dr.

Bartlett said abruptly, stepping aside. "Dinner is about to begin."

I felt a bit bewildered as I tried to figure out what had just happened between Dr. Brown and Reverend Perkins. But Dr. Bartlett ushered me toward the back of the house.

"We're dining outside. It's such a lovely night."

I felt perplexed. Late September in London was too cold for an outdoor dinner.

Then, when I saw where Dr. Bartlett was taking me, I realized that "outside" was not quite an accurate term for the dinner setting. He led me through the drawing room to the two great French doors I had seen Max exit through the last time I was at the house, and then into a sort of magnificent hothouse containing nothing less than an indoor forest. It was bordered by high stone walls covered with ivy. Exotic flowers blossomed from the greenery in orange, pink, and yellow puffs.

I looked up and saw a glass dome high above us and the clear, starry night sky beyond. The dome must have been at least level with the fourth story of the house. Birds dashed back and forth under the dome. Many were rainforest birds—toucans, parrots, and others that I could not identify. Undoubtedly many had been brought here by Dr. Buck.

Trees, many of which were tall with thick leaves and not native to England, had been planted throughout the area. Small monkeys dangled and jeered at us from above, and snakes slithered along the ground. A very large fountain stood immediately in front of the forest, and a long table sat just in front of the fountain. A few torches surrounded the table for lighting, but beyond that, past the fountain, the only light in the entire place came from the moonlight above.

Everyone except for Dr. Bartlett's housemates and myself were already seated, ready to dine. A giant platter of stuffed roast mutton and bowls of bread and baked beets had already been placed on the table. Dr. Bartlett guided me to an empty seat at the end of the table, near Simon and William and just in front of the fountain. Aside from Dr. Bartlett, Dr. Buck, Reverend Perkins, and Dr. Brown (I had not seen Max Bartlett anywhere), there were three other young physicians whom I did not know so well: Colin, Alistair, and Branwell. William stood quickly when he saw me approach.

"You look beautiful," he said, pulling out my chair for me.

Simon nodded; his sea-glass eyes emitted only a polite gesture of greeting. I briefly wondered if he had noticed me in the same way that William had.

As I had observed before, in the course of the dinner Dr. Bartlett and his housemates seemed to have no hired servants—not even one. Dr. Bartlett himself, or Dr. Brown, removed dishes throughout the meal; Reverend Perkins and Dr. Buck refilled wine and water glasses. Dr. Buck, I imagined, was the sole gardener of the surrounding forest. He rose at least twice to shoo away curious monkeys.

The conversation among the guests mostly involved

medical-related issues—specifically, the benefits of the profession's recent merger of practicing medicine and conducting surgery. I listened to this conversation carefully, but when the subject turned to politics, I became bored. I cared about political issues, but I found debating them useless.

I took a look at the stunning fountain directly beside me. Nearly concealed in patches of dark green mold on the round stone base of the fountain were the engraved words *A Posse Ad Esse,* followed by the symbol of a chalice.

My surprise and confusion at this recurring symbol—whether in my visions or in the utility room painting at the hospital—struck me like a thunderbolt. What did it mean? *From possibility to actuality.* Was there something significant about the inscription?

My thoughts were interrupted when Dr. Brown and Reverend Perkins brought out dessert: pineapple ice in champagne glasses. I tried to focus on the conversation. Unfortunately, it had become monopolized by Alistair, a Conservative who viewed the poor as "idle," and Colin, who believed more government money should be given to the parishes.

The noise of the fountain just behind me and the increasing intensity of the conversation at the other end of the table isolated William, Simon, and me at our end.

"Ridiculous," William muttered. "More money will not fix anything."

Simon disagreed quickly. "We spend so much money

on wars, on these brutal battles around the world, but we let England's poor fall by the wayside."

"I agree with you, Simon. But you think too highly of people. You think that the poor, just because they are poor, are *good*. Frankly, the East End riot I witnessed last week was a demonstration of bloodlust and ignorance."

Simon was not finished. "I find the wealthy disgusting, too. I am *from* a wealthy family. We accumulated our fortunes only a few decades ago—through the slave trade."

He took a drink of wine as a *bit,* just a bit, of pink colored his otherwise white face. "Sometimes I feel as if my very life is atonement for their sins."

William smirked at his ancestral guilt. "You place too much blame upon yourself. I prefer to help people when I can, but otherwise, I find nearly all people, of *all* classes, disgusting."

"You're a cynic. You lead a small life."

William's face flushed at Simon's comment.

I felt surprised that Simon had actually pushed the matter. I realized, at that moment, that although elusive and cool, Simon had all of William's intensity. But while William fought with fire, Simon fought with ice.

"William, it is exactly your cavalier attitude that maintains the ongoing problems that confront us daily in Whitechapel," Simon continued.

William responded angrily. "And you, dear Simon, are doing everything you can to fix these massive problems during your nighttime surgeries at the hospital, are you not?"

I stared hard at William. "What are you … ?"

"Inappropriate, William," Simon said. His voice might have smashed porcelain.

I thought of that night at the hospital, when I had walked in on Simon and Dr. Bartlett after they had performed a surgery. No one else at the table was paying attention to us, so I asked, quietly, "What kind of night-time surgeries?"

Simon kept his angry eyes on William. "Often, many of our second-floor patients have been brought in suffering from crude, unsafe abortions. Dr. Bartlett has, for many years, been working to better and more effectively provide safe abortions for women. This is, of course, illegal, but I have taken care of infants afflicted by their mother's diseases—syphilis, gonorrhea. Both Reverend Perkins and I have found dead, abandoned infants on the steps of his parish church in the middle of winter. So, yes, I believe that it's morally necessary for me as a physician to know how to perform the procedure safely."

William snorted.

"Have you performed abortions?" I asked him.

William seemed taken aback. "On occasion, and only when necessary. I have performed them on some of Christina's friends. But I certainly do not need to be tutored in the matter."

None of us said a word for a few minutes. I knew that I was supposed to be shocked by what I had heard from Simon, but I wasn't. I saw the moral complications of the matter as Simon described them.

Suddenly, at that moment, someone removed the headband from my hair. Rough hands, pungent with the scent of Oriental cigar, covered my eyes.

"Who has snatched your lovely headband? Is it a monkey perhaps? One that likes sparkly things? *Lovely*, sparkly things."

Max.

"Cut it out, Max," William said.

The hands lifted from my eyes, but the headband had disappeared.

"Give it back," Simon said, wearied.

"Or what?" Max said gruffly. "Will you and Dr. Siddal *duel* me for it?"

"Just give it back." William took a sip of water. He sighed. I knew his thoughts were still involved in the argument he had just had with Simon.

"No."

It was an invitation.

For me.

The torches had burned down, and the clearing had become darker than it was when dinner began. Most of the party had started meandering back into the house, although Dr. Buck was leading Alistair and Colin toward some of the trees near the front of the area. He seemed swollen with pride over his hothouse collection.

Max locked eyes with me, turned, and walked back into the forest, disappearing into the darkness.

"Abbie," William said quietly. I could tell by his expression that he thought very little of Max Bartlett.

"He'll get tired of the game in a bit and toss it back to you, Abbie," Simon said.

"Funny thing about games," I said, rising from my chair. "I usually win."

William shrugged and casually helped himself to another piece of bread.

I followed Max, alone. I told myself that I needed to retrieve the headband, but once inside the trees, I admitted to myself that I found him alluring.

Everything in the forest was even darker than in the clearing. The fountain sprayed behind me, and the monkeys screeched from treetops. Narrow trails in the dirt wove in various directions around the thick trunks. Although the whole place was enclosed, I began to panic a little, feeling a bit of the same fear that I would have felt if I had truly been lost in a forest at night. Even the stars above the glass dome did not seem to be separated from me by glass.

"Max?" I could barely hear my voice amidst the monkey cries.

I felt a thick leaf or shrub brush against the back of my neck.

I whipped around.

Nothing.

Arabella.

I thought I had heard my name, but from where, I could not tell. I decided to go right, and plunged down a trail into a thick plot of trees. I then took a narrow trail left.

The place was enormous, larger than I had first imagined. I speculated that I must be near the back wall, but no wall came into my sight.

Something large and furry landed on my shoulder. I shrieked just as the monkey leapt off, and it was then that I felt propelled through the darkness until my back was pressed up against a large tree trunk.

"Abbie." The whisper came inches from my face, and I saw Max in the darkness, shirtless. His chest and shoulders were muscled, glistening in the muggy hothouse. There was something feral, uninhibited about him in that moment.

My panic dissipated into intoxicating pleasure; he was close enough to kiss. I swallowed as I fought against all of my conflicted feelings: desire, fear, a peculiar curiosity.

Without a word, he moved even closer, and, stroking some loose hair away from my forehead, he placed the headband back into place. With the movement, a dark place on his upper right chest, which I had thought was a shadow, became clear in a spot of moonlight.

I gasped. It was a tattoo of the chalice, with the words *A Posse Ad Esse* across it.

This was why he had brought me back here. To show me this. *Why?*

My throat felt parched and dry, and I could barely hear myself as I asked, "What is it?"

He didn't answer, but smiled widely, and his green eyes flicked and glimmered in the darkness. As he leaned closer to me, I felt the warmth of his chest through my bodice.

I trembled as he brushed his lips, feather-light, against my cheek, along my jawline toward my left ear. My unanswered question roared inside me and, vaguely, I felt as if I should push him away, but I did not. I was too incapacitated by desire.

Then he whispered, "Goodbye, dollygirl."

Horror suddenly overtook me, and I staggered. He flashed a wide, satisfied smile and disappeared into the forest.

I sucked in air; my chest heaved. Dizzied, lightheaded, I clutched the tree behind me. I vividly remembered the young pickpocket's changed expression after giving me my brooch back, and the cheeky "dollygirl" comment he had made before running away. Max's use of the same phrase terrified me now, for reasons that I didn't fully understand.

What did he want me to know?

Who was he?

Simon, William, and Branwell found me just as I had regained my composure. I steadied my breathing, but still felt my face burn.

"All is well," I said casually, adjusting my headband a bit.

There was an awkward pause before Dr. Buck stepped out from behind a tree, holding one of the torches from the dinner table.

"Dr. Buck is about to show us one of his most remarkable collections," Simon said, taking my arm.

Dr. Buck adjusted his spectacles and held out the

torch. "Do please let me go first. This place can be a bit of a maze at night."

He stepped ahead of us onto the path.

"Miss Sharp, I think you might find this interesting. It is a *private* exhibit. As I have told the others, you must never discuss it with anyone. I only show it to my dearest friends. If you betray me, it might"—he waved one hand in the air like a magician while he pushed a thick branch out of my way with his other hand—"*disappear.*"

My curiosity mounted.

"Watch the pond." Simon guided me around a small pool of water as we turned a sharp corner. The pond was only about six feet wide. I saw silver fish flash under the water's surface.

A strange *dee-doo, dee-doo* sounded from nearby. It was high pitched and jarring.

Dr. Buck mounted the torch on a nearby iron pole. "Behold: my prize pet."

My heart rose to my throat. Inside a small fenced enclosure was a bird, about three feet tall with a thick, short, curved bill. It sported some of the loveliest plumes I had ever seen. I gasped; it was as if an illustration from a beloved book of my childhood had come alive before me.

"Is it really?" William asked.

"Unbelievable." Branwell stepped closer and reached out to touch the bird's head.

Quoting the very book that was on my mind, Lewis Carroll's *Alice in Wonderland*, Simon recited: "'There was a

Duck and a Dodo, a Lory and an Eaglet, and several other curious creatures.'"

"Yes," Dr. Buck said in a low voice. "It *is* a dodo bird."

"But these birds have been extinct for more than a century," I said.

"Yet here is one before you, alive and well," Dr. Buck replied.

"How and where did you find him?" William asked.

Dr. Buck smiled. For an achieved naturalist, he looked impish, cryptic in the torchlight. "Oh, I've had him for a few years. Found him in the native environment where he supposedly disappeared, the island of Mauritius in the Indian Ocean."

"Is he the only one?" Simon asked.

Dr. Buck seemed determined to remain mysterious. "For now. But trust me, when he dies, he will not be the last."

None of us understood his meaning, but I think we all knew that he would not divulge any more information that night.

I still had another question as I stared at the magnificent bird, which strutted about uttering low coos and *deedoos*. "Might I see him again?"

"Oh yes, any of you are free to see him anytime. A small handful of people in London do know of his existence. But he is not yet ready to be exhibited to the scientific community. He must stay here now, under the cover of my forest."

Dr. Buck's mouth creased open in a smile as he dropped a pile of dried pumpkin seeds into the palm of my hand. The dodo stopped strutting and its black marble eyes rolled in my direction. With gentle stabbing motions, it ate the seeds from my hand.

I felt overwhelmed with emotion as I fed the dodo. It was a magnificent impossibility.

"What do you know of Max? Besides the fact that he's Dr. Bartlett's nephew," I asked Simon, nonchalantly, as we rode back to Kensington in his carriage that night.

In the darkness, his eyes met mine. He was curious, but I knew that he, unlike William, would not ask any prying questions.

"Honestly, very little. I think he travels frequently, along with Dr. Bartlett and the others. But often he comes in and out at Dr. Bartlett's gatherings. He's elusive. A bit odd."

I settled back in my seat and tried to process what had happened between myself and Max in the hothouse. The chalice symbol, my visions, Max's whisper in my ear … even the existence of the dodo bird. I knew there were connections I needed to make, connections that my mind could not yet comprehend.

Sixteen

"Arabella? *Arabella*, are you listening to me?"

At breakfast the next morning, I was so preoccupied with the events of Dr. Bartlett's dinner party that I had stopped listening to Grandmother.

"Yes, I'm sorry." I took a sip of hot tea and refocused. In spite of all that was on my mind, I did not want to be rude.

"I was *saying* that I am going to have the walls on the first floor repainted and new wallpaper added in the parlor and this room. I'm also having some renovations done on the second floor."

"Why? Everything looks fine." I surveyed the walls—all the paint and wallpaper seemed immaculate as usual.

"*Why?*" Grandmother looked at me as if I were a half-wit. "Because they look *terrible*."

"All right." I shrugged a bit.

"I am telling you all this because the work is going to be so extensive that we will have to be out of the house for a few weeks. The noise, the paint and glue odors, will not be healthy for me, you, or Jupe. Lady Violet has generously allowed us to stay with her during that time"

I did not feel very happy about this, and Grandmother caught my scowl.

"This living arrangement will only be for a short time. Mariah will be there."

I perked up a bit at this. With great effort, I resumed talking about the renovations.

Grandmother never brought up anything I did in Whitechapel anymore. If she did not outright regret allowing me to work with Dr. Bartlett, I think that my "moral education" had not had the effect she desired. Rather than increasing my gratitude for the life of leisure she had provided for me, I had become preoccupied with my work at the hospital. Also, although she had said very little about it, I knew that my acquaintances bothered her, particularly the friend who was a Rossetti relation. This, in her eyes, was a reckless act that might have devastating ramifications on her social network. All these concerns had become etched upon her face day by day—her worry about me, her worry for herself, and her worries regarding her social position in a fickle world. In the morning light of the dining room, I saw all of these worries in the fur-rows between her brows.

I listened to her detail the impending renovations for as long as I could stand before excusing myself. I told her that I would be at the library for a few hours, and that, yes, I would be back for late afternoon tea.

As I walked rapidly in the direction of the British Library, I thought about everything that had happened to me since arriving in London and coming to work at Whitechapel Hospital. The first two months had been filled with rou-tine, dull days spent with Grandmother and her friends. Then the chase with the pickpocket—the instance when I had that first vision—changed everything.

I reflected on the order and subject matter of the visions. The very first vision was of the chalice and the ritual of the robed, hooded men. Then I had visions on the nights of the Ripper murders—both of the chalice and of the murderer. I also had a vision of a victim's corpse—Annie Chapman, I think. All of my visions, therefore, involved either the chalice symbol or the Ripper murders. I now knew that the chalice symbol was somehow con-nected with Max, and with Dr. Bartlett and his friends, given that it had shown up at the hospital *and* on their fountain. *A Posse Ad Esse: From possibility to actuality…*

But I couldn't fathom what the chalice and inscrip-tion symbolized or how they might be linked to the

Ripper murders. Of course, I had no evidence that they were linked to the murders at all, except that my visions of the chalice always seemed intertwined with my visions of the murderer.

I bit my lip as I crossed the street. If Mother had seen visions or been psychic, as I now suspected, somehow I had attained her abilities upon coming to London. I would have given anything to ask her about my visions— I didn't know how much to trust them, and I would not have taken them so seriously if they had not been so clearly linked with real happenings.

Once in the library, I sat at a desk with a large stack of books under the glass dome of the Reading Room. I began researching symbols, specifically chalice symbols, and found that the chalice was often linked with the Holy Grail, the cup supposedly used by Jesus at the Last Supper. Often, the Grail is linked to communion and eternal life—immortality.

A Posse Ad Esse.

From possibility to actuality...

I felt crazy for thinking it, but I had seen a dodo bird— supposedly extinct—alive and well and walking about in a London hothouse. The chalice symbol on Max's chest, in the painting at the hospital, and on the Montgomery house fountain *meant* something. It somehow united Max, Dr. Bartlett, and the other housemates. If they were all united around this image, I wondered if they were part of a secret group. Could they somehow be seeking immortality? After all, the chalice *was* linked to immortality.

Could they somehow be immortal?

I felt ridiculous for even thinking this, as it seemed to defy reason. But the thought did haunt me.

Regarding the Ripper murders, even if Dr. Bartlett and his housemates were in some sort of society or organization—which certainly was no crime—I didn't see how they could be linked to the murders. I certainly couldn't understand why they would be involved in the murder of Whitechapel Hospital patients. Dr. Bartlett himself had discussed the "bad publicity" the murders would bring; killing Annie Chapman and Polly Nichols, his own patients, would not make sense. He seemed like such a dedicated physician... I simply could not picture it. And apart from the visions, of course, I had no evidence. Even Abberline did not suspect Dr. Bartlett; indeed, he had told Dr. Bartlett immediately after the Polly Nichols murder that he was not a suspect, and then made him one of Scotland Yard's primary medical consultants in the investigation. Abberline had essentially told me that he suspected one of the other physicians at the hospital. He had, after all, questioned Simon and William several times.

Simon and William.

I shook my head. There was no way either of them could be the Ripper. I could not believe it.

"Abbie *Sharp*." I felt hot breath in my hair and whipped around to see Mariah's beautiful face above me. She wore a dark blue walking dress and a wide-brimmed hat.

"Lady Westfield told me that I might find you here. What *are* you doing, walled up in the library on this lovely fall day?"

"Just reading." I quickly closed the book.

"Well, stop, this instant. Let's go to Harrods. I have some shopping to do for the wedding that will never happen."

"What time is it?" I asked.

"One o'clock." She put her arm out, smiling.

I could not believe that I had been here for three hours now. I gave my books one more glance; the chalice research had captivated me. As I took her arm and walked away from the Reading Room, I thought that an afternoon of normalcy—a short shopping trip with a friend—might be exactly what I needed.

I arrived home that late afternoon in a much better mood.

Ellen greeted me almost as soon as I opened the door with a small envelope. She had made a clumsy attempt to reseal it.

I frowned at her as I took the note.

Ellen's face paled. "I hav' some work to finish in the kitchen, Miss." She curtseyed and left.

Why did Richard not greet me this afternoon? I read the note:

Dear Miss Sharp—

Please do come to Whitechapel Hospital tonight if it is not a problem. I am amalgamating/cleaning

the pharmacy. Your help [and company] would be
warmly welcome.

—Most Cordially,
William

Grandmother was out all afternoon and would then be taking dinner at the St. Johns' house, so I spoke to Richard before I left, assuring him that though I might be late, I would be leaving and returning safely in the St. Johns' carriage. I knew that he would communicate the message to Grandmother, clearly and without any of Ellen's drama. I knew Grandmother would not worry about me if I was in Simon's company, and I felt relieved that I would not have to argue with her.

At nearly eight o'clock, I heard the St. Johns' carriage stop in the street, and I felt relieved that Simon had received my message requesting a ride to the hospital with him. I had not sent it until five o'clock.

As we left Kensington, I saw Grandmother's carriage still parked in front of the St. Johns' residence.

"I see that Grandmother is still at your house."

Although I had noticed Simon's home before, I studied it closely as we rode past. It was taller and grander than Grandmother's. The outside had been painted an unblemished white color and the windows, tall and wide, were framed by inky black shutters, each displaying gold latches for when the windows were shut from the outside. The bushes had been trimmed to perfection, and I saw not a single weed in the lawn. It looked cold and formidable.

"It is so ... " I tried to think of something nice to say. "Grand and well-kept."

Across from me, Simon's well-formed mouth smiled. I could never fool him with a false compliment. His elusiveness shielded others from his own thoughts, but his gaze missed nothing. I could not hide even a very small lie. Mercifully, though, he made no comment on my falsehood.

"I enjoyed dining with your grandmother tonight. She is an interesting woman, actually. Most of my mother's friends would not allow their daughters or granddaughters to have a 'working class' experience in the East End. And yet ... she does not seem immune from the social preoccupations that my mother exhibits."

I stared out the window. Night had settled in; the gas lamps on the street glowed in dewy brightness.

"She has known Dr. Bartlett for many years, and she trusts him," I explained. "But, as I've mentioned before, her main reasons for allowing me to work are more selfish. She wants me to have a greater appreciation for my Kensington life."

I kept looking out the window, hoping that the disdain in my voice was not too thick. I felt fondly toward Simon for his silences, for his total absorption of my words and expressions without inquiry into more than I was ready to give him.

I glanced back, through the darkness, at Simon's ivory face—so perfect, with only a few blond locks escaping across his forehead.

"But it has not had the desired effect?" he asked, though I knew he already knew the answer.

I smiled. Shook my head.

"Why are you returning tonight?" he asked. It was a baited question.

"William sent me a note. He is cleaning the pharmacy and requested my help."

At the mention of William's name, Simon's expression veiled.

I felt oddly exposed, and I blushed.

Gracefully, Simon changed the topic to discuss the hospital. "Dr. Buck and Dr. Bartlett left London today. They are giving a joint lecture at Oxford on Monday. They'll be back on Wednesday, but in the meantime, some of us are working extra hours."

As we walked into the hospital, Simon told me that he would be working on the first floor. I knew that the first floor was overwhelmed, particularly the nursery. Two days earlier, I had witnessed a set of twins born to a fifteen-year-old mother. Miraculously, the twins and the mother lived, though the infants required round-the-clock care and a supplemental wet nurse.

"Do you need my help?" I asked Simon as he prepared to make his rounds.

"No, go ahead, the pharmacy is in very poor order."

I paused, thinking I might be more useful on the first floor.

"William is waiting." Simon nodded toward the stairs.

I did not miss the hint of discord in Simon's voice.

I ascended the dark stairs, not seeing any light past the second floor. When I stepped onto the fourth floor I was shrouded in darkness except for a single stream of light coming from the laboratory at the end of the hall-way. I heard bottles rattling and crashing amidst mild curses. I prepared myself for William's intensity. Although he attracted me, he was always a force I had to brace myself for.

He was on his knees in the dust and dirt when I found him. He wore a pair of reading spectacles. A box lay before him, filled with empty and near-empty glass bottles. The large closet had been lit by several candles set on various shelves.

It was evident that the pharmacy had not been cleaned or organized in ages. The bottles were sloppily arranged on the shelves, some so near the shelves' edges that they looked as if they could fall over at any moment.

"I will never understand," William said, pulling more bottles off the shelves, clattering them loudly in the pro-cess, "why so many nurses insist on returning *empty* bottles to the shelves."

He held up an empty glass bottle for me to see. "I mean, what good will this do for anyone?"

I noticed, in the candlelight of the pharmacy, that even though William was still unspeakably handsome, he seemed paler than before. Even rage could not darken his cheeks. I guessed his poor coloring resulted from some sort of exhaustion. Perhaps he had been working too many hours.

"Sometimes I feel as if Josephine and Mary are the only *competent* nurses left in this hospital."

His eyes flashed toward me. "Sorry, Abbie. I do not think of you as a nurse, so I'm not implying that *you* are incompetent. You are more of an honorary physician."

I said nothing. It was impossible to respond when he was in such a mood. Taking a nearby broom into my hands, I began sweeping the floor.

He thrust some strips of paper at me and a jar of glue. "Please ignore the floor for now and glue these strips to the bottles. We need to put new labels on everything."

He continued to curse and complain as I began putting on the new labels. I wondered if he had quarreled with Christina. But his mood was getting under my skin, so I stopped what I was doing and glared at him. It was my turn to be angry.

When he saw my expression, he stopped and ran his fingers through his sweat-drenched curls. "I'm sorry. It's just…"

"Why did you ask me to come here?"

I knew now, intuitively, that he had not just asked me here to help with the pharmacy.

After a moment of indecision, his brows furrowed, William kicked a box of empty medicine bottles aside. He glanced around the laboratory and quietly shut the pharmacy door, closing us inside. He lowered his voice to a near whisper.

"Abbie, I wanted to see you tonight, but there are things that I cannot tell you."

"*What?*"

He ran his fingers through his curls again. "I cannot tell you some things because I cannot understand them all myself. There is a large, looming puzzle that needs solving."

My heartbeat quickened. William's words seemed to mimic my own recent thoughts. Had he also noticed the chalice symbol and inscription, not only here at the hospital but on the fountain, and perhaps in other places? Did he have knowledge or evidence about the murders? Part of me wanted to tell him everything. Perhaps if I told him of the visions, about Max's tattoo, about my research, we could piece together these clues. But I still feared confiding in anyone about the visions; I still felt terrified of looking insane. Also, William had not told me nearly enough for me to assume that his anxieties and questions were remotely related to my own.

In that second, I cleared my mind and decided that William was still too much of an enigma for me to confide in him. I would keep my thoughts to myself.

"You're not making any sense," I said.

William's face brimmed in frustration. "I know." He closed his eyes and paced a few feet. "I want to tell you more, but I do not want to loop you into any mess that you would be safer staying excluded from. Please don't ask *any* questions."

His eyes were pleading, so I nodded.

"I cannot tell you much, but some information has arisen ... " His voice trailed off.

My heart quickened again, and I wanted desperately to know what was going on.

He continued his agitated pace. "The bottom line is that I must go abroad to look into some things."

My mind swirled with questions:

For how long?

Where exactly?

Why?

The last question I thought might burst out of me:

Will you miss me?

"Here is what I can tell you." He stepped forward. The pharmacy had become warm; the candles' heat had no vent, no outlet. And some of the bottles, I thought vaguely, might be flammable. We would have to open the door soon. William whispered so softly in my ear that I could barely hear him.

"There are dangers here in London, even in this hospital, for us. You need to be careful."

He *had* to be talking about the Ripper murders. I felt dizzied, as if I were on a cliff, about to plunge forward. William's closeness to me also brought about a thunderbolt of feelings, new and indecipherable.

A candle singed the fourth finger of my right hand.

"Ouch!"

William jumped back a little.

"It's fine," I said quickly. The tip was only reddened. "This has to do with the Ripper murders, doesn't it?"

"I said to not ask me questions." William stepped forward again.

"You cannot expect..." I whispered. We were both speaking in whispers now. "You cannot expect to drop such information on me—that I'm in 'danger' and that you are leaving—and then forbid me to ask *anything*."

He sighed and relented a bit. "Yes, it is about the murders. But I cannot tell you more. For your own safety. You have to trust me. And, like I said, I don't understand everything myself. When I get back, I should be able to tell you everything."

The air was heavy with questions—not only about William's mysterious journey, but now, I sensed, the invisible questions about us. What did we mean to each other? I felt as if I stood on the cliff's edge again, and I still feared the fall.

I heard my voice crack as I asked, "How long will you be gone? You can at least tell me that."

"I don't know exactly. Maybe a few weeks. But the reason I'm telling you all of this is to warn you to *be careful*. You *must* trust me about that."

Did I trust him?

Did I love him?

I felt such confused feelings; hot tears stung my eyes. Ashamed, I turned away, facing the shelves of freshly filled bottles, their new labels inches from my nose.

"Abbie..." William's finger pushed aside some loose strands of hair around my temples. He stood directly behind me, stroking my ear with his fingertip. My lobe tingled. I felt my chest heave. "I *have* to leave. But, truthfully, my biggest drawback, my biggest weight, is going to be leaving you here, knowing some of what I know."

Then why wouldn't he bloody tell me what he knew?

I turned to face him. "Will you be safe abroad? Aren't you in danger also?"

He ignored my question. "Will you just believe me and be careful?"

The air had become intolerably hot. I felt a drop of sweat slide down my forehead.

"Yes, yes."

William's eyes burned into mine for a few seconds before he relaxed. It seemed he felt that he had communicated to me a little of the seriousness of my situation.

"We won't talk about this again … at least not tonight," he whispered. "From the moment I open this door, we must not speak of anything that I have said. I have simply told Dr. Bartlett that I have an ill relative I need to be with on the Continent. I told him that I hope to return before too long."

His expression changed, and I thought for a second that he might laugh. I did not know what was so funny.

William explained. "We had better open this door before we burn ourselves to death in here. And it does not look good to have ourselves shut in here for so long. Sister Josephine would be quite put out."

He opened the door, effectively sealing our conversation in the pharmacy.

Then he took the box of empty bottles into the utility room in the adjoining laboratory. I heard the bottles being thrust around in the sink. As I glued labels to the jars and relabeled the bottles, tears slid down my face and my hands trembled. I felt deeply affected by something. But I could not sort out my feelings. I felt fearful, for him and for myself. Confused about what was going on, and if I was doing the right thing by not telling him about the visions. But then again, he was withholding information from me.

I tried to dry my face with my apron. I took a few deep breaths. William had not returned to the pharmacy. I did not want him to see me crying.

"Abbie."

It was too late.

He set the box of dripping bottles down.

"Don't cry." He said this in a voice he had never used with me before. It was a voice he reserved for hushing infants in the nursery. I had heard him use the tone with his aunt a few times, that evening when I had visited.

I turned around, past the point of caring if William saw me cry. He wiped the tears from my cheek. His finger brushed the tears away as he would remove a gnat, an eyelash. Before I knew what I was doing, I kissed his finger.

"Oh God," I gasped. The cliff again. I had fallen.

William jumped back, jolted, and stumbled a little against the shelves. At that point, a bottle from the rows of herbal medicines crashed to the floor.

"I'm sorry." Overwhelmed with embarrassment, I knelt and began wiping the strong-smelling herbs and glass fragments into my hands. I hardly knew what to do with the irrational surges of emotion coursing through me.

Then came a horrible moment where we both looked at each other. William, who was always so transparent, became closed off. A sealed book. I felt terrible that my action might have caused him to react in that way. So I returned my focus to scooping up the particles on the floor, and William remained still, frozen, with his back against the shelves.

"These herbs are certainly contaminated now. I am sorry to have wasted them." My voice cracked.

William said nothing as he knelt beside me to help scoop up the pieces, and I was afraid to look at his face.

The situation began to feel a bit ridiculous, and I laughed a little amidst tears.

He established eye contact with me, and smiled.

"Don't worry, Abbie. *I* was the one who knocked the bottle to the floor." He laughed a little.

There was a moment of awkwardness, neither one of us knowing how to move on from what had just happened. But slowly, tediously, we meandered back into small talk and the immediate tasks at hand. We worked late into the night. William was thorough and meticulous. The hours ticked away. The pharmacy closet gradually returned to order.

By the time Mary showed up at the pharmacy door, it was well after midnight. She seemed a bit hurried. In her hands she clutched a piece of paper that she thrust at William. I knew she was still a little angry at him for locking us in the closet during the riot. I made a mental note to ask her about how Scribby was doing when I got the chance.

"Dr. St. John needs these medicines. *Soon* if possible."

"Does he need my help?" I asked.

She eyed William and then me. "He might. If you can pull yourself away from Dr. Siddal."

William merely smiled at Mary's sarcasm. "I'll be fine here. Abbie, go see if you can give Simon a hand."

After Mary left, William put Simon's requested medicine bottles in a small box for me.

I began to descend the dark stairs with the box of bottles in my arms. My time with William had been emotional and puzzling. I felt a rising fear, and I wondered about the web in which we were caught up. I also worried that my feelings for William were too strong. I blushed as I thought of my actions in the pharmacy—to act as I had was unlike me.

I had almost reached the second floor landing when the vision struck me. I clutched the banister to keep from falling and dropped the box, shattering the bottles upon the stairs.

In my vision, Liz Stride laughed near a streetlamp in a small courtyard somewhere. I saw the long shadows of a wrought-iron fence pass across her face in the lamplight. A figure, shrouded in a black cape and wearing a tall dark hat, gave her small bag. She ate from the bag. She laughed and stroked her hair. A bright red carnation had been pinned to her greasy dress lapel.

She was about to die.

I had to move. Fast.

I felt my way down the staircase. The vision stayed with me, pulsating up and down within my consciousness of my immediate surroundings.

He was with her—the Ripper. I had to find her.

I ran down the stairs and out the front door of the hospital, searching my mind. Whenever the vision mushroomed up, I clung to it, trying to pinpoint Liz's destination.

Where were they?

If I could just see a landmark in my mind, a business name or a street sign.

Liz's nearly toothless smile flashed in my mind.

She was still alive.

They stood just inside a fenced court on a dark street. *Where? Where?*

While running away from the hospital, I heard a few shouts behind me but ignored them, grasping at the vision. My brain hurt as I stretched to see beyond Liz's face, to see and hear her surroundings. In the vision, I heard a train. Guessing that she must be near the railways, I began running in the direction of Commercial Street.

As I ran, I realized that I had no idea how to protect Liz or myself. I had no plan except to fight. I didn't even have a weapon. My stomach sank in fear.

After I had run a stretch of Whitechapel Road, I came to Commercial Street. Along the way, I passed cottages, warehouses, pubs. Few East Enders were out. Once I passed the last pub on Commercial, the streets were mostly abandoned, and I heard the increasingly close rattle of a train. I had no idea where they were and hoped that I was close to their location.

The vision swirled in my mind again—a street sign, first blurry and then clear: *Berner Street.* They were one block away—very close.

Silently, taking care not to make noise, I eased quickly through a connecting street—more of an alley in its darkness and smallness—and paused against the side of an abandoned sweatshop. The entire time, I tried to remain in the shadows.

I stepped carefully onto the next street. It was Berner.

The hair stood up on my neck when I saw Liz and the Ripper. They were directly across the street from me, about fifty yards away in a darkened courtyard. The vision had stopped now that they were in front of me. I remained in the shadows of the sweatshop and squinted, trying to see their faces. But I could see very little.

It was then that I heard Liz bid the stranger goodbye and turn away from him. She had not quite reached the streetlamp when he lunged from behind, pulling her back into the shadows.

No! I tried to scream, but only a croak escaped from my lips.

He must have cut her windpipe before she could cry out. I heard the knife slashing through fabric and then skin.

My stomach wretched and before I could stop it, a soft splash of my vomit hit the concrete at my feet.

The ripping noises stopped.

The shadow across the street looked up, directly at me. The rest of his figure was too shrouded for me to see anything else.

He straightened up.

I gasped and backed into the shadows of the sweatshop.

When I looked in the Ripper's direction again, he was gone. This frightened me almost more than seeing him across the street.

He might be anywhere.

Noise broke out from somewhere in the depths of the courtyard where the body lay. It was the creaking of a cart, perhaps a railway worker's cart, bringing supplies to an early morning shift.

I was torn. Part of me felt as if I should run to Liz; I hated leaving her on the street. But I knew she could not have survived that attack, and in the back of my mind I thought I should run back to the hospital.

The person pushing the cart stopped as his cart hit the body. It made a soft thud.

"Dammit, you drunken … " The cart-pusher must have seen blood, because within seconds he shouted, "*God!*" and then "Police! Police!"

As I cowered near the building, I felt a bit of relief at the whistles of constables. The man with the cart shouted to them.

"Body here! *There's a body here!*"

But I seemed too far away from the comforting noise of police whistles and shouts. The Ripper had seen me, and I felt as if I was still in danger. I stood near my puddle of vomit, afraid to scream. I had just witnessed the speed at which he could murder and escape. If he was anywhere near me, no constables, even if only yards away, could reach me in time to save me.

Several policemen had already arrived on the scene.

"She's still warm!" someone shouted. "He can't be far."

Then I heard Abberline's voice. "Search all the surrounding buildings!"

Someone grabbed me from behind, pulling me back into the shadows, and then thrust my back against a closed door at the side of the sweatshop.

I tried to scream, but a hand clamped tightly over my mouth.

I saw William's face, inches from my own.

"Don't speak," he mouthed, though no sound came out. "He's here."

Rainwater dripped from the broken guttering above us into a nearby puddle. I tried to see beyond William, to see *anything*. My eyes ached with the strain.

I heard footsteps—steady, sharp.

He had to know we were there. He must *know.*

My vomit lay only a few feet away. It was then that I heard splashing sounds, very light ones, in the puddle of rainwater.

Then I saw him.

The Ripper stood in front of a doorway, not facing us, but wiping his hands on what looked like a handkerchief. Though he was so close we could hear him breathe, I could not see his face; he was only a darker outline against the already dark night.

William smashed me flatter against the door. My chest was pressed so hard against his body that I could barely breathe.

I held my breath when the Ripper paused, still in the doorway, his back toward us. At that point, he tilted his head slightly, very slightly, toward us.

He knew we were there.

William tensed.

Then he turned and walked away from us. I heard his steps proceed, unhurriedly, away from Berner Street.

After several minutes, William relaxed. He released me and I reeled.

"Are you all right?" he asked.

"He murdered Liz. Liz Stride." I was breathless, trying to push away the image of her murder.

"Liz?" William said. And then, suddenly, "My *God*."

Lights were quickly going on in the windows of the houses behind the courtyard. And I heard shouts and orders coming from the street. They were searching the homes and buildings. Abberline's force thought the killer might still be there. They had no idea that he had already eluded them.

"Come on. We have to tell them which direction he went," I said.

"It won't do any good. The police cannot and will not catch him."

I looked at William, not knowing what he meant. But it did not matter. I had to talk to the police myself. I hated involving myself in the investigation; I had sworn since my meeting with Abberline to keep uninvolved with Scotland Yard. But this time, I had *witnessed* a murder, of a patient *I* had cared for. I owed it to Liz to try to do whatever I could to help in the investigation. The least I could do was tell them what I had seen and that the Ripper was no longer anywhere near Berner Street.

I pushed past William, but then stopped in my tracks. The puddle of rainwater was clouded with blood.

My voice came out hoarse. "He washed his hands, or possibly the knife, in this puddle."

"Abbie, *why* were you out here?"

I had no logical answer. *Should I tell him about the visions?*

Suddenly another image rushed over my mind, so quickly and with such force that I doubled over. I thought I might wretch again.

"He's not *done*. He is not done!"

"Abbie? What's going on? Are you sick? What do you mean ... " William seemed more fearful now than he had when the Ripper was standing near us.

To my horror, I saw Cate Eddows in my mind, a smile on her face as she greeted someone. The shadowed figure placed a small bag, identical to the one offered to Liz, in her hand.

"We *have* to find her. He's going to kill her!" I yelled.

William looked at me as if I were out of my mind. I ignored him and tried to focus on the vision, which had left me as quickly as it came.

"We need to get you back to the hospital. You're not thinking clearly. You might be in shock."

A square—an open square—appeared in my head. Flagstones. Mitre Square!

I began to bolt in the direction the Ripper had gone.

"Abbie, *no!*" William held my arm in a vice grip and blinked at my rage. "Let's stop this nonsense and go back to Whitechapel Hospital. I cannot leave you alone on the streets now."

I saw that he was not going to let me go.

He should have known better.

"I'm sorry William."

I disengaged his grip with a sharp kick to the groin, followed by a single kick at his chest. I heard a small crack and winced, knowing that I might have broken, or at least cracked, a rib.

He doubled over in pain. But I knew that he would be fine. Eventually. I bolted in the direction toward Mitre Square.

As I ran, the vision returned.

Cate still had no idea that she was in danger. Underneath her mold-stained black bonnet, she smiled. I noticed, as I had when I'd brought her medicine in the hospital one time, that she had a prominent scar on her lower jaw. I saw the back of the caped figure, who, maddeningly, never clearly revealed his face to me in these visions. And I saw what she did not—a knife in his hand, gleaming.

I sucked in my breath in horror as I saw the Ripper snatch her into the shadows before she could make a sound.

I had reached Church Passage, which opened out into Mitre Square. I stopped halfway down the road, knowing that I no longer needed the vision when the crime unfolded in my immediate vicinity. And this time, the Ripper was doing his bloody work even closer to me. I dared not step out into the court. I heard him breathing. I heard the ripping of skin, the wet tearing of organs. I clamped my hand over my mouth, fighting the overwhelming feeling of fear, of nausea. Of loss. He gutted his victims as if they were animals in the slaughterhouse.

I tried to back away, silently, back up into Church Passage. I held my breath when my heel accidently kicked a bottle, sending it loudly against a brick wall. This time, the Ripper did not stop at the sound. I felt horrified when I heard him emit a chuckle. I was certain, at that point, that the Ripper knew I was near him.

It seemed as if the visions were nothing less than invitations. I shuddered.

After what must have been only five minutes but seemed like an eternity, he stopped. The sounds ceased completely. I heard him leave, this time not with steely steps but with swifter, silent movements. I heard the air catch under his cape, and he was gone.

Everything remained quiet as I crouched against

a building. As before, I hesitated, having no idea which direction I should run.

Other footsteps, not the Ripper's, entered the square; the footsteps of a night watchman. I heard the rattle of a whistle and more footsteps, panicked now. A shout: "For God's sake, mate, come to my assistance! It's another murder."

Then someone grabbed my shoulder, throwing me face-first against the wet, dirty side of the building. I smelled the tangy, yeasty odor of blood and heard the chuckle I had heard only minutes earlier.

He was behind me now.

I felt oddly giddy, caught off-guard like this. It would be very difficult to fight. I wondered how Grandmother, amidst her real sorrow at my death, would handle the despair and humiliation of me being murdered in a little dirty passage by the Ripper. Killed in the same manner as the common prostitutes.

I thought about all of this with bitter humor as I felt the knife stab into me.

Then all became blackness.

Seventeen

Heaven was pretty much as I always thought it might be, if it existed at all.

I found myself lying on my back at the bottom of a pond of cool, clear water. The shock of the cold water was a pleasant sensation; my skin, indeed every part of my body, felt—*sensed*—more acutely than ever before. Looking up through the wavy surface of the water at a late afternoon sky, I watched kingfishers cut through my view, slicing through the air just above the water with unbelievable force. Everything seemed colorful, alive—not the slightest bit dreamlike. I began swimming upwards.

Up.

Up.

As I broke the surface, the sharp ammonia smells of

Whitechapel Hospital assaulted my nose. I now lay not on my back in the pond, but on my stomach, face down. I could not move or even speak. My muscles seemed dead.

It was then that I felt searing pain in the back of my right thigh, just below my buttocks. I realized I was lying under a light blanket on the third floor operating table. In my peripheral vision, I saw a small amount of early morning, pumpkin-tinted sunlight seeping through a window.

The Ripper. The pain reminded me of what had knocked me unconscious. The last thing I remembered was the smell of the wet brick wall, the blood odor of the Ripper, the thrust of the knife. I began to hear my heartbeat pound in my ears. *Was he nearby?* I panicked, trying to move, but remained paralyzed.

I felt better when William's voice broke forth from the other side of the room. "*Dammit,* Simon. Do you think you might wrap me up without breaking another rib?"

"She kicked you quite hard," I heard Simon say, more than a hint of amusement in his voice. "This left vertebral rib is broken nearly clear through."

"How is she?" William asked.

"She will be all right. The stab wound did cause quite a bit of tissue damage. She will not be able to work for several weeks."

Dear God! I wondered, in my paralyzed state, if I was blushing. Though I felt the blanket covering me, I could not tell if I was even dressed. I felt rising embarrassment that the wound Simon had stitched was so high on my leg. This worry was compounded by Simon's verdict that I would need some recovery time from the wound.

It was then that I noticed my finger, against the bedsheet, could wiggle a little. I was about to try to speak, but decided to remain silent. I felt certain that neither Simon nor William would tell me all I wanted to know about what had happened last night, or why I was still alive.

"I am angry at myself for letting her go off like that," William said.

"Drink some cool water. You've looked like a ghost since you got back."

I heard the soft rush of water pouring into a glass.

"Thank you. She ran so fast. With this broken rib, I could not catch up. I ran around for thirty minutes, calling her name like a madman. You have no idea my relief when you told me she was alive. Before she ran away, she was talking incoherently—somehow she *knew* he was going to murder again."

"She *knew*?" Simon's voice sounded sharper than I had ever heard it.

"She did."

I hoped that I did not suck in my breath when I heard William's water glass shatter against the wall. "She might have been killed."

"William." Simon voice came out gentle.

"Don't try to be my *priest* now. I should have locked her up, stuck her in a bloody kennel. But instead I let her get away from me. She might have been killed."

Silence.

"In fact, she *should* be dead now. It does not make sense why he left her alive. Why he left me alive. I told you—he was right behind us near Berner."

I heard the dry slicing of scissors through cloth bandages before Simon spoke, his tone even. "Keep your voice down, William. I gave her an extra dose of chloroform, but she should be waking soon. Besides, we do not want anyone *else* to overhear us."

I felt their eyes on me.

"What happened, exactly?" William asked. "You still have not told me how you found her."

There was a long pause. I strained to hear Simon.

"She was dropped off at the front doors in a pauper's coffin, a pinewood box. It is identical to the ones the morgue uses to bury unclaimed corpses, the standard kind we have sent here by Dr. Phillips for many of our deceased patients."

I had been dropped off in a coffin!

Simon was quiet for a minute before he continued, softly. "After you both ran out of here, I was attending to the first floor but was so distracted by the thought that she was out there, I had trouble pulling myself too far away from the front doors. I was at the doors instantly when I heard the box thump against them—that was shortly after two o'clock."

"So *you* found her?"

"Yes." Another pause. This one longer than the last. "You should heal in a few weeks. Don't strain your chest too much. And please, put your shirt on. Anyway, the lid fell aside when I opened the front door. My first thought was that she was dead. She lay face up. Her face was so white, she looked almost bloodless. Her clothes were bloodstained. But when I checked her pulse, I felt that she was still alive."

"My God."

"I carried her discreetly up here. It was then that I saw that the wound was not fatal, though it bled profusely. I had Mary begin cleaning the wound so that I might stitch it. While she was occupied in that task, I disposed of the coffin."

"Was she … ?" William's voice trailed off.

I heard the sound of surgical tools clinking on a tray.

"No. There were no other injuries." The clinking stopped. "I told Mary that Abbie had been stabbed by a deranged vagrant when she stepped outside to dump out a pail of water."

"So, are you certain that it was *him*?"

"The wound is perfectly consistent with those of the victims. It was most certainly the same knife, a surgical, thin six-inch blade. Branwell was at the morgue this morning and saw the bodies. These murders are very similar to the other two. Both patients left, voluntary discharged, yesterday. Both were disemboweled. The Ripper spent more time with Cate. Took out all of her intestines, laid them neatly beside her shoulder, removed the left kidney, mutilated her face. He cut off her nose."

"Disgusting. This is *maddening*, Simon. We've talked

of some of my theories. I know you have difficulty thinking ill of anyone, except perhaps the rich."

Simon cleared his throat a little before continuing, "You know that I am shocked by the unfolding of these events as much as you are, William. I see enough sense in what you have told me lately to agree to keep this conversation between ourselves—to agree not to go to the police with what happened to Abbie. But I know your tendency to be impetuous and hotheaded. I do not want you to make any premature enemies for us."

"Agreed."

I wondered what they had discussed that would make them such sudden and unlikely allies.

"So, you are leaving for France tomorrow?" Simon asked.

"Avignon, specifically. The safe is there."

The safe?

Someone, either Simon or William, began sweeping up the pieces of the water glass.

I had heard enough. Clutching the blanket around me, I said with my best attempt at a groggy voice, "Might I have some clothes?"

Simon was with me in Grandmother's parlor to tell her that I had been mugged in Whitechapel the night before, stabbed as I left the hospital.

When Simon and I had left Whitechapel early that

morning, the police and the press had begun descending upon the hospital in swarms. Like flies. But I was home now, facing Grandmother and away from the crowd.

She was disturbed as she sat across from me, her eyes glassy with tears. Otherwise, her entire demeanor seemed perfectly put together, her dress crisply ironed, her hair smooth. Oddly, in that moment, I knew that she loved me.

"She *will* be all right?" Grandmother asked shakily.

"Just a flesh wound. The police apprehended the mugger immediately."

Grandmother's face tightened, frightening me.

"I am *fine*," I said, reassuring her. "I will be able to return to the hospital in a few weeks."

Her face hardened; I had said the wrong thing.

Simon cast me a look. "It will be at least *four* weeks before she should return to work at Whitechapel Hospital."

Grandmother seemed to accept this. Particularly since it would give her a month to attempt to persuade me (or manipulate me) to not return at all.

My wound throbbed so much I could barely walk. Still, I *would* get better. I needed to get better. Apart from my desire to heal and return to work, my experience with the Ripper—and what I had seen him do to Liz Stride and Cate Eddows—had sparked a flame within me to stop him.

Part III

"Unjust! Unjust!"

—*Jane Eyre*

Eighteen

On Monday morning, we moved into Lady Violet Chanderly's house, and my first two weeks there were terrible. I felt totally preoccupied with the murders, with what had happened to me, and with William, wondering whether or not he was all right. But I could do nothing, absolutely nothing, as I was entirely bedridden. The wound had not only cut deeply into my hamstring, but I acquired a mild infection so that whenever I tried to stand, shooting pain coursed from my thigh to ankle. Once the infection set in, I couldn't walk, let alone take stairs, so I was essentially confined to my fourth floor bedroom at Violet's house.

It was during this time that I came to appreciate Mariah even more. Her bedroom was just down the hall from mine and she visited me almost daily, bringing me magazines, gossiping about the goings-on of the house. It was through her that I learned that Lady Violet Chanderly was actually deeply in debt, displaying expensive furnishings while unable to replace badly rotting wall and floor structures throughout the house. Her husband, Sir Bertram, was a drunk and heavily addicted to laudanum, and spent most of his days in his large library doing absolutely nothing. Violet went to great lengths to keep his addictions a secret. They had nothing except their name.

"So there you have it," Mariah said, tossing the end of her cigar out the window. "One of London's finest families, batty, and only a few steps away from the poorhouse."

Mariah and I were the only occupants of the fourth floor, which allowed her to talk freely with me about the Chanderlys' dysfunctions, and to smoke.

I lay propped up in bed reading *Wuthering Heights*. It was hard for me to focus. I had planned to start walking around my room the next day; I figured the wound would heal better if I had a little exercise on top of the extra rest.

Mariah exhaled loudly, walking away from the open window and sitting on my bed. "Only a few more weeks until I can leave here for good, never look back. Break away from this life and start my life abroad as a writer."

I had reread the same paragraph in my book at least three times in the past few minutes, such was my restlessness. "You're still planning on running away?" I asked.

"Undoubtedly. The night before the wedding. Then it's off to Paris."

Mariah had told me very little about her paramour, Charles. I had the feeling *she* didn't know much about him. She slipped away several nights a week to see him. She knew, I think, that it wouldn't last, but she thrived off romantic peccadilloes. An elopement before her marriage would be quite the scandal, and, I was sure, break her away from the Chanderlys and stuffy Kensington for good. And she would make it as a writer—in Mariah, I saw a bit of a rising star. I had read some of her writings, and she was quite good.

She chattered a bit about her planned elopement and told me about the latest book that she had written, a mystery novel.

My mind wandered. *Mystery.* I felt caught in such a puzzle regarding my feelings for William and the truth behind Dr. Bartlett and his friends, especially whether they played any role at all in the Ripper murders. But for now, I was stuck in bed recovering, caught in Kensington purgatory.

By mid-October, I began walking around my bedroom a little. The pain was still sharp, but much less than it had been two weeks before, and the infection had healed. I focused on completing small tasks; specifically, it had occurred to me that I might give Mary some of my dresses. She was poor, and I had so many. I began separating them out by colors: two black dresses, a brown one, a mint green one. I bit my lip knowing that it might be a bit of a fight to get her to take them, but I knew, in the end, she would.

A knock sounded at the door.

One of Lady Violet's servants entered with an envelope. My heart quickened, and I hoped that the letter was from William. Perhaps he was safe, back in London.

But it wasn't from William.

A newspaper cutting fell out; it detailed the state of the Ripper investigation. As I skimmed through the article, I saw that dozens of suspects had been brought in for questioning, including some of the morticians examining the bodies, seven young men from prominent families, and, of course, many physicians, surgeons, and medical students. As I scanned the article, I recognized many names including Dr. Bagster Phillips, but neither Simon's nor William's names appeared.

To my disgust, next to the article was a published sketch of one of the murder victims. The illustration, graphic and detailed, displayed one of the victims with blood pouring from her stomach onto the street. Though I knew that the press had a tendency to dramatize or sensationalize events, I found such a portrayal disrespectful to the women, and I knew that had the Ripper's victims been anyone other than the prostitutes, such a picture would never have been published.

Following the graphic illustration and story about the murders was an article about Whitechapel Hospital itself—about the many services the hospital provided for the Whitechapel district. The sender had cut off part of that story, clearly wanting me to read the article regarding the investigation. My anger and irritation increased when

I realized the identity of the sender. Abberline's card, complete with his name and the address of Scotland Yard, had been tucked neatly inside the envelope.

Why was he sending me this?

Furious, I thought of how Abberline's men had recklessly searched Londoners' homes and businesses in the vicinity of Liz Stride's murder while the Ripper had already left the area to pursue another kill that same night. Where were the police when the Ripper stabbed *me*, stuffed me in a coffin, and dropped me off at the hospital? I had, by now, lost any respect that I might have had for Scotland Yard. They were ineffective and bullying. Meanwhile the Ripper was still free, still at liberty to murder.

Part of me felt tempted to throw the letter, card, and newspaper clipping into the trash, but then, a second later, I thought it might be time for me to set up a meeting with Abberline. I wasn't, and didn't plan to be, a pawn in his investigation. Perhaps I hadn't made that clear enough before.

I cooled down gradually as I finished setting aside the dresses. By the time Mariah stopped by my room for afternoon tea, my anger had subsided a bit. My intended trip to Scotland Yard gave me even more inspiration to get better. I would attempt to walk downstairs the next day.

That night, I awoke in the curtained darkness of my bed with a desperate wish that I had been dreaming when I had heard the chuckle—the same one from my nightmare, from that night in Church Passage.

But this time, I had heard it in my bedroom.

My heart raced. *Was he in my bedroom?*

No. I told myself. *You were dreaming. You've been having nightmares lately. You've been anxious.*

I heard a footstep.

Someone *was* in my bedroom.

In horror, I saw a place on the drawn bed curtains ripple delicately, not by a breeze, but as if a finger had slid gently down the velvet surface.

I held my breath.

After lying frozen for several minutes, not moving, hearing nothing, I made a rash decision. I threw back the curtains.

As I scanned the room, everything seemed dark and quiet. The fire had died down. The windows were shut.

Then I saw that my bedroom door was open. Wide open.

I had not actually locked the door, but it seemed odd that it would have blown open on its own.

Cautiously, I got out of bed and went to close it.

The hall was completely black except for a stream of moonlight. Then I saw that the door at the end of the hall was open. Squinting a bit, I saw a steep set of stairs through the door; they must lead to the attic. My heart beat faster, as I doubted that anyone would need to be up there at this time of night.

Ashamed at my terror, I left my room, shut the door to the attic firmly, and returned to my room, shutting—and this time locking—my bedroom door.

I did not sleep the rest of the night.

They were almost imperceptible, but I heard tiny scratching noises coming from the attic, directly above my head.

Nineteen

The next morning, Grandmother stopped by my room to let me know that Simon would be at the house for dinner. In spite of having had very little sleep, this was my impetus to make it down the stairs.

I had many questions for him and hoped that we would have a chance to talk alone. I felt desperate to know about William, whether he had heard from him. I also hoped that perhaps Simon would tell me what William sought in the safe abroad.

In the late afternoon, I descended the stairs slowly. The trip was not as difficult or as painful as I had anticipated, and I knew that I would probably be walking easily by the next week.

Mariah had gone to the opera with Cecil, so dinner

was quite dull. It was only me, Violet, Grandmother, and Simon. Simon was all grace and politeness to the two women, but a few times our eyes met, and I knew he wanted to speak to me.

Sir Bertram was away from London for a few days, so the library was empty that evening. After dinner I retired there, hoping that Simon would soon be able to pull himself away from Violet and Grandmother before too long.

Although still limping a bit, I walked slowly around the library to pass the time and to exercise my leg. Bookcases with ladders covered every wall, except for the bottom half of a wall with a great fireplace. The ceiling, three stories above me, had floral designs cut into the plaster. I felt too agitated to read so I paced a bit, then sat on a nearby sofa.

When Simon finally came to the library, he sat next to me on the couch. Formal. Polite. Statuesque.

"Simon, where is William?" I asked almost immediately. "And what is he doing?"

If Simon was surprised by my directness, he showed nothing.

"He is on the Continent. In terms of what he is doing, Abbie, that I cannot tell you."

Ever since the Ripper had attacked me and I'd returned to Kensington, I had been forced to process everything alone. I felt haunted by the visions and my suspicions. So in spite of Simon's secrecy, I decided to tell him everything. I did it quickly and quietly, before thinking too much about what I was doing. I told him about what had happened in

Church Passage, of the visions that I had had in connection with the murders. I even told him about the chalice visions, and then the chalice image I had seen at the hospital, and how Max, that evening in the hothouse, had shown me his chalice tattoo.

As my words poured out, I realized I was crying a little. To tell someone everything brought me a certain amount of relief, but at a great risk. The visions, particularly, might not sit well with rational Simon.

Simon remained perfectly composed at my statements.

His silence was maddening. He was not looking at me as if I were crazed, but the silence made me nervous.

"Talk, please," I pleaded. "Have you seen the chalice picture at the hospital, and on the fountain?"

Another long, unbearable pause. I could read nothing from his expression.

"Yes," he said evenly. "I have seen it in both those places."

"The tattoo?"

Simon said nothing, but handed me a handkerchief.

"And dear *God*." I wiped my eyes. "Please tell me you don't think I'm crazy for having the visions. I haven't told anyone about them yet. My mother, I now think, might have seen visions too, and now that these have come to me ... I'm afraid."

"It is all right, Abbie." His voice cooled me like running water. "I do not think you crazed. In my work, I have seen very ... strange things. The human brain is still very unknown, and as a priest and physician, I see so many dimensions of the psyche. In fact, ever since that night at Dr. Bartlett's party, when I found you collapsed upstairs, I have suspected this."

"*See*," I said quickly. "We're all caught up in this. We have to share *everything* if we're going to make sense of anything."

He looked into the fire as he said quietly, "William shared some information with me, something that might shed light on these Ripper murders, and confided in me about his trip. Normally we don't speak to each other much, but to his credit, as your friend, he wanted someone working at the hospital who was also your friend to watch over you in his absence."

Suddenly Simon turned to face me, his ice-blue eyes penetrating. "He was going to tell you everything regarding his trip, our suspicions. I told him that I suspected you were having visions, and that he could tell you he was leaving, but nothing else. When he told me on the night of the double murders that you seemed to see visions, this confirmed my suspicions."

The realization swept over me and I felt stricken. Their secrecy had something to do with the visions. "They *are* real, then, and have something to do with why you cannot tell me more," I said. "Is my mind contaminated in some way?"

Simon looked around the library and lowered his voice to a whisper. He leaned closer to me, his breath like a brush of silk upon my temple. "There is nothing wrong with *you*. But we are *all* in danger. Not just William, but you and me, even possibly now. You must be wary of the visions. If you have any more, send me a message quickly."

"What are they?" My voice cracked.

"Be careful, Abbie, and we should not talk about this right now. Just keep in contact with me."

I hardly knew what else to say. We were silent for a few minutes. We tried to talk about the hospital—about the even heavier police presence since the recent murders. He asked about my leg; I told him it was healing well.

But the air was heavy and all of our subsequent conversation felt stifled, unnatural.

Then Simon suddenly smiled, leaning back on the sofa and focusing on the ceiling high above us. He seemed to be debating something in his head. Abruptly, he looked at me, something of mirth in his expression. "Have you picked up any of the novels in here yet?" he asked.

"No, not yet. I have not been in here before now."

"So you know nothing about the famous Chanderly library?"

"No," I said, completely unsure what was coming.

"I feel indecent doing this, but it is quite an extraordinary secret."

He stood and gestured for me to follow him to the nearest wall of the library, the wall with the fireplace.

"Have you noticed *this* on any of the other books?" Simon pointed to a tiny whisk of white chalk on the spine of a volume of *Oliver Twist.*

"No."

"Take the book off the shelf and open it."

I obeyed. My mouth dropped open at the illustrations and photographs. I felt my face turn hot in a blush as I turned page after page, each photograph seeming more indecent than the previous one. After my initial shock, I let out a laugh. There was not a single word from *Oliver Twist* on any of the pages. I glanced at all the books around me and saw that many with respectable titles had the tiny white mark.

"So all of the marked books have these photographs and . . . illustrations?"

"Yes."

I couldn't believe it. I remembered my conversations with Mariah about the Chanderlys' problems, but concealed pornography in the library seemed a bit much.

Simon continued, his voice even. "Sir Bertram has one of the largest, most extensive pornography collections in England. Possibly in all of Great Britain. This is general knowledge in Lady Violet's society, though the women never speak of it." He smiled gently. "In terms of the *unmarked* books, Sir Bertram does have a spectacular array: Shakespeare, Chaucer, Jane Austen, the Brontës. You just have to be certain to check the spine. Unmarked spines are decent; marked ones are not."

I wondered out loud why sophisticated Mariah never told me about this.

"Perhaps she assumed that you already knew." Simon leaned back against the bookcase and stared at me, a curious expression upon his face. I heard the fire crackling loudly in the background.

The diversion had made me feel better, but the questions still roared in my head.

As if reading my mind, Simon said, "I will tell you more when *I* know more and when I know that it is safe. I have not heard from William, but if I do, I will tell you. Do not try to visit Whitechapel Hospital or go anywhere near the East End."

"What ... " Alarm coursed through me. I could not imagine giving up my work at the hospital.

"You can return to work later, but it is not ... safe for you there right now."

"Is Dr. Bartlett ... ?" The questions I had about Dr. Bartlett, his friends, and Max stayed with me.

"Dr. Bartlett knows that you're recovering from the mugger's attack. I don't want to say anything now. But I just don't think it would be wise for you to be near the hospital. Be careful everywhere, but stay near Kensington."

"I don't know how much longer I can stand this. I *have* to know what's going on, and I hate just sitting around here."

"It won't be much longer."

A servant entered the library to attend the fire.

"I promise."

When Simon left a few minutes later, I had a horrible feeling that much was going on around me yet I could do nothing. It was the worst sort of helplessness. *One thing at a time*, I told myself. First, I had to get my strength back. If I didn't do that, I would never be able to leave this house.

I tried to go to bed early that night, but everything

from my conversation with Simon kept me awake. At nearly eleven o'clock, I heard Mariah's door open. She must have taken one of the back servant stairs, because when I left my bed and went to the window, I saw her leave the house with someone. Nosy about this Charles, I tried to see his face, but I couldn't.

Eventually, I fell asleep.

Sometime, not very long after, I sat up in bed, my heart pounding. The scratching noise from the attic above had woken me up. I felt tempted to peek out in the hallway, to see if the attic door was open again, but I chastised myself. The Ripper murders had made me paranoid and fearful. It was probably rats.

Another week passed. Simon stopped by twice for tea, but each time, Grandmother and Lady Violet were there, so there was no time to talk. I had been diligent about walking around the house and climbing up and down the stairs. Because of this, my leg was almost entirely recovered.

Finally, a week later, on one of the few evenings when Sir Bertram was out, I retired to the library to look at some of the Chanderlys' "unmarked" collections. I began browsing a Shakespeare collection just as a late October storm raged outside. The wind whipped and whistled against the outside of the house while gusts screamed down the fireplace, swirling some of the ashes out onto the hearth. I walked to the fireplace and pushed the ashes back into the fire with my boot.

The instant I finished this task, I heard the library door open. It was Simon.

His voice was soft as down. "Abbie, I was only just able to leave Whitechapel, and I wanted to talk with you before another day passed."

I turned from the fireplace and felt my insides tense at his voice. Something seemed thick in the air. Awkwardly, I stepped away from the fire's heat, my back to a bookcase.

He stopped, as if the words had become too heavy to speak.

Then, in a rush, he kissed me. My head slammed back against the books on the shelf behind me. I kissed him back, vaguely wondering if the books against my hair were marked or unmarked.

My mind turned to a summer when Mother and I had lived in Scotland. I was six years old and had wandered into a meadow behind her employers' home. The grass had been tall, nearly as tall as I was. I had felt taken by surprise when a small cloud of yellow butterflies burst out before me. The absurdity and delight of this memory struck me.

Then, amidst the blooms of pleasure and mirth, I sensed something amiss. I knew that after this moment, for better or for worse, my friendship with Simon could never be exactly as it had before. I felt a lump in my gut, knowing that I did not love him, but I could not bring myself to pull away from his kiss.

It was Simon who ended it. He rested his forehead against my own and stroked my throat with his fingers.

"I have fought my feelings for too long," he said. "I had thought I could do without matrimony, without love. I am too busy. But we fit perfectly, Abbie, and our dedication to the profession goes hand in hand. I have every confidence that you can and will find a way to attain admission to medical school. Then we can continue to work in the Whitechapel area after you complete medical school, or we can go anywhere that you might wish."

I stared back at his handsome face, and I imagined the life he proposed to me.

It did seem perfect. Even Grandmother would approve of the match. But I could attain all that Simon suggested without his help, without marrying him. The only reason I would marry him would be if I loved him. And that was not how I felt, at least in that moment.

A crack of lightning sounded from outside. I had to give Simon an answer, but I did not want the kissing to stop.

"I cannot marry you."

"Why?"

"I don't love you. We don't know each other."

As I spoke the words, I realized the truth of what I said. There was something not quite flesh and blood about Simon. Even in that moment, he was an enigma to me.

I thought about William. I didn't really know him, either, but there was more transparency about him. Furthermore, the very fact that I thought of William during this moment with Simon helped me sort through my feelings.

"We have many years." Simon leaned in to kiss me again.

"I'm sorry, but I still say no."

"But we are so dedicated to the profession."

His words helped me pinpoint another unsettling part of the proposal. "You seem to want a companion for your work rather than a lover, a wife," I told him. "I consider you a friend—a dear friend, Simon—but I do not know you enough or love you enough to marry you. So, my answer must be no."

I hoped that my words didn't hurt him too much. His face remained expressionless. I admired him so much: he was driven and had strong character. But I simply could not accept a proposal from him, and I had to remain firm in that.

Another flash of lightning.

Simon's glassy eyes momentarily searched my own. I remembered how well he could discern my thoughts. I knew what he suspected, and I winced under the gaze. But if he wondered if William was a factor in this rejection, he said and asked nothing.

"I'm sorry, Abbie." He turned to leave.

"Don't be." My words sounded weak as cobwebs.

But he did not turn around again as he left the library.

That night, I felt awful. I had a terrible time falling asleep.

Still, I knew that I had made the right decision. At least for now, I could not make a promise of engagement to Simon. That much was very clear. But I mourned the loss of my friendship with him.

A tinny noise, sounding like a scrape of metal, jolted me away from my thoughts. I had locked my door, but I felt certain that I heard my doorknob rotate. I peeked through the curtains and saw, in horror, the knob turning slowly one way and then the other.

It stopped.

My blood ran cold, but I told myself that it was probably nothing—a servant accidently thinking that my door was the one to the attic. But as I tried to fall asleep, I heard the faint scratching noise begin from the attic above me. I pinched myself to make certain that I was awake.

I was.

Then, unmistakably, the scratching turned to footsteps above me. They were slow, faint, deliberate. Someone was up there.

I chastised myself, thinking that I was letting superstition affect my reason. After all, Mariah had told me that many of the floors needed to be reinforced. The floor structure might be particularly creaky after the earlier thunderstorm.

I turned fretfully in my bed, sleeping very little.

The next morning when I awoke and came downstairs for breakfast, I felt tired and glum, and sitting at the far end of the long dining room table, heard very little of Violet and

Grandmother's conversations. Mariah, because she kept late hours, almost never came down to breakfast.

One of the servants presented a note to me. It was only when I thanked him that I saw who it was.

"Richard!" I said, excitedly. I hadn't seen him since we had left Grandmother's. "I didn't expect you to be here."

He cleared his throat and said quietly, "I am only needed to supervise at the house during the hours when the workers are there. I decided to help out here a bit. For the company."

"Of course." The conversation at the far end of the table had stopped, and I saw Grandmother's eye upon me. Lady Violet looked at me as if I were a wolf child. *Chatting with a servant—unacceptable.*

I groaned. "It's good to see you, Richard."

He bowed and left.

Tearing open the envelope, my eyes watered when I read the contents.

Dear Abbie,

I do apologize for any awkwardness that might arise from my proposal last night. I misread your affections for me, and I am sorry about that. Do not let this affect our friendship or your adherence to my warnings. I still admire you and care for you warmly.

—Sincerely,
Simon

The strokes had been written in a careful hand. I felt a wave of sadness as I carefully folded the letter and left the dining room. I felt Grandmother's eyes on me as I left.

Twenty

On Saturday, I felt suffocated. I had to get out of the house.

I told Grandmother that I was going on a walk and left before she could question me. I took the four dresses, folded in a large bag, and started out early, just after breakfast. I felt mildly guilty, as Simon had warned me not to go to the East End, but it was broad daylight, so I walked a few blocks and caught a carriage.

Once in Whitechapel, I left the carriage and, clutching the bag close to me, walked until I found Miller's Court, right off Dorset Street in the Spitalfields district of the East End. The area seemed even more poverty-stricken than the nearby Whitechapel Road. The air on Dorset reeked of urine, vomit, and spilled alcohol, and when I entered

Miller's Court, I saw enormous rats scurrying through the passage even in the noon hours.

"No, I won't accept them," Mary said when I opened the bag and laid the dresses out for her to see.

The place where she lived was a small, single room with one bed and a fireplace. In spite of the fire, the room was freezing. One of the windows had been broken, a rag stuffed into the pane's hole. The bed in the room had only two very thin blankets. Mary was alone when I found her, and I saw embarrassment on her face as she let me in. I knew her financial situation was strained, but I had no idea how much.

"I'll just leave them here. Give them to someone else if you don't want them," I said, turning to leave.

"Take them with you. I'm doing fine."

At that point I felt irritated. True, I had never lived in a room like this, but I wished she could know that I was not always so privileged—that there had been times, particularly between Mother's governess jobs, when we had no money. I wish she had seen my life in Dublin, the youth I played with in the streets, the orphans and pickpockets. I wanted to tell her about all of this, but it seemed foolish. She could only see me as I was now—Lady Westfield's Kensington brat granddaughter.

"Fine. I'm trying to help. It's a simple matter. I was going to get rid of some dresses, so I thought I would give them to you."

She still looked angry.

"Take them, Mary," someone said behind me, and I

jumped. Scribby stood in the doorway with a bundle of firewood under his arm. When Mary crossed her arms, her shawl fell a bit and I saw how sharp her shoulders were.

"Thank you, Miss Abbie, for helping Mary get that hospital job," Scribby continued. "Mary knows"—here he cut her a hard glance and began feeding some wood into the fire—"how fortunate we three are to have jobs at all, being immigrants."

I saw, then, tears in Mary's eyes, and she bit her lip. I looked away quickly, knowing how proud she was.

"Thank you, Abbie," Scribby said again, very kindly. He was walking well now, but I saw that the lower part of his leg was tightly bandaged. "Mary appreciates the job and the clothes. The fact is, we will be able to afford to get better rooms at some point, but we're sending money to her family. She has a sick younger sister, so we're pretty poor right now."

Without glancing back at Mary, who was saying nothing, I nodded, said goodbye, and left.

First thing on Monday morning, I went to Scotland Yard.

Walking through the maze of offices, I found Abberline. His office door was open and he sat behind his desk. The odor of dirty teacups and pipe smoke immediately assaulted my nose. The large highlighted map behind him now had four red pins, marking the site of each Ripper murder.

"I thought I had made my answer clear," I said, placing the card and newspaper clippings on his desk. "Why did you send me these? Do you think you can bully me into playing along with your investigation?"

He looked up, his face pale, his eyes bloodshot. He seemed surprised by my sudden presence. Weary and unprepared. The case was becoming a great burden to him, I could tell, but I pushed all my sympathetic thoughts aside.

"Miss Sharp. Do sit down."

"I prefer to stand. Now, why did you send me this *after* I told you that I wanted to play no part in spying on my friends? I work at Whitechapel Hospital, and I won't be a pawn in your investigation."

Everything I said was true, but what I didn't say was that I believed his inquiries were futile. I thought of the chalice symbol, of my vision of that odd ritual, of Max's tattoo, of all the pieces that didn't fit together yet. I remembered the police chasing Scribby, the heavy police presence in the hospital, and I suspected that Scotland Yard's search was going in the wrong direction. Their investigation and tactics would be fruitless. And given my cryptic conversation with Simon in the library, I feared that something larger was behind all of this. With all that I might have before me, that was something I had to figure out on my own. I did not need Scotland Yard's watchful eye upon me.

Abberline looked stunned, for once unable to speak.

"Will you leave me alone now?" I asked once more.

There was a small hesitation; he looked as if he wanted

to say something before deciding against it. "Yes. Certainly, if that is what you wish."

"It is. Good day, Inspector Abberline."

"Good day."

That was, I felt certain, the last I should hear from him. He was used to getting his way. I just had to act a little galling, a little troublesome, and he would leave me alone.

By Tuesday evening, I felt particularly agitated. Mariah had been out so frequently, with Cecil or with Charles, that I didn't see much of her. I had hoped that she would stop by my room that evening. I hadn't seen Simon since his proposal the week before. I missed his friendship, and I felt lonely. William still loomed in my thoughts, and I would have given anything to know where he was. Eventually I resolved to go to bed early, and at some point, after several hours, I fell asleep.

A giggle woke me. It came from somewhere in the hallway. Then silence.

My first thought was that Mariah had come back from a rendezvous with Charles drunk. She also might have Charles in her room. *That* was more likely. Whatever she was doing, it was none of my business, so I turned over and tried to sleep again.

More silence. I began to think that I might have dreamt up the giggle.

Then there was a loud bang. The attic door had slammed opened.

I bolted upright in my bed.

I heard it—the trudging footsteps. This time they were not above me in the attic, but came from the hallway. I heard them very clearly—too clearly.

Just as I calmed myself with the certainty that I had locked my door, I peeked through my bed curtains.

My bedroom door was wide open.

I commanded myself to stay calm and took deep breaths as I put on my slippers and rose to close my door. I reached the open doorway. Just as I began to shut the door, something white flashed past me in the darkness.

I swallowed and suppressed a scream. Then, as I reached out to pull the doorknob and shut myself in my room, I saw it—the bottom trail of a white nightgown ascending the attic stairs.

Of course. It was Mariah sleepwalking. She must have been the one making the noises above me those nights. I felt so foolish, thinking of my mind's absurd and terrible fantasies.

I didn't want her to fall down the attic stairs or to get hurt on something up there, so I took a candle from my room and went to find her. I would speak to a servant in the morning about securing the attic door.

When I reached the top of the steps, I could no longer see her. The attic was larger than I had imagined, a huge, mazelike place that seemed to sprawl over the entire house. I could not locate Mariah anywhere.

The only light came from the moonlight breaking through a few high, small windows near the ceiling. Cobwebs swooped across everything like drapery. Sheets covered old furniture, creating enormous white lumps in the darkness. I saw empty portrait frames, old portraits spoiled by burns and spills. I saw wooden chests and piles of foul-smelling clothes.

The slough of a foot from several yards away caught my attention.

"Mariah." I spoke quietly, stepping toward the sound.

When I stretched my candle out in front of me, I saw that nothing had been placed in the large middle section of the attic floor. I wondered if that was one of the weakened structures of the house. Only spiders scuttled through the thick dust in that square portion of floor.

"Mariah." I hoped to find her quickly and lead her back to her bedroom.

I continued walking, seeing what looked like the back of a large dark wig poking above the back of a sheet-covered armchair.

"Mariah." I sighed in relief.

Her head did not turn.

Perhaps she had fallen asleep in the chair.

"Mariah," I said again when I reached the armchair. I laid one of my hands upon her shoulder.

The head turned toward me.

I screamed.

Twenty-one

The body was Mariah's, but it was not Mariah's gaze that met my own.

I stared in disbelief at the eyes. They were not the vague eyes of a sleepwalker. Somehow they shone not with Mariah's spirit but with cunning, with bloodlust. I thought of my visions, of the pickpocket's changed expression, and then of Max's "dollygirl."

Although my bewilderment and confusion mounted, I suddenly knew who the Ripper was—and he had found a way to meet with me.

"Hello, Abbie."

In horror, I recognized the strong, tinkling ring of Mariah's vocal chords, but they were now distorted, made rude by the parasite inside her.

My horror quickly gave way to rage. "Leave her alone. Leave us *all* alone!"

I wanted to strike out, to hurt him. After all, he did not have his knife now. I could fight him. But to do so would mean injuring the body of Mariah.

"How are you able to do this?"

I heard the cluck of a tongue as "he" stood, positioning himself toward me like a coiled snake. I backed instinctively away.

"I have no plans to hurt you, Arabella Sharp, at least not tonight." He stepped forward.

I now heard the familiar sloughing sound, the scraping of Mariah's slippered feet moved by the heavy force that possessed her.

"Who are you?" I asked, but his name was on my lips.

He did not answer, just continued to move forward.

I did not believe in spirits possessing people; I did not believe even now, with this "creature" before me.

Yet I was seeing it with my own eyes.

I still could not speak his name out loud. But if this was truly Max, how could he not be limited by a body?

The hot wax from my candle dripped onto my finger. The sting reminded me of what I must concern myself with right now: *survival*.

"Go away!" I shouted, thrashing the candle toward him as he advanced. I stopped the flame just before it met my friend's body. I could not hurt her.

The being paused, laughing softly—that chuckle from my nightmares. His predatory gaze proved such an awful contrast to Mariah's lovely figure. The violation disgusted me.

"Let us talk, Abbie Sharp."

It was an invitation that I could not stomach.

"Leave her *alone*! Leave Mariah *now*!"

He paused in his advance, cocking his head to one side. My heart pounded in my ears.

"I'll oblige your request, *Miss Sharp*. Your friend can have her body back."

He bowed slightly, mockingly. I wondered what he was up to. As I watched, he leapt back with unnatural force, landing, on his feet, dead center in the middle of the empty section of flooring. The boards creaked loudly under the thud.

"No!"

"Goodbye, Abbie." The eyes flickered a bit. "For tonight…"

I ran to where the boxes and furniture stopped, just on the perimeter of the space. I knew this part of the attic must stretch over the library—if the floor gave out, Mariah would fall three stories to the library floor.

"Abbie?" Mariah was confused and sluggish.

I could see that she had no idea where she was.

"Don't *move*, Mariah," I pleaded, in what I hoped was a calm voice. She could not weigh much. I estimated her to be only ten yards away from where I stood.

I stifled a scream when the entire floor under Mariah trembled, as the beams under the floorboards shifted.

Dear God. It was more unsteady than I had thought.

In Mariah's expression, bewilderment gave way to understanding. But she was not one to panic or to go hysterical, and, after taking a deep breath, she took two steps cautiously toward me.

"You were sleepwalking. Just walk *light-footed* toward me."

She took three more steps.

The groaning again. Then a violent cracking noise.

A few more cautious steps. More cracking. She was only about three yards away now.

"You're almost here, Mariah. Take my hand." I stretched out my arm toward her.

I breathed a sigh of relief. She would make it.

But then, all at once, the floor gave way, starting from the center of the section and rippling outward—instantaneously creating a large crater. I heard the sounds of crashing beams and floor pieces falling far down onto the floor of the library.

"Jump!" I screamed at Mariah. But the flooring under her gave out so that before she could make the leap toward me, she slipped, and clutched onto a dangling piece of flooring.

"Hang on, Mariah!" I shouted.

Anyone but Mariah would have fallen already, panicked. But Mariah, even as she dangled above a three-story drop, remained focused, struggling to pull herself to safety.

"Hurry, Abbie! Get a sheet. Something. *Anything.* I can make it up. But my *hand*—it will slip soon."

I glanced around and saw that the nearest piece of draped furniture was too far away to grab in time.

"There isn't time, Mariah. I'm going to anchor myself and give you my hand."

She was so close to me.

Lying on my stomach across the sturdy flooring, I buried the toes of my slippers into the floorboard seams so that I could inch forward.

I slid on my belly toward the edge of the crater. I could then see more clearly—both my friend and the scene beneath her.

Far below, Sir Bertram was still on his sofa, just beyond the enormous pile of wood, floor beams, and clouds of dirt. He was looking up at us in a drug-induced stupor. I'm certain that he thought the entire scene far above him was part of a laudanum nightmare.

Servants began to swarm into the library.

"*Help!*" I screamed down at them as they stared at us in disbelief.

Then, miraculously, I strained myself downward and clutched one of Mariah's hands as she clung to the beam with her other hand.

"I won't die, Abbie." She fixed a hard look upon me.

"No, you won't."

She seemed reassured as she let go of the beam to grab my hand with her other hand. I knew that if I had both of her hands, I could gingerly ease her from the pit.

As I tightened my grip on her hands, I strained backwards.

Lady Violet had arrived on the scene below.

Her scream did it.

Mariah slipped from my grip and plunged toward the splintered pile three stories below.

I lay frozen in place on the attic floor.

My thoughts tunneled toward a chamber that ran deeper than the pit in front of me. Mariah's last look of horror when she fell would be forever cemented onto my consciousness. Her death was a great loss, a waste.

If she had never known me, she would still be alive. I thought of the patients at Whitechapel Hospital who had been murdered. I had known most of them. William and Simon were already in danger.

Was Grandmother in danger? Would all those that I love die?

Richard was the first to find me in the attic, and he gently pried me off the ground before placing a blanket around my shoulders and leading me away from the crater. I told him in words that did not seem to be my own that Mariah had sleepwalked upstairs, that I had tried to save her but she had fallen through the floorboards.

He hushed me gently as he led me down the narrow attic steps.

Grandmother and several of the servants ran to me when he brought me downstairs, but I could not bear any words of consolation or give any out myself. I felt detached, exhausted.

Cursed.

Twenty-two

I stayed in bed until late the next morning, unable to move. I couldn't sleep. I couldn't cry. Fury overwhelmed me, along with the grief and guilt. It had been over a month since the Ripper had attacked me in Whitechapel, and now he wanted to show me what he was capable of, what he could do. That he could not be limited even to a body. I felt certain now that he had possessed the pickpocket, that he had lured me to the hospital. And now he had possessed Mariah.

I thought of Max's mysterious tattoo, of his connection with Dr. Bartlett and the other housemates, of his apparent possession of some sort of supernatural powers. But *why* was he terrorizing me? Why did he not just kill me? What did he want?

I heard the morgue carriages pull away with Mariah's body, and hammering sounds echoed from somewhere downstairs. Fleetingly, I wondered if there would be an investigation, and then remembered that everyone thought this was a terrible accident. *How many more people had to die?*

Grandmother knocked on the door around noon. She wore black and held Jupe in her arms. To my mild surprise, she said nothing about me still being in bed; I had thought that the stress might make her particularly fussy. Instead, she sat in a chair by my bed and said nothing for several minutes. Her eyes looked puffy; I knew she had done her mourning in private.

The hammering sounds grew louder.

"Lady Violet demanded that the library be boarded up for now. It is too terrible."

I said nothing; I just lay on my bed staring at the ceiling.

Grandmother stroked Jupe's back. "I inspected our house with Richard yesterday. The renovations are nearly finished. I told Violet that we would return home today so that we would not be any trouble to her."

She then spoke a bit about how nice her house looked. But as she continued, almost to herself, I knew her thoughts were elsewhere.

Then suddenly she became quiet. I felt her eyes on me. And I broke my gaze from the ceiling to look at her.

"I watched Mariah grow up," she said suddenly, distractedly. "She never sleepwalked."

I snapped fully out of my reverie. *Was she just thinking out loud or did she have other suspicions?*

Unable to read her expression, I said nothing. I couldn't have told her the truth of what I had seen anyway.

With Jupe still in her arms, she stood up and smoothed the bedcovers around me. This was her awkward attempt at being compassionate.

"The funeral will be Friday afternoon, Arabella."

Then she left.

I stayed in the bed all afternoon, watching the day progress. Afternoon slipped into dullish evening as shadows lengthened across my room. With every passing hour my anger rose, dominating even my feelings of grief. The Ripper had taken over my friend's body to get to me. It was unfair. Awful. Mariah had been a beautiful girl, an aspiring writer, bright, vibrant, driven. She was a mere stepping stone for the Ripper, a piece in the puzzle he had laid out for me.

I jumped, startled, when one of Violet's servants knocked on my door to help me collect my things. Grandmother's carriage already waited outside.

The moment we returned to Grandmother's house, I went straight to bed again without a word to anyone. I stayed in my bedroom all day on Thursday, both mourning for Mariah and trying to figure out what to do. Unable to sleep on Thursday night, I stared at my freshly painted ceiling. I *had* to know what was happening. I couldn't put it off any longer.

Moonlight broke through my curtains as the night

deepened. Dr. Bartlett's Montgomery Street house, with its gallery, its eccentric occupants, and all of its mysteries, beckoned me. Grandmother's house was quiet—everyone was asleep. Silently, I got out of bed, dressed, and slipped out the front door, in the pitch of night.

Part IV

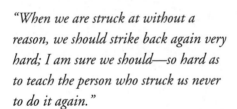

"When we are struck at without a reason, we should strike back again very hard; I am sure we should—so hard as to teach the person who struck us never to do it again."

—*Jane Eyre*

Twenty-three

As I walked the long stretch of Montgomery Street, the air whipped cold and sharp at my face. It was a dry, freezing night. Dead leaves, riding the gusts, swept across the street before me. Not a single person was out. Abandoned boarding houses and shells of workhouses lined the street. There were no working streetlamps, and I saw no one. In the distance, Dr. Bartlett's house loomed before me. With the windows all curtained and dark, it looked as if they were not home.

All the better. I could have the freedom to explore the house myself.

Thankful for the high winds, I tiptoed soundlessly to the front door. It was unlocked. Carefully I turned the knob and pushed the door open an inch. I could see nothing but darkness inside.

You are insane, I told myself as I nudged the door further open. Why would it be unlocked? Perhaps they were gone and someone had broken into their house. Then again, they might be home, asleep, or in some other part of the house. Either way, I slipped through the door.

I saw the soft glow of the jellyfish from the drawing room aquarium, but not a single light was on in the house. The stairs rose into darkness before me, and another hallway shot out to my right.

I heard voices, soft chanting, coming from somewhere in that hallway.

My heart stopped. Déjà vu swept over me as I remembered my vision of the hooded ritual. The voices were so muted they had to come from behind something, either a wall or a door down the hallway. Carefully, I crept toward the sound, feeling ahead of me to make certain that I didn't fall over any chairs or bump into a sconce. As I proceeded, the chanting grew louder, so I knew I was closer. A tiny stream of light shone ahead of me, and I saw at the end of the hall two large, steel doors, medieval-like in structure. Architecturally, the doors did not fit in with the rest of the house. The light was coming out of a large keyhole in one of the doors.

Kneeling on the ground, I peered through the keyhole and covered my mouth to keep from gasping. I saw a windowless room, lit only by candles and torches. Some mats and rugs lay at the perimeter of the room, but other than that, it was empty of furniture. Robed figures stood in the center, chanting in Latin. I couldn't make out all of their words, but I did hear *A Posse Ad Esse*. Then I saw a flash of silver—the chalice being passed from hand to hand.

I couldn't quite see the faces clearly, but I knew it was Dr. Bartlett and his housemates. It was some sort of organization, some sort of brotherhood ritual.

The chanting continued, seeming to roar in my ears as I studied their figures, unbelieving. Then I noticed that there were only four figures. One was missing. Someone wasn't in that room.

At the same moment I thought this, I felt the sharp point of a knife against the back of my head. As my blood ran cold, I stood up, tensing, and slowly turned around.

It was Max.

With one finger over his lips, he signaled that I should be quiet. He moved the knife point to my throat and ushered me ahead of him. With the blade now against my back, he forced me down the hall, past the stairs, and into the drawing room.

I was backed up against the jellyfish aquarium, the knife at my throat again. This blade was thin, sharp, surgical-like. Perfect for tearing organs. It was his killing blade.

"I thought you might come here tonight. I had a premonition," he said.

I glared at him. "What do you want? What is that ritual? That *thing* Dr. Bartlett and the others are doing in that room?"

The leopard-green eyes flicked in the darkness. I thought of cut gems.

He chuckled, amused. "Are you actually going to listen to me tonight?"

Fury flooded through me, and I lunged forward. Almost without moving, he pushed the knife harder into my throat. The pinch was unbearable; I felt wetness, and I knew that I bled a little.

"I wouldn't recommend that, Abbie Sharp," he said calmly. "If you want to live to hear the answers that you seek."

"*You*. It was *you* in the attic last night."

He gave a little bow. "Indeed. I found your friend quite charming. But she knew me by another name—Charles."

I caught myself just before I tried to attack him again.

"Temper, Abbie. Remember your temper."

"Why couldn't you just talk to me, as you are now? Why did you have to kill her?"

Max stepped closer, the knife still against my neck. Then, in the darkness, he put his forehead against my own.

Instantly I saw what was happening in that room, had a closer view of Dr. Bartlett chanting under his hood, slowly passing the chalice. The vision whirled through my consciousness, and then away just as Max pulled his head back.

I stared at him, dizzied, questioning.

"You and I share a gift, Abbie. A remarkable gift. We are seers of things: past, present, sometimes future. We are some of the very few who possess this power. You can see things on your own, or see others' memories or visions as you did just now. Touch makes the visions come more easily, but I don't have to touch you for you to see what I'm thinking. Your gift is that remarkable. The first day we met, I cast you a vision, and you became aware of your gift. It had been dormant before then. Many of the visions you had after that were through your own powers, but some, I sent you."

I thought of how I had seen him crawling down buildings, the possessions, the pickpocket, and Mariah. I almost couldn't hear myself as I spoke. "But it's not just visions. It's more. You can possess others' bodies. You were in the pickpocket's body . . ."

He winked. "Once again, you can do so much more."

"So what does this have to do with what's going on in there, with that ritual?"

"*Immortality*, Abbie Sharp. It has to do with immortality. The philosopher's stone—an element in the elixir of life—was discovered centuries ago by Robert Buck. Along with Julian, Marcus, and John, he formed the Conclave. That ritual in there celebrates the true Holy Grail, the gift of immortality. We drink the elixir on this date, once a year, and can live . . . forever."

I had had suspicions, but knowing that I had been right—that they were old, *centuries* old—was overwhelming. It went against reason, against everything in my known world.

"You are . . . " I swallowed.

Max whispered in the darkness. "The others are four

hundred years old. I'm a bit newer, a later addition. I'm—the enforcer, you might say."

I could speak it now. The words burned my lips as I whispered them.

"You're the Ripper."

His eyes shone, and I had my confession. "Yes."

A roaring pause. I thought of all the murdered patients. I thought of Mariah, of the dead.

My vision blurred with tears. "Why?"

"The Conclave promotes the greatest good for England: The greatest political good. The greatest social good. The East End is forgotten, abandoned. All I did was ... bring some attention to it."

I remembered Perkins's letter to the newspaper; I remembered the whipped-up public frenzy, the journalist frenzy ... the extra supplies, the news coverage, the money donations, the volunteers. Even the sensational flourish—the organ mailed to the police. This kind of murder mystery would naturally enthrall a London public raised on penny-dreadful novels. This *had* all been planned. The lives of each victim had been taken for this purpose.

"But Polly, Annie, Liz, and Cate. They were all *people*. They had done no wrong. They were patients at Dr. Bartlett's hospital. And he knew about all this?" I knew he must have. But I still fought against believing it.

"He *sanctioned* it," Max replied. "Abbie, you are being short-sighted."

"It was wrong," I said.

Max sighed, as if my comment wearied him.

"The rest of the Conclave will be resting soon—usually we rest after taking the elixir. But, here's a proposition: you share my gift. The elixir brings out my gift even more—I can leave my body, possess others, even defy gravity. I can *climb walls*, Abbie. For some reason the elixir empowers my body's energies—both physical and mental. You, because you are also psychic, might be able to do all this too. I will help you learn all of it, if you take a drink. The elixir makes everyone who drinks it immortal. But you and me..." He paused and I saw the jellyfish shapes from the aquarium behind me flit across his face. "It makes our type *shine* as immortals."

"But how did you know that I was psychic? How did you know to find me, specifically?"

"Interesting that you should ask. We have long toyed with adding a new, younger member for the Conclave. For years, Julian has suggested that we might possibly add a woman, to have a female perspective in the group. He heard from your grandmother that Caroline had had a daughter, now returned to London. I watched you; Abbie, for two months I watched you. You seemed a perfect candidate—raised by an educated mother, newly arrived in London. Disoriented, restless, with only one still-living relative. Young. Trainable. Risk-taking... I saw that particularly when you chased the pickpocket into the East End. I also saw, then, that you were psychic. At that point, Abbie, we knew you were the one."

What were they going to do? Were they going to force me to take the elixir, to become one of them?

Max lessened the pressure of the knife on my neck. A bit. "You should know that we're in a small muddle with one of your friends."

My heart quickened.

"Dr. William Siddal." Max watched my expression, but I kept my features still. "I killed one of his relatives who found out about us several years ago—a physician, if I remember correctly."

Polidori! William's great uncle.

"But unbeknownst to me, he had written everything down and put it in his family's safe in Avignon. Siddal knows of the papers' existence. As does St. John, now. Not good for either of them."

So that was what William sought. Papers detailing the identity of the Conclave. Proof of the existence of the philosopher's stone.

Max looked carefully at me. I panicked momentarily, remembering Simon's concern about my mind. If Max could cast visions for me, could he also read my thoughts? But almost instantly, I knew from his expression that he could not.

The chanting had stopped.

Max cast a glance back out of the drawing room.

What next? I tensed, waiting. Thinking.

"You can go." He dropped the knife, stepped back.

I froze, wondering if this was a trick.

"Marcus Brown will meet you in Hampstead Heath, near the ponds, tomorrow afternoon at five o'clock. Your friend's funeral should be over by that time, and the Heath is within walking distance of the cemetery."

I felt a shiver run through me, thinking how much Max knew of my daily life.

"Why is Dr. Brown meeting me? Why don't you just tell me what I need to know about the elixir now?" I asked stubbornly.

Max smiled, gazing at me as if I were a child who did not understand him. "As I told you before, I'm just the enforcer. Officially inviting you into the Conclave is not my role. Marcus is our politician, our diplomat. He'll offer you our terms and discuss the elixir."

I started to leave the room. Then I stopped dead in my tracks, turning around to face him.

"You'll leave William and Simon alone."

It wasn't a question. It was a command. I remembered Mariah's face before she died—I couldn't bear losing either of my other friends.

He nodded. "As long as you—or they—don't do anything stupid."

I stared hard at him before turning to run out the front door.

"And Abbie … "

"What?" I looked back.

"A Posse Ad Esse."

"In the midst of life we are in death…"

The priest's words rang out evenly at Mariah's funeral. The weather could not have been more bleak. Rain poured through the canopy of trees in Highgate Cemetery in great sheets, splashing between the crowded umbrellas held by the attendees at the service.

Very few people had come. I stood beside Grandmother, Catherine, and Violet within a small crowd of strangers.

A long, lean figure in black cut into my periphery.

Simon.

He stood under a giant oak tree, a bit away from the funeral, holding only an umbrella.

When the muddy dirt was cast onto the coffin, the funeral attendees gradually left the graveside. I walked over to Simon. As I approached, Simon stared in the direction of the burial, not at me.

I wondered what he was thinking at that instant.

When I reached him, we did not say a word, but instead silently eased ourselves toward one of the many little paths in Highgate.

My mind flashed back to the time I had been here with William.

Simon and I had said nothing for several moments, but I wanted to break the awkwardness. I needed him as a friend.

"Simon … about … "

He knew instantly of what I spoke because he interrupted me, saying, "Please, Abbie. It is done. We will never speak of it again. I am merely your friend now."

I felt such mixed emotions. On one hand, I felt affection for him, relief that he desired our friendship as it had been before. But also, strangely, I felt irritation, anger even. I wished that he might give away some *hint* of his true feelings.

I could not dwell on this. We had more pressing matters to discuss.

"You know how she died?" I asked.

"Sleepwalking, I was told."

We had come to a giant mausoleum in an area of the cemetery referred to as Egyptian Avenue. We stepped inside the mausoleum for shelter from the pouring rain. The dark entryway was cold, damp, black. I shook off my umbrella, and Simon leaned gracefully against the stone wall near a tomb. I noticed, a bit painfully, that Simon kept a greater physical distance from me than he had in the past.

"It's not true, is it?" he added softly.

I shook my head. The tears poured out this time. As my guilt over Mariah's death returned, my emotions unloosed. I could hardly look at Simon now, fearful for him. He was caught up in all this because of me.

He moved forward, then stepped quickly back. I think he had meant to embrace me but decided against it.

Taking a deep breath, I told him every detail of what occurred in the attic—and that Max was the Ripper.

Simon said nothing; he simply watched me as I spoke. His face glowed in the darkness, resembling one of the marble angels on the Highgate tombs.

The rain continued in torrents, just outside of our shelter.

"And that is not all, Simon…" I paused, wondering what he suspected.

"What else is it, Abbie?"

I stared up at him, unable to speak for a moment. I couldn't bear thinking of him dead.

Then I told him all that Max had told me last night about the Conclave's history, and that they wanted me to join them, and why. Simon kept his composure even when I told him about Max knowing of William's trip and the existence of the papers.

I was breathless by the time I finished.

"They want me, Simon, as an immortal member of the Conclave. I don't really have a choice."

I almost told him about my impending meeting with Dr. Brown, but then stopped myself. Simon would forbid me from going.

Don't do anything stupid, Max had said.

Feeling the full burden of what was before me, I chuckled, a little wildly, tears still on my face.

"Do you have any idea of when the official invitation might come?" Simon asked.

"I have no idea," I lied. "I think we have some time. After the yearly ritual, the Conclave takes some time to rest. Have you heard anything from William?" I added quickly.

He shook his head.

Max would have to leave William alive at least long enough for him to return with the papers—so that he could destroy them. Those papers were the only evidence of the Conclave's existence. But I still worried for William. I had seen what Max was capable of.

"Are you still at the hospital frequently?" I asked Simon.

"Yes. But Dr. Bartlett and Dr. Buck have only been there sporadically of late. Of course, now we know why." He sighed and sank deep in thought.

It was three o'clock. I had only two hours until my meeting. I had to find a way to get away from Simon.

"I think I need to be alone for a few minutes," I said.

He looked at me, and I feared he would not leave me.

"I'll catch up with Grandmother. I promise."

"Abbie."

"*Please.*"

He stared at me a moment in the tombs' shadows, indecisive. Then he quietly left.

Silence.

After Simon left, I watched the rain pour around me with such force that it would be nearly impossible to walk out into it now. I thought of the dead bones in the coffins all around me. They all had oblivion; they all had peace. Mariah was among them now.

I needed to think. Two more hours. I doubted Dr. Brown would kill me in broad daylight in the Heath. And he certainly wouldn't offer me the elixir today. It was my understanding that there would be some sort of ceremony.

Exhausted, frustrated, I collapsed against one of the tombs and then sat on the damp floor. I stared ahead, hypnotized by the pelting rain. The time passed and the temperature dropped, but I felt numb to it all.

I thought I imagined it. I thought I heard William speak my name from far away.

"Abbie."

I had barely heard it, above the roar of the rain, and I froze, unable to move. Unbelieving.

"Abbie."

I heard the voice again, and I stood. I whipped around to face the entrance of the mausoleum. I had desired him so strongly in his absence that when I saw him, I feared it was a vision.

But he wasn't a vision. He stood before me in flesh and blood, dripping wet.

"You are back," I said. I swallowed, still unbelieving.

"I am."

Now, faced with the possibility of death for him and for me, I knew exactly what I wanted. Before I could think on it further, I ran to him and kissed him. In that moment, I felt alive, trembling more than I ever had in my life. I felt dizzied, particularly when William returned the kiss with a vigor that equaled, or possibly surpassed, my own. We fell back against the iron grating of a crypt. My face wet from his, I felt frighteningly unbridled.

The time was passing quickly before my meeting.

Summoning all of my strength, I pushed him away from me.

I told him everything I had just told Simon. As I spoke, I saw a bag at his feet. In my earlier frenzy, I hadn't even noticed it. "Your uncle's papers! Are the papers in there? Tell me, quickly, have you read them? Do they tell us anything that I have not already told you?"

"Yes, I've read most of them. They reveal just a few more details. During the time Polidori worked as Lord Byron's physician in the Alps, he became acquainted with the Conclave—their British neighbors also staying in the Alps at that time. He became suspicious that the group might be something more than the eccentric scholars they put themselves forth to be, and one night he searched through Dr. Buck's lab, finding his private notes. He found out the Conclave's secret—that they had discovered the philosopher's stone and had created the elixir of life, and that they killed to protect themselves. Knowing that he himself would probably be killed, Polidori wrote down everything he knew and sent it to Avignon, where our family solicitor put it unopened into a safe. Max killed Polidori without having any knowledge of the papers. That was a colossal mistake for Max."

"So how did you learn of their existence?"

"Christina. No one had opened the papers until my father happened to clean out the safe about the time he met your mother. He read through them, and consequently often sought out Dr. Bartlett's lectures—to see him, to see the other members of the Conclave. He brought along other artists, including your mother, to these lectures; she like the other artists would have been ignorant of my father's investigative motives. He told no one about his discovery until closely before his death, when he wrote down his own notes and added them to Polidori's. He had the papers sealed again and sent back to Avignon. On his deathbed, he told Christina about it—about the Conclave. She, only half-believing him since his mind was so riddled by drugs, never brought it up, even when I began working directly with Bartlett and Buck in Whitechapel. But when the murders occurred, she became suspicious, worried for me. I didn't believe it; it didn't seem possible. But finally, I agreed to go retrieve the papers."

"And your father never did anything to stop them?"

"He was an artist—he had no idea how to stop a group of politically sanctioned immortals."

"Politically sanctioned?"

"Dr. Buck was an alchemist for Queen Elizabeth when he discovered the philosopher's stone through his experiments, created the elixir, and told the queen of its existence. She sanctioned Dr. Buck, along with three others, to form the Conclave, a group consisting of a scholar, a theologian, a scientist, and a physician. She made them swear an oath to her to keep the elixir secret and to use their immortality for the public good of England. The downside of this is that the Conclave kills to protect themselves from those who become too suspicious of their identity. Or, as in these Ripper murders, they are willing to kill for the public good. Their discoveries in science—vaccines and medicines, for example—have saved many lives, but at a cost. They are great humanitarians, but in order to continue as they have, they lost respect for *individual* lives. The betterment of the masses always trumps those of the individual."

"Max—they took him into their group years later, as their protector and assassin."

As I spoke, the rain abated, I knew the time was pressing near when I would have to leave William. I needed at least a half an hour to get to the ponds.

"Yes. Rossetti's notes don't reveal much about Max. The Conclave took him on in the early nineteenth-century, probably for his psychic abilities. For some reason, when he took the elixir, he was sort of an aberration; he could do and see things the others couldn't. And Rossetti's notes explain something else—why your mother suddenly eloped with Jacque Sharp. My father sent your mother away probably to protect her, and … "

William paused.

"What is it?"

"My father is your father. He probably also wanted to protect you. Your mother's elopement with her friend Sharp was last-minute. Sharp would have known you weren't his own."

This didn't come as a surprise; actually, it was more of a confirmation of what I had already suspected, and I felt an odd numbness. I should have been excited to know my parentage, but I wasn't. Even if Gabriel Rossetti sent my mother and me away to distance us from the Conclave, he still abandoned us.

"Abbie? What are you thinking?"

I shrugged. "Nothing. That it doesn't really matter even

if he is my father. And … " The meeting loomed before me, and, with what was to come, this might be my only opportunity to make my confession.

"And what, Abbie?"

"That I love you." I kissed him again, warming. A distant church bell tolled the four-thirty hour and I knew I had to leave.

With the break in the rain, I heard a footstep on the stone floor. I gasped, pulling myself away from William as I saw Simon, standing there in the mausoleum.

"William, how nice, you have returned." His tone was bitter, acidic.

William said nothing, and I moved away from him. Awkwardness and anger hung in the air.

"And how extraordinarily responsible. You left this bag of papers near the doorway. Decades-old, sought-after by an immortal assassin, and you leave them here, to um … entertain Miss Sharp."

I eased backward, toward the entrance. William would not be able to hold his temper long in the face of this.

It was my chance to flee and make my meeting. I heard William shout at Simon as I slipped through the bushes, darting away from Egyptian Avenue and out of the cemetery in the direction of Hampstead Heath. I didn't hear them shouting my name, but even if they saw that I was gone, Highgate Cemetery was a difficult place in which to see very far. It would be almost impossible for them to follow me.

Once out in Hampstead Heath, I found the park

virtually empty. The rain had subsided momentarily into a dewy mist, some of it settling into a fog that blanketed the mirror-still ponds. A man tossed a ball for his dog; a very small group of children, bundled for the chilly weather, played nearby with their nanny.

At exactly five o'clock, just as I walked away from one of the ponds near a small copse of trees, I heard my name spoken. Dr. Bartlett and Dr. Brown were suddenly beside me.

"Miss Sharp," Professor Brown said, in his most pleasant tone.

It was an odd little rendezvous. They looked well, quite well. It must have been the elixir. To any passersby, they might have been my uncles, accompanying me on a stroll.

I watched the dog fetch the ball from across the largest pond.

"Go ahead," I said, pulling my coat tighter and facing both of them.

"Dr. Bartlett wanted to be here with me," Dr. Brown said, cheerfully.

"I am fond of you, Abbie," Dr. Bartlett said. "And I am very impressed by your work at the hospital. Imagine lifetimes of doing all that we do there. Think of how much you might learn. Accomplish."

I saw an odd yearning in his expression. Both Dr. Brown and Dr. Bartlett were greedy for me, and ever since my talk with Max, I knew the real reason they wanted me—for my gift. I wondered if they expected me to aide Max in his dark deeds.

"So, what is it?" I asked. "This philosopher's stone.

Please explain." I needed to know the details, and, admittedly, I was curious.

Dr. Bartlett continued. "Robert Buck, after many, many years of trying, finally created the formula for the philosopher's stone, necessary for the elixir. It was an extraordinary discovery. He tested it on animals first, and then consumed it himself. Through his tests, he learned that drinking the elixir once does not make one permanently immortal; rather, it must be consumed once a year to maintain the effect. Hence, our ritual."

"And then you never die…" I said, feeling a twinge of yearning even against my will.

Dr. Bartlett cleared his throat. "You *can* die—the elixir doesn't prevent that. We can die by accident, through physical trauma. But we do not age, or become ill. The elixir keeps us from dying of *natural* causes."

"I see."

The wind picked up; the tree leaves rattled hard above us.

Dr. Brown spoke next. "We're here to ask you to join the Conclave. As you observed last night, we have already conducted this year's elixir ritual; Max guards the house during the ceremony, and his ritual occurs later. We plan to offer you the elixir tonight, and then after that you may take it yearly with the four of us."

"And if I choose not to?"

They were both silent. But I knew. There was no real choice.

I felt seduced by the idea, drawn to being immortal.

But they were murderers. I had seen them kill, brutally. I lost my friend to them.

No Abbie. You can't be in league with them. Leave them. Now.

"No. I do not accept."

I turned before I could see their expressions, walking fast past the ponds across the grassy park. The wet wind beat at me hard and I clutched my coat closer. Thunder roared in the distance as a storm blew in. I increased my walk to a furious pace.

Now I had to warn William and Simon. And we had to come up with a plan, because we were as good as dead.

Twenty-four

I had only walked about a mile out of the Heath when someone from behind grabbed my wrist, hard.

"What were you *thinking?*" William demanded. His face was furious as he spun me around. "Where were you? We've been looking all over for you! Why would you leave us when you know that they're after you?"

I shook William off me. "I had a meeting with them in the park. I knew you would never let me go alone, so I went by myself to meet them. I said no. *I refused their offer, William.* I hope you know what this means for us."

I saw Simon standing behind him. If they had quarreled, Simon was now perfectly composed.

"So what do we do?" William asked. "Max could show up any time."

"I don't know. I *don't know.*"

Grandmother. She would be back in our house tonight. Although I often went out during the day, to go to the library or on walks, if I didn't come home tonight she would certainly call the police. I also thought of Max. Who knew how many people he might kill to get to me?

"We can't flee," I told William. "Apart from Max finding us, we have to stop them. So that no one else dies. And we should warn Christina. Max knows now that she knows of the papers."

"Abbie's right," Simon said.

Max could be trailing us right now. But at least we were alert; I felt as if Christina and Perdita were sitting ducks in their house. Max could already be there.

"And Christina's friends," I said.

"Fortunately, all of them are living on their own now. So this is a rare occasion where it's just Christina, Perdita, and me," William said quickly.

Evening was setting in. The rain had stopped, but the wind and rumble of thunder had picked up. Christina's house was only a few miles away, but time was of the essence. Immediately, we caught a carriage. We were only a few blocks away when the traffic became heavy.

William, agitated, began cursing, swearing. "Let's get out and run for it!"

Then the vision hit me, and I saw a shadowed passageway. The flounce of a mint-green dress.

Mary! I realized in horror. Max was following her.

No. No. No.

"Mary! He's after Mary!" I yelled. "Stop the carriage."

"A vision?" Simon asked.

"Yes, *yes*. He's behind her. Following her now. He's going to kill her."

I jumped out of the carriage. There was no time to explain. I began running hard and fast toward the East End, hoping that Simon and William would follow me, be able to keep up with me.

I heard William shouting my name from far behind me. "Abbie!"

When the vision came again, I saw a door—Mary's front door.

As the vision broke into my consciousness again, I could see that Mary still had no idea Max was behind her. She was singing, and then humming a tune. The words to her song came out in her thick Irish accent, which I knew she always took great pains to cover on a daily basis. Lost in her song, she had no idea he was behind her.

He is behind you. He is behind you.

I ran faster, until my chest felt as if it would explode.

I'm coming, Mary. I'm coming.

I ran hard, only concerned with getting to her.

I heard a key in a lock. The key paused.

She knew. She knew now he was behind her.

I heard a muffled scream. It was too late. He had pushed her into the room and slammed the door shut.

"*No!*" I yelled out loud.

I ran. I was almost there.

Just as I reached the Miller's Court alleyway, I heard

the slam of a door, saw a shadow disappear with unbelievable speed into the dark.

I stood in front of her door.

"Mary." My voice croaked.

I opened the door. Everything in the small, single-
room dwelling was dark except for a roaring fire in the
fireplace.

Then I saw it—a mangled mess in the bed. The fire
roared high in the small fireplace. In the flicker of the fire
flames, I saw the black shine of blood.

No. No. I felt cold. I felt frozen. I could not even vomit
as I did when I witnessed the murders of Cate and Liz.

Someone pushed me back into the wall. I vaguely
wondered if it was Max.

"Abbie! Abbie!" William shook me. He was enraged,
his face flushed. "What are you *doing*? What are you
doing? You should have waited for us to catch up!"

He had not seen the bed yet.

"It's Mary. Mary Kelly. He killed her."

William followed my eyes to the bed. Simon was
already there, holding a lamp across the bed. He said
nothing.

"God *dammit*!" William exploded.

He turned back to me, his eyes wide.

I began to regain control of my senses. Swallowing
hard, I said, "He's angry. Max is mad that I refused their
invitation. He is trying to compel me to join, now, showing me what he's capable of."

As with Mariah, guilt nearly overcame me. Mary died because of me.

But I also felt hate.

William looked as if he was going to say something, then decided not to. Instead, he hugged me hard.

"William." Simon's voice broke through in the darkness. "Come here."

William walked over.

I followed him, standing at the foot of the bed and trying not to look at the body, which had been mutilated more than the others—beyond recognition.

"This is not Mary Kelly," Simon said. His white fingers teased some blood away from the scalp. He held the lamp closer to the body.

"The hair is black. Mary had lighter hair."

Liliana. I pushed past William and Simon, looking at the hair myself. The corpse was not Mary's. But the corpse wore the dress that I had lent Mary.

Mary was the intended victim, but Max had just murdered Liliana.

"Simon is right," I said. "This is Liliana, her friend. She must have borrowed Mary's dress." I felt a little guilty at the mighty relief that washed over me that the dead woman was not my friend.

Then my thoughts turned back to the still-living Mary.

"We have to find her. We have to find Mary. She must leave London, *now*. Everyone must be made to believe that this is her. If she is seen alive, she will be killed—Max is on a killing spree. Christina. *Grandmother*," I said, almost hysterically. "They could both be in danger. We need to act fast."

"I'll go find Mary and Scribby," William said quickly. "You and Simon go warn Christina."

"But Grandmother…"

"I'll go to Kensington," Simon said immediately. I'll tell your grandmother that you're working with Christina at New Hospital tonight. That they were short-staffed. That way, she won't call Scotland Yard."

I knew Simon was such a favorite with Grandmother that he just might be able to convince her to be all right with that.

"Good, but Grandmother is still in danger…"

"I'll speak to Richard," Simon said.

"What can Richard…"

"You obviously don't know your butler well," Simon said cryptically. His mouth curved, very slightly.

"What?" I asked, perplexed, but he said nothing; his eyes shone a bit.

It was then, in the roaring firelight while we still stood over the corpse, that I saw William gazing at us. His normally flushed face paled with some sort of realization as he looked at Simon, and then at me. But he remained silent.

"So I'll go to Christina's," I said. "I'll warn her, and we can all meet up there."

"Absolutely not," William said. "You can't go alone."

"We *have* too! People's lives are at stake and we're wasting time."

Simon hesitated in the doorway, but he knew I was right. He nodded at me and left.

"No." William grabbed my arm, but I shook him off.

"Just go find Scribby and Mary. Hurry! I'll see you at Christina's shortly."

I sprinted away without another word.

I ran fast, and caught a carriage after a few blocks. As it sped away, I saw the moon rise high over the Thames, bright even amidst the rolling thunderclouds. Night had arrived, and I didn't know if I would see another morning.

Twenty-five

hristina! Christina!" I shouted as I burst through her front door.

All was silent except for Hugo's barking from far above me, up in William's bedroom where it seemed the dog must be shut in.

"Christina!"

No answer.

I walked through the dining room. A note for William awaited him. It was from Christina—she had gone to work at New Hospital that evening.

A sense of foreboding washed over me. Apart from Hugo's barks, something seemed eerie, too quiet, about the house. When I ran to the parlor, I found it empty too, excepting for the parrot Toby in his cage. A fire roared in the fireplace, illuminating Polidori's face.

Gazing up at the portrait, I considered William's handsome great uncle in a new light.

"You knew," I whispered. "You knew about all this."

A loud noise came from another part of the house, near Perdita's bedroom.

My heart pounded in my chest.

As I stood frozen, I tried to think rationally. It was probably Perdita; she could have made the noise. She was almost blind and had poor hearing; she might not have heard me shouting.

Nonetheless, I removed a poker from the fireplace as I crept out of the parlor, into the hallway toward her bedroom.

The bedroom door was slightly open.

Softly, so that I would not scare the old woman, I knocked.

"Perdita?" I whispered, tightening my hold on the poker but concealing it in the folds of my skirt so as not to frighten her.

The door creaked as I pushed it open. The room was small, with very few furnishings. A thin stream of light from a streetlamp broke through a crack in the drawn window curtains, illuminating the bed. A figure lay under the bedcovers. My stomach churned when I saw the pillow covering the face.

I approached the bed cautiously and removed the pillow. Slamming my hand over my mouth to suppress a scream, I leaped back from the bed. The old woman's cataract-covered eyes stared, lifeless, up in the air. The frozen expression on her face was one of horror.

Max!

Then the vision came over me with great force, a vision of the chalice with the *A Posse Ad Esse* inscription. I fell to my knees, my kneecaps hitting the wooden floor painfully. The poker fell from my hand. This vision was strong and my insides felt on fire. I tried to fight it, to bring myself out; Max could be anywhere, and likely in this room with me. My fear for William and Simon escalated. I hoped they would arrive soon.

I screamed as the vision dissipated and I felt myself lifted with great force.

"No!" I yelled.

Max threw me hard onto the bed. I tried to fight him before he could get me pinned. I kicked, spit; I clawed at him, but he was too fast, anticipating all of my movements. Within seconds he was on top of me, immobilizing me. I wished I could move, even a little, as Perdita's body had jolted into mine during the struggle.

"You killed her, an old woman! And you *killed* my friend!"

Max just smiled in the darkness; it was a satisfied smile. Everything was going his way.

"I heard that you refused Marcus's very polite, *very* generous offer. I was incensed. It was perhaps beneath me, but you see, Abbie, I am a slave to my senses. That is my Achilles heel, some would say. You needed some heavy persuasion—so I thought I would start with your nurse friend."

Horror washed over me. Max had super-human speed, and I feared for Simon and William—perhaps we had already fallen into a trap where he had killed them first and then met me here to terrify me into joining the Conclave.

"Simon and William! Where *are* they? *What did you do to them?*"

Rage surged through me. Max's face was only inches from my own. I lunged upward, biting his cheek hard. I tasted blood.

That made him angry.

I tried to push aside all the visions swarming through my mind of the murders, of how swift he had been in his kills, of what had just happened to Liliana in the bed in a matter of minutes. And now I was in bed with the Ripper. I screamed as, in a single movement, he twisted both my arms above my head, pinning them to the bed behind me with one hand. Shooting pain coursed down my shoulder blades, and, in horror, I realized that somehow Max had brought my skirts high to press a knife blade hard against my thigh. He was on top of me, and I knew, in that moment, that I was completely in his power.

The wound on his cheek was a dark half moon. It would scar. "You're *not* in a position to fight me, Abbie Sharp."

I glared at him and felt tears come to my eyes as the pain in my thigh intensified. Any moment the blade would break through my skin.

He brought the knife up slowly to my face, running the blade along my cheek. I smelled the rusty scent of blood.

I fought a consuming horror as I realized the full extent of what was happening. This wasn't a second chance. Max had already killed William and Simon. I had refused the Conclave's offer, so now it was my turn. I remembered the corpse on the bed. Mutilated beyond recognition. Max enjoyed this; he would take his time torturing and killing me, a perfect way for him to spend the hours until Christina returned and he could then kill her. After that, everyone who knew the secret and the existence of the Conclave would be dead.

My mind raced, panicked, as I tried to think of a way to escape.

With great force, I bucked my whole body up against him, although I knew the momentum would be useless with his position on top of me. His weight crushed me, and I felt only a little relief as he arched upward, moving the knife slowly from my cheek downward toward my right breast.

I shuddered as he began, almost playfully, cutting the buttons away from the front of my dress. "You are allowed one question. *One* question only."

He stopped, smiled. Met my eyes. "And I think I know what you're going to ask."

"What did you do to them, to William and Simon?"

Against my will I began to cry, hoping that their deaths had been fast.

"They're alive."

My heartbeat quickened as I felt my hopes soar.

"For now." His look was sharp as he cut away another button. "And I am not going to kill you, at this time. The Conclave has decided to give you another chance. Your *last* chance, Abbie Sharp. The others are collecting William and Simon, and they should soon be at our house. You have a meeting with Julian, Marcus, Robert, and John there, tonight."

He paused, cutting away another button.

"If you refuse this time, your paramours die. *You* die."

"And if I accept, you will let them live?"

Max brought the knife downward, back to my upper thigh. I braced myself for a cut, but he just pressed the blade hard against my skin.

"We might negotiate."

"Leave Christina alone. She knows nothing."

His eyes glinted at the lie.

"She's safe for now, Abbie. We'll see how you behave."

I thought about trying to attack him again, but I knew I had to be more cautious now that William and Simon were Conclave prisoners. One wrong move could be disastrous.

He finished cutting the last button off the front of my dress. I knew he had to keep me alive, but I did not know what else he intended to do. Fear coursed through me. He wanted me to be afraid. With great effort, I steadied my breathing and met his eyes. It was a challenge.

"Abbie." He moved the knife upward to my throat. "I loathe leaving you now, but I must. I have some further Conclave business to attend tonight."

"More *killing*," I spit out.

He pushed the knife harder into my throat and tears slid down my cheek at the sharp pain.

"No more questions. The others are going to handle the killing tonight if you refuse. They did it for three hundred years before I came onto the scene. However, if something happens and I have to step in, it won't be pretty. So no foolish rescue missions, Abbie Sharp. You have a choice—to live, immortal with us, and *possibly* save your friends, or to die."

He released some of the pressure of the knife at my throat.

"You are to leave, to go straight to our house. And trust me, love, I'll know if you don't make it there. Everything depends upon you tonight."

He was silent, contemplating me in the darkness. I held my breath, trying to guess what his next move would be.

He kissed me hard, violently, forcing his tongue into my mouth. I struggled and tried to scream. I smelled, tasted, the blood from his cheek wound. The contact caused my mind to ignite, swirling and enflamed as I saw the chalice, the words, burned into my mind. As before, this vision was so strong it pained me.

Max pulled away, his smile brilliant in the darkness. "It beckons you, Abbie. Goodbye."

He was gone, disappeared into the darkness. I was alone, frozen, lying on my back on the bed, the dead woman beside me.

I felt trapped. A mouse in a cage. I had no plan. No plan whatsoever. But there would be no chance to save William and Simon if I didn't get to Montgomery Street.

Twenty-six

After hastily pinning together my dress, I began walking in the direction of Montgomery Street. It was a long walk and fog had settled all around. I still shivered from my experience with Max. He said he had some Conclave business to attend to, but he could be anywhere, even near me now, making certain that I arrived. I felt weary, exhausted. But thinking of William and Simon, that there might be a possibility of saving them, drove me on.

I had to go, try to bargain for my friends' lives. But I was aware of the only acceptable condition for their lives, the price I must pay. Even then, their lives might not be spared. After all, I was bargaining with murderers.

A cat ran across the street in front of me and I suppressed a dark chuckle. *Nine lives.*

I knew that Simon and William's only chance for survival depended on me taking the elixir. As I approached the house, I asked myself what I feared about this option. Of course, I could not remain with the Conclave, tolerating their murders. But I could perhaps flee from them, taking the elixir formula with me. I contemplated living out immortality in my own way. I remembered Mother's death, how she had wasted, suffered. I thought of all the illnesses, the deaths, the stillborns at the hospital. Perhaps I could have lifetimes to learn to help people *without* murdering.

The Conclave house was directly before me.

I ascended the steps, and I knew, even as these thoughts raced through my mind, that I could not drink the elixir. In consuming it, I would set myself above the rest of the human race—I could cheat death, cheat aging. It was an unfair advantage. And the persistent, unalterable fact remained: everyone could not live forever.

Dr. Bartlett opened the door almost immediately.

"Abbie, I am delighted to see you. Come, come in out of that cold."

It was as if I had arrived for one of his dinner parties. He was all cheer and good humor.

I scanned the house. Light streamed down the stairs. From the dark drawing room I saw the phosphorescent patterns of the jellyfish aquarium dancing along the walls.

"Where are they, Dr. Bartlett? Simon and William. Where are you keeping them?"

"Our meeting first, Abbie."

I felt my fury rise. He was all politeness when we all knew that my life, as well as William's, Simon's, and Christina's, was at stake. I followed him up the stairs and past the closed door to the gallery. As I walked, wondering where they held Simon and William, I had a sudden racing fear that my friends might *not* be alive. Perhaps the Conclave had lied to me in order to lure me here for this meeting.

The hall wound sharply to the right and then to the left again as we approached a door at the end of the corridor.

Dr. Bartlett opened the door, which led into a large room furnished with only an enormous, slablike table, a suit of armor, and a fireplace. The entire Conclave, excepting Max, sat at the table, their eyes upon me.

I panicked a bit. I had no idea what I would say, and so much depended upon me knowing for certain that William and Simon were alive.

"Do be seated, Miss Sharp," Dr. Buck said, gesturing to an empty chair across the table as Dr. Bartlett seated himself to the right of Reverend Perkins. Reverend Perkins's eyes bore into me. If it were up to him, I would be dead already.

After a very odd exchange of pleasantries where an outsider would never have guessed that the outcome of the meeting might be my execution, Dr. Buck cleared his throat quietly.

"I understand that our offer was not accepted."

I started to speak, but he raised his hand, silencing me.

"We are giving you another chance, Miss Sharp. We

thought you should meet with all of us, once more, before making a decision."

"Did you order Max to kill my friend Mary and an old woman?" I asked. "Then you kidnapped William and Simon. To threaten me?"

Dr. Buck and Dr. Bartlett met eyes quickly before Dr. Bartlett stated, "Max has his own methods."

"But his murders are ordered by *you*, and it was you who took William and Simon against their wills."

They all remained silent, unwilling to acknowledge that they persuaded anyone by these means. Dr. Bartlett lit a pipe.

They looked like ordinary, professional, middle-aged men. Still, I did not understand why I had not seen more of their peculiarities when I first met them. Earlier today, in Hampstead Heath, the light had been too hazy to see it clearly. But now I saw, in each of their eyes, pieces, layers of the history they had witnessed, sweeping like ocean waters back and forth over a wrecked ship. This was the aspect about them that made them seem not quite human.

Dr. Brown spoke first, kindly waving his hand as if brushing away a leaf.

"None of that matters, Miss Sharp. The point is, are you or are you not willing to join us? This is an extraordinary opportunity, and we are giving you a second chance to make a decision."

"A *last* chance," Reverend Perkins growled.

I was silent. I had learned about the workings of the philosopher's stone from Dr. Brown and Dr. Bartlett the day before, and my decision had been made. I had no more questions—no other way to stall them. The crackling of the fire in the fireplace deafened my ears.

"I want to see William and Simon before giving you any answer."

"They are fine," Dr. Buck said. "Safe. And as you know, we are open to ... "

"Max said that you might negotiate with me for their lives."

"We might ... " Dr. Buck began.

"I insist on seeing them *now*."

Dr. Brown started to say something, but Dr. Bartlett cut him off. "It's quite all right. She can see them. John, you have the key?"

Reverend Perkins sighed loudly and stood up.

While the rest of the Conclave stayed in the room, Reverend Perkins led me back through the winding hallway and down the main staircase. He took me back down the corridor to the room where the ritual had taken place. The enormous doors were closed. Reverend Perkins took out a set of keys and unlocked them.

The room was dark and bare except for a few lit candles on the floor; I did not even see the chalice. William and Simon sat in chairs, back to back, in the opposite part of the windowless room, their hands cuffed together and also to the chairs.

They were alive.

"Might I have a moment with them, alone?"

Perkins's eyes veiled, hardened. But he shut the door, leaving me alone.

I rushed to them, frantic, desperate. I had to free them.

"William!" As I came close to him, I saw that his right eye was purple, darkly bruised, and almost bloody looking.

"William thought it would be a good idea to fight John and Robert when they came to take him away," Simon said dryly. "He only regained consciousness a few minutes ago. Of course, it could have been worse. They had guns."

I tugged at the cuffs. Both of their wrists had been bloodied after struggling against the cuffs so vigorously.

"I'm fine." William said almost irritably, and with renewed energy began trying to free himself. "What's happening? What have they said to you?"

"I have only a few moments with you," I whispered. "They're giving me a second chance to join them, and I demanded to see you, to see that you were alive, before giving them an answer. Is the cuff key with Reverend Perkins, on his key ring?" I asked Simon quickly.

"Yes, he locked the cuffs when they brought us in here."

I cursed under my breath. Sweat dripped down my face and I was close to a panic.

"Do you have anything I can try to pick the lock with?"

"A pocketknife. We've been unable to reach it, but it is in my pocket," William said.

In a second, I retrieved the knife and began working at the lock. I tried to keep my back to the door. For all I knew, Reverend Perkins was watching us through the keyhole.

"My aunt. Is Christina safe?" William whispered.

"Yes, for now. Max promised to leave her alone. But..."

"What is it?"

"Perdita, William. She was dead when I arrived at the house."

"*Damn!*" William hissed as his face contorted in pain. "Get these cuffs *off!*"

"Keep your voice down and let Abbie work," Simon said quietly.

I was having no luck getting the lock open.

William was incensed now, swore profusely, and began jerking his hands against the cuffs in an effort to free himself.

"Hold still—I can't do this at *all* if you don't hold still." I whipped my head around to glance at the door. Reverend Perkins could come in again at any minute, and time was running out.

"This has to end *now*," William continued. "Abbie, they killed your mother."

"*William*," Simon hissed.

I froze. A cold chill swept through me, and I stopped picking the lock. The pocketknife still in my hand, I stood, facing William.

"What did you say?"

"William," Simon said angrily, "this hardly does any good..."

"She deserves to know." William met my eyes. "There was more in my father's notes than I told you, but I thought it might be too much for you, too overwhelming. Dr.

Bartlett fell in love with your mother from the first moment he saw her, that day at the operating theatre. He convinced the others that they needed a woman in the group. Caroline was educated and beautiful; she would be an asset to them as an immortal, as the psychic, the artist of the group. They gave her the offer. When she refused, they only allowed her to live because she was pregnant, the hope being that she might have a daughter with her same gift. Gabriel sent her away with Jacque to protect her. Max probably killed Sharp and let Caroline live only long enough to raise and educate you, the thinking being that you would be most like her if she raised you herself. He was probably the one who killed her, too, once you became a woman. It wasn't dysentery. He undoubtedly poisoned her."

Her visions. I remembered how they had increased in the weeks before her death. My mother had known the Conclave was coming for her during my entire childhood—and then, in those weeks before she died, she had *seen* them.

And Dr. Bartlett had been in love with her. This explained the lingering looks, why he called me "Abbie" while the others called me "Miss Sharp." Why he had sent Max to seek me out, specifically, to see if I also was psychic. It also might explain why they were so willing to give me a second chance.

I was Dr. Bartlett's second chance after he did away with Mother.

"Abbie," Simon said gently. "It's the truth. I'm sorry."

Oddly, I didn't cry. I only felt fury. A consuming fury.

"Abbie, are you all right?" William asked.

William and Simon could not help me now, not as long as they were locked up like this. And I had no immediate way of freeing them.

"I'll be back," I said, turning from them.

"Abbie? Where are you going?" William demanded.

I didn't answer him as I clutched the pocketknife tighter, concealing it in the folds of my skirts.

"Abbie, *don't* be stupid. You need us."

"Don't do this alone," Simon added.

"Abbie! *Abbie*! Get back here." Now William was desperate.

Ignoring them, I joined Reverend Perkins in the hall.

"I hope you're satisfied now, Miss Sharp," he said as he locked and bolted the door again.

I followed him, formulating a plan as we ascended the stairs. My best chance to eliminate the Conclave would be to kill the members one at a time, and I had to keep them separate. They could overwhelm me if all together.

Reverend Perkins would be the first to go.

I removed the knife from my skirt folds and felt my palms sweat. It would do no good if the others heard him cry out. Severing his windpipe would ensure his silence.

I steadied myself.

One. Two...

Catapulting my whole body against him, I knocked him to the floor and collapsed on top of him. Then immediately, before I could think too much about what I was doing, I plunged the knife into his throat, feeling it cut muscle and then bone. I turned away, hearing only a gurgle. Then nothing.

I stood up, quaking all over as I forced myself to look at him, to make certain that the blow had been a fatal one. His enormous hands reached toward his bleeding throat. He could not make a sound. Reverend Perkins had hated me more than the others, and I watched his angry stare until he gasped his last breath.

The door to the conference room slammed open and urgent voices sounded from far down the corridor. The others had heard Perkins fall.

I bolted into the gallery, slamming and locking the door behind me. The moment I shut it, I heard them outside. They had found John Perkins's body and immediately began trying to break through the gallery door.

Feeling a bit like a trapped rat, I panicked when I realized that I had dropped the knife in the hallway. I frantically scanned the cases of weapons—the spears, the guns, the knives. I considered the guns, but I could not be certain whether they would work or not, whether they were loaded or not. A second later, I pulled a handkerchief from my pocket and, covering my fist, punched through one of the cases and took the bowie knife.

Excellent for skinning and tearing organs.

As I held it, I estimated the force of my momentum; I considered the curved blade, the heavy handle. If I could send it spinning, I might be able to make a kill.

The door frame cracked a bit as the men outside pushed against it. They would be through at any moment.

There were no windows in the gallery; I backed up against another door at the far side of the room.

Then the gallery door burst open and I faced them across the room, the knife poised in front of me.

"You killed my mother." My voice quivered and did not sound like my own. I shook with rage.

"She had a choice, Abbie. A fair one."

"Did she?" I spat. "What, join your group or die? The same choice you're offering me? What kind of choice is *that?*"

"It was an offer," Marcus Brown said, taking a step forward. "Off the table, now that you've killed John."

"Stay where you are!" I warned him, before turning my attention back to Dr. Bartlett.

He laid one hand on Marcus Brown's shoulder. "In a minute, Marcus. Your mother," he continued, turning to me. "With her gifts, once she took the elixir, might have been anything."

"What? As your immortal *love puppet?*"

A chilling coldness overcame his expression. I suspected that my statement affected him more deeply than John Perkins's death had. His response came out severe and cold, as if he were issuing my own execution order. "No one can live, knowing the secret. It is part of the rules— four centuries worth of rules."

My mother might have been just another casualty to them, but to me she meant something. They had not seen her suffer and die. They had not loved her as I had. They had robbed me.

Robbed me of too much.

Dr. Brown pushed past Dr. Bartlett. "Miss Sharp, this has gone too far. Stop this foolishness. Drop the knife and surrender to us." He spoke kindly, politely, even as he was crossing the room to kill me.

The great politician. The murderous politician.

The politeness infuriated me, and I decided that their gentlemen's rules were at an end.

"Your Conclave can go to fucking hell!"

I slung the knife forward. It stuck hard in Marcus Brown's heart.

Without wasting another second, I plunged through the door behind me, locking it. I found myself in yet another gallery lined with cases, a door slightly ajar at the far end.

I needed another weapon.

Trying to ignore the shouts, and then the great thuds against the door, I ran toward the cases.

In these cases there were no weapons, only rows and rows of shrunken heads: the skin was dark, leathery, obviously stretched and then boiled. The eyes had all been sewn shut. The hair on the heads was all different colors—blond, black. I swayed as I saw a streak of auburn locks. In my horror, I tried to tell myself that Robert Buck had collected these heads from gravesites around the globe. But I knew of his anthropological curiosities, of the people that the Conclave had killed over the years. I swallowed as I contemplated how far Robert Buck's experiments might have gone over the centuries.

There was nothing in this room to help me, so I ran toward the other door. Along the way, I threw myself against the cases, crashing them to the floor in the hopes that the mess would stall the Conclave.

Running into the next room, a laboratory, I slammed and locked the door behind me. There were no more escape routes. I would have to face them in here.

I began flinging open cabinets, looking for a new weapon. Test tubes and fluids crashed around me. In the darkness, I slammed into the dissecting table and my hip throbbed in pain.

I heard their voices and the sound of crunching glass. Robert Buck and Julian Bartlett were in the gallery.

My odds would be better if I could create some sort of diversion. A large vat of formaldehyde caught my eye.

As I heaved it toward the door, I spilled half of the vat's contents. The formaldehyde spread across the floor quickly. I dumped the remainder of the contents along the edge of the floor and across the surface of every counter-top, taking care to keep the solutions off my skirts.

Just as I grabbed the nearest Bunsen burner, Robert Buck and Julian Bartlett broke through the door. Buck slipped immediately, falling, just as Bartlett braced himself on the slick floor. His eyes met mine as I lit the burner and tossed it onto the ground near me. I then leaped into the dry, middle part of the laboratory. Flames shot across the floor and up the countertops. The laboratory would be engulfed in flames within minutes, and then the house.

Julian Bartlett shouted something to Robert Buck and

started to fight the fire. Buck, standing again, grabbed me hard as I ran past. I kicked him sharply in the ribs but could not disengage myself. I fought hard against him and we fell together, tumbling out into the gallery.

Shards of glass crunched under my back and cut into my arms as we rolled across the floor. I tried to ignore the shrunken heads that kept bumping against my body, focusing instead on keeping Buck from pinning me. He slammed my head hard against the side of one of the felled cases. Then once he was on top of me, he put his hands around my throat, choking me. Flickers of light began to appear in my peripheral vision. I was losing consciousness.

I dealt a mighty kick upwards into his sternum, and heard a crack. That was enough. He released his grip and I slid out from under him, dizzy but standing.

Heaving and choking, I stumbled out of the room as smoke began pouring out from the laboratory, engulfing the galleries. I hoped that Dr. Bartlett had been overcome by the flames and smoke. That would leave me just Robert Buck to kill until I could find Max.

Buck stood up and I ran from him into the first gallery, ducking, trying to keep my head away from the smoke.

Pulling the bowie knife from Brown's body as I ran out of the gallery, I almost tripped over Perkins's body at the top of the stairs. *The handcuff keys.* Keeping an eye out for what was behind me, I struggled to get the keys unhinged from his belt. My hands trembled and I felt myself crying as I fought to free them. Buck would be upon me anytime.

"Abbie *Shaaaarp!*" I heard him roar from the gallery, just as I freed the keys and ran down the staircase.

There was no time to free William and Simon—there were at least thirty keys on the ring and I had no idea which, if any, would work on the handcuffs. I certainly didn't want to lead Robert Buck to them, so I ran in the other direction, into the drawing room.

Large sheets covered all the furniture. All the fish aquariums were now gone except for the jellyfish globe aquarium, which rested upon a large cart with wheels. The top had been removed.

Venomous. Can kill someone within minutes.

I still had the knife, but an easier means of killing Buck occurred to me.

Pushing all of my weight against it, I rolled the giant globe aquarium on its wheels toward the side of the entrance to the drawing room. Then, standing on a chair, I steadied my breathing and waited. I heard the stairs creaking. He was coming.

I held my breath as I placed my back against the aquarium. Timing would be everything. Then, if this didn't work, I still had the bowie knife.

I focused on the silence, listening for Robert Buck's breathing as he approached the room.

The second he entered, I threw my back against the aquarium. With a great crash, it toppled over, emptying its contents onto him. I would have fallen along with it, but I grabbed a nearby window curtain, catching myself just in time.

I leaped off the chair and stood nearby, watching, the knife ready in case this didn't work. Robert Buck was screaming and thrashing on the floor, his spectacles falling off. Jellyfish clung to his body. His neck began swelling immediately, turning red and then purple as he suffocated.

Smoke poured down the stairs. He was dead. Julian Bartlett, if alive, would have come down the stairs by now. I started to maneuver past Buck's body, careful of the jellyfish, to get to William and Simon.

Then I heard the crashing footsteps upstairs and a voice calling for Robert Buck.

Julian Bartlett was still alive.

I also heard roaring flames as he ran down the stairs. The fire had spread. Then a bullet hit the wall behind me. Bartlett had seen me, and he had a gun.

Sprinting back into the drawing room, then through the French doors into the hothouse, I found myself enshrouded in early morning darkness. The fountain was empty and the place absolutely silent. There were no shrieking monkeys, no flying birds.

I ran fast past the fountain into the forest, knowing that I had to take cover before he caught up with me.

I was not a moment too soon. The hothouse doors slammed open just as I reached the trees.

Once in the wooded area, I planned an ambush. If I could take him by surprise, kill him quickly, then free Simon and William, we just might make it out before the house burned down.

The tree nearest to me had a thick branch about ten

feet off the ground. Silently, clenching the knife blade in my teeth and plunging the keys into my right boot so that I would not lose them, I climbed up.

I heard his footsteps. He was closer than I had thought. I eased further out on the branch.

He stood directly underneath me.

He had been my supervisor, my mentor. But now, as Mother's murderer, he had to die. Slowly, silently, I removed the knife from my mouth and clutched it hard.

I inched forward a bit more. Dropped.

But he stepped aside and spun around, aiming the revolver at me as I hit the ground painfully. I rolled sharply to one side just as the dirt exploded in the spot where I had been.

I stood and charged at him with the knife before he could fire again. But with frightening ease, he caught me and spun me against him, holding my body and my wrists in a vice grip. Before I could take another breath, he had taken my knife and placed it against my throat.

I struggled, but he held me too tight.

"It has come to this. *This.*" He pressed the knife harder.

He seemed calm, calm even though I had killed the others, calm even though he was about to kill me now.

"You've created quite a mess for me, Abbie. Ruined so much of what I have worked for four hundred years to build. They are gone now."

It was a cool reproach, yet stern and controlled as if he lectured a child.

"You know, Abbie," he whispered softly, soothingly, in

my ear, "I thought Caroline Westfield was extraordinary, that she wanted to do extraordinary things. But she disappointed me and turned out to be sadly ordinary."

"*You...*"

"Hush, Abbie."

In that moment, I felt overwhelming panic. He had immobilized all of my limbs, had me locked against his body. I had come so close to surviving, to saving William and Simon. If I died now, they would both die, very soon, in the fire.

I almost choked as the vision washed over me. Julian Bartlett's touch, my emotions, must have triggered it. I saw my mother's face, as she stood in front of the Conclave in that meeting room—the same room where I had been. I saw the sharpness in her expression, her defiance. She had just refused the elixir.

The vision, a split-second lightning flash, left.

Mother's face had done it. I had to finish this.

With a crazed burst of energy, I threw Bartlett off me, snatched the knife from him, and kicked him to the ground. I had knocked the wind out of him, but nonetheless, I placed my boot hard on his chest.

"No, Julian. Mother *was* extraordinary. *You*, on the other hand—"

I cut his throat.

"—Are just *too old*."

He died without another word, those unfathomable eyes finally lifeless.

When I reached the drawing room again, smoke had

already poured down the stairs and through most of the first floor. It was hot, difficult to see. The smoke burned my nostrils, my throat. My fears rose for Simon and William. Covering my nose and mouth with one hand, I crouched low and hurried through the drawing room, careful as I stepped around Robert Buck's body.

The floor creaked above me. It could collapse at any moment. The fire had spread so quickly, and Montgomery Street was so empty, the house would likely be burnt to the ground by the time the fire department arrived.

I reached the large doors to the ritual room and pulled away the first bolt. My hand trembled as I tried five different keys in the lock. None worked. After ducking to the floor to gulp fresh air again, I stood, tried the next key, and thanked the gods of luck that it worked.

As I burst through the doors, I saw that although the room was smoky, the doors had sealed away most of it.

"Abbie!" William yelled. "Bloody hell, you're alive! I heard the gunfire, the yelling. Then the smoke came."

Smoke was now filling the room.

"I have the keys, but *dammit*, I have no idea which one—"

I screamed when I heard a ceiling collapse somewhere on the first floor.

"One of the keys is a bit shorter than the others, with a small notch on the top," Simon said coolly. "That's the one to the cuffs."

I found it.

"Thank you, Simon, you're amazing as always." I unlocked the cuffs.

"Hurry! *Hurry!*" I yelled, although I hardly had to say that. William grabbed me, pulling me hard out the doors, Simon just behind us.

The heat was unbearable now. My eyes burned, watered. I tasted ash. Fortunately, once we made it to the hallway, the front doors were immediately in front of us.

We broke through them, into the embrace of the early morning air.

Twenty-seven

The house burned quickly, to ashes, after we left. Because of the fast-moving flames, and because of the isolation of the street, the fire department in fact did not arrive until it was leveled. Simon, William, and I watched from the distance, just to make certain. In the end, even the hothouse was no more.

It was almost three o'clock in the morning, and still very dark, when we arrived at Christina's house. She had returned from New Hospital already, and we found her sitting in her parlor, Hugo at her feet. She was pale, ghost-white in fact, and I saw her hand tremble as she raised her steaming teacup to her lips.

"He was here. Wasn't he?" she asked.

I sat beside her on the sofa while William and Simon sat across the room.

I nodded.

"I just arrived and found her in the bed." Christina wiped a tear away from her eye. "She has no living family. No friends but us. We can bury her on our plot."

None of us said anything for quite a while. Then she finally looked up, focusing on us for the first time. I knew we looked a sight. All three of us had torn clothes; we were dirty, covered in ashes. The front of my dress had come open again, and I saw, in the firelight of Christina's parlor, that I had dried blood smeared across my dress and on my hands from the killings.

"How very rude of me," she said shakily, standing up. "You all look terrible and exhausted."

After she brought us tea, she expressed her regrets.

"I never really believed Gabriel's story of the Conclave. I should have said something when you began working at the hospital, William. But truly, I thought it was nonsense. You have been in such danger."

We immediately told her all that had happened. How they were all dead now except for Max. How, except for him, all evidence of the Conclave was now destroyed.

"And Polidori's papers?" Christina asked.

"Robert Buck took them from me just as he and John kidnapped us at gunpoint. I'm sure they burned with the rest of the house," William said.

"Mary and Scribby?" I asked him quickly. "Were you able to find them?"

William nodded. "Easily. I actually found them returning from somewhere, only blocks from Miller's Court. Max would have killed them, too, if they had come back any earlier. I convinced Scribby that he did not need to see the mutilated body of his sister; they should be on their way back to Ireland. They have a lot of unanswered questions for us, of course. But I convinced them to leave immediately—that Mary's life depended upon it."

I shuddered. The mess in that bed would be forever burned into my mind.

"And what about Max?" Christina asked.

"He told me that he had business to deal with." I told them about how the jellyfish aquarium had been on wheels, how of all the animals and birds were gone from the hothouse.

"They might have planned on moving abroad again," Christina suggested. "That was one of the ways they apparently kept their immortality secret. They've been in London now several decades without aging. It would have been about time to move on."

"I think it's likely that Max has left London, taking the animals somewhere," Simon said. "But when he hears about the loss of the elixir, of the deaths of the rest of the Conclave, he will be furious."

"But he's free. The Conclave is gone. He doesn't have to work for them anymore," William pointed out. "There's a chance he might move on, leave us alone."

"You're being naïve, William. You're forgetting the minor detail of the elixir." Simon spoke irritably. "He hadn't had his ritual yet. He needs it every year to maintain his immortality. We just robbed him of that."

Simon was right.

"We don't know when Max might be back," I said quickly. "We'll have to stay on alert. And when he comes back, we'll deal with him. But I'm not going to live in fear."

"Neither am I," Christina said. "He might be back tomorrow. He might be back next year. We'll be prepared, but life has to go on."

She took another sip of tea, and I saw the quick glance she snatched at the Polidori portrait. We sat in silence for several minutes, a heaviness weighting the air.

Christina lent me a dress and I cleaned up in preparation for returning to Kensington. There was no way I could return to Grandmother's with my dress torn open and blood smears everywhere. I dreaded the upcoming weeks with Grandmother; that morning, especially, new arguments over my plans to attend medical school and William and Christina's continuing presence in my life were battles that I did not feel like having. They would be best saved for after I had had at least a full night's sleep.

While Simon readied the carriage for us and Christina had Perdita's body taken away, I had a single stolen moment with William. As soon as we were alone in the parlor, I embraced him.

I was shocked when he pulled away.

"What happened between you and Simon in my absence?" he demanded.

At first I thought he was joking; then, I saw from the angry shine in his eyes that he was not.

I couldn't lie. "It doesn't matter. I had made you no promises."

Then I felt angry. Annoyed that after everything we had been through in the last day and night, *this* was his concern.

We stood for a few minutes in angry silence, alone in the parlor in front of the Polidori portrait. I felt frighteningly, deeply in love. But the realization that love was faulty smacked me hard. I knew Mother had loved me, but our relationship had had so many cracks, so many mysteries. Grandmother loved me, but she was still fierce, controlling. Annoying, in fact.

Why did I expect William to be flawless?

Still, I didn't have to tolerate his absurdities.

I sighed and shrugged, turning to leave the parlor.

But then he pulled me back, snatched me to him. Kissed me. With his jealousy still present, the kiss was possessive as well as passionate. All thunder and sharpness. And there, in Christina's parlor, amidst the faint odor of must and bird feathers, I embraced him back and eagerly returned the kiss.

"Abbie!" Grandmother shrieked angrily as Richard let Simon and me into the house. From the front hall, I saw breakfast still laid out in the dining room, only half-eaten.

Amidst Grandmother's cries that I was "selfish," "rude," and "improper" for putting her through so much following a funeral, I felt my stomach growl and my mouth water at the smell of hot bread and bacon. My hunger nearly overwhelmed me in that moment. As I kept my eyes on Grandmother, I tried to ignore a small exchange between Simon and Richard—Simon silently pushed some banknotes into Richard's hand; Richard pushed Simon's hand and the money away and shook his head. My curiosity about Richard rose a bit. I would have to ask Simon about him later.

Meanwhile, Grandmother was still lecturing me so sharply that my ears rang. After the previous night, I had no fight left, so I merely continued with the apologies. Then I felt myself flush in frustration when Ellen arrived on the staircase landing to watch the scene.

It was only after his odd exchange with Richard that Simon finally stepped in, speaking to Grandmother in his most graceful voice. "It was an emergency, Lady Westfield. As I told you last evening, they were short-staffed and Christina was desperate for help. Abbie's generosity saved us last night, possibly saved patients' lives."

Grandmother could never resist Simon, and I felt myself smile. Simon was a smooth liar for a priest.

"Well . . ." She stammered for a minute, obviously embarrassed at her earlier rage. In spite of everything, I wasn't angry. The "mugger" attack upon me several weeks ago, and now Mariah's death and funeral, had been difficult for her. In spite of Simon's contrived excuse for my absence, I knew that she had dire fear of me being too far away from her. I was all she had left in the world.

With great effort, Grandmother forced herself into a more composed and polite state. "Simon, you must stay for breakfast. I insist."

He stayed. I had never appreciated a morning in Kensington so much. And I ate like a ravenous beast.

I went to bed early, in the afternoon in fact. The moment I got back to my room, I thought of my mother. I had experienced such complex feelings for her: Loyalty for her in the face of the Conclave. Frustration, anger even, that she had not prepared me to confront her past in London. She had known that Max would come for her one day, that the Conclave would likely draw me to them. *Why had she not said anything?* But as I lay there in bed, I thought long and hard about what she could have done. What she could have said that would have helped me, prepared me more for the Conclave. I had no answer.

I fell asleep quickly, and slept soundly and without nightmares. Still, at some point, I dreamt about a real occurrence from the summer I turned sixteen. It had been one of the hottest and driest Dublin summers ever; the entire summer, I had felt sweaty and sticky. In the dream, dust swirled through the street and I felt a coat of grit in my teeth and hair.

Surrounded by a crowd of youth, I was in an alley,

knife-throwing at our wooden targets. I felt the handle, the blade. It was the last round of our competition—if I made this shot, I won. I focused, inhaled. Every other noise from the alley, from the street, sank to nothingness in my head. I had practiced at home, practiced even in this alley, until calluses formed on my right palm.

The sling, the hit. And then I realized that I had hit the target. *I had won.* This was the last round in our competition, and out of everyone, I had won. I felt elated. There was no real reward, other than added respect from my hard-to-win Dublin friends. But it was a great triumph for me. After the praise ceased and the hits on the back stopped, as the crowd dispersed and everyone went back to their parents' houses, I retrieved my knife and turned to leave the alley.

I saw Mother standing at the alley entrance.

The dusty, sun-streaked air made her appear hazy at first, and then clearer. She wore the prim governess dress that never quite seemed to suit her. A dark cloud cut through the sky above, shadowing her face as we stared at each other. I feared she was angry at me. I was late returning.

But an odd flash of contentment, then splendid approval, washed over her face.

"Time to go home, Abbie," was all that she said.

As I woke up, in the periwinkle glow of dawn, I knew Mother had done what was best—she had left me alone. The education she had given me was all that I needed before my return to London and subsequent fall into unknown waters. She had taught me to think critically and to be open to new ideas. The Conclave was like nothing I could expect or imagine, and my survival depended upon my learning and adapting along the way.

This wave of understanding washed over me, and I felt peaceful. Soon I fell back asleep and did not wake up until late morning.

Epilogue

A day later, I sat looking out my bedroom window at Grandmother's house. Pigeons, doves, sparrows dived in and out of spires and gabled towers in the near distance, flying black specks as the sunset ensued in a coppery flash. In spite of not finding Max yet, I felt hopeful, in that moment, as I had never been.

I leaned further out so that the wind whipped at my hair, and I inhaled a faint whiff of baking pies, the sharp tang of smog. I would begin, immediately, applying to medical school, and in the meantime continue to work alongside William and Simon at Whitechapel Hospital.

I bit my lip; my return to the hospital was not a subject I had yet broached with Grandmother.

Richard knocked at the door. I had asked that whenever possible, he bring me my mail rather than Ellen.

"Miss Arabella. This arrived just now, attached to a very large package downstairs."

He handed me a small envelope. He paused before leaving, eyeing me curiously. "I am glad that you returned to us safely."

His statement was odd; I wondered what Simon had told him the other night. Richard might know or suspect that we had not been at the New Hospital, that something else was going on. Nonetheless, he remained the poised butler, his expression fond and kind.

"Thank you, Richard."

I hoped he knew that I meant it.

The moment he left, I tore open the envelope with my letter opener. But before I could read the note inside, I heard a blood-curdling scream from downstairs.

My first thought was that it was Max, finally returned to take his revenge. I dropped the note and ran, taking the sharp letter opener with me.

I reached the staircase landing and froze. Ellen had already opened my package.

Grandmother, her face stricken as if she had seen the devil, was standing in front of an enormous portrait—Dante Gabriel Rossetti's missing Lamia portrait featuring my mother.

I gasped, my emotion overwhelming. Mother's hair was down, and long, way past her waist. Rossetti had captured the gold flecks amidst the red color of her hair perfectly; it was the hair I had brushed daily throughout my childhood. In the portrait, she sunbathed upon a rock near a beach, her body totally naked, her face and breasts very human, but her feet dragonlike. Translucent, sea-green scales covered her legs and her arms, and great claws extended from her fingers. She was monstrous and beautiful. Cryptic, and yet authentic.

I heard a thud behind me as Grandmother fainted.

I pulled myself away from the portrait to attend to her. Richard returned with the smelling salts and she revived immediately.

"Destroy it!" she cried. "Take it out to the back and destroy it, Richard."

"No, no, don't you dare!" I shouted at Grandmother. "It's *mine*. Christina Rossetti promised it to me, and if it goes, *I* go. I'll put it in my room, in my closet even. No one needs to see it. But it's mine."

Grandmother knew it was mine, and she could say nothing. She stared at me, her eyes flaring. She stormed off to the parlor. But I knew I had won. I knew, in spite of all her raving, that in the end, I was more important than her pride.

After Richard helped me carry the enormous portrait to my room, I picked up the envelope; I had nearly forgotten about it upon seeing the portrait. I assumed that perhaps Christina had found the painting somewhere. Or maybe it was William who had located it.

I pulled the note from the envelope and read.

Dear Abbie Sharp,

This has been great fun. But all is not over. I do think this belongs to you. Enjoy. Au revoir.

—M

About the Author

Amy Carol Reeves has a PhD in nineteenth-century British literature. She published a few academic articles before deciding that it would be much more fun to write about Jack the Ripper. When she is not writing or teaching college classes, she enjoys running around her neighborhood with her giant Labrador retriever and serial-reading Jane Austen novels. She lives in Columbia, South Carolina, with her husband and two children. *Ripper* is her debut novel.